VICISSITUDES:

the ups and downs and changes experienced in a lifetime

Debra L. Ice

Braydie Codell Publishing
Jacksonburg, West Virginia

ISBN-13: 978-0615424231

Published by: Braydie Codell Publishing
            Jacksonburg, West Virginia

Cover Image: Photo of autumn leaves in West Virginia was taken by Debra Ice while ATVing with husband.

Acknowledgements

Appreciation and much love go to my husband Tom, to our children Tommy Ice and Janell Work, to the memory of my deceased brother Rick Lloyd, to my sister Candi Gordon, and to my best friend Kathy Phillips, for supporting and encouraging me through much more than this project. A heartfelt "thank you" goes out to them for being patient through all my years of talking about wanting to become a published writer. Years that span the decades is a long time to listen to the ramblings of a procrastinator who lacks self-confidence. Because this simple body of work was such a long time in the making, and because I didn't want to spend another decade querying agents who likely would return rejection notices, I also thank everyone for understanding why I decided it was time to give myself some peace of mind, to bring this body of work to an end, and to move on with my life. It seemed the timeliest way to achieve my dream was to self-publish.

To my friend and author Millie Covey Fry, who unexpectedly walked into my life one day: You've been a source of great inspiration and encouragement—quite the mentor—and I can never thank you enough for your kind words and continued support. To Terrie Dansereau and Gary Bennett, who share my love for writing: I hope to see your publishing dreams come true. To Dr. Terry Craig: Thank you for taking time from your busy schedule to read and encourage me on what turned out to be the infancy of my completed manuscript. To a very dear friend Linda Kirk: Thanks for reading a different bit of my work and for asking when you'd have a chance to read more. Even if you were only trying to be nice, your words were encouraging.

For almost every time I went to the local hardware store since beginning my manuscript: Thank you, Rick Barr, for being thoughtful enough to ask how my book was coming along. The fact that you didn't laugh when I told you I was writing meant a lot to me.

Dedication

This book is dedicated to the memory of my beloved grandparents, who—as I remember them—were patient, wise, compassionate, and selfless. They were simple country people with an abundance of common sense who understood the truly important things in life—and who put that understanding to meaningful use. If they're still watching over me: Thank you for giving my siblings and me a safe place to land. Your walk was much greater than your talk, and you'll always be remembered with love.

Preface

Right up front: This is an autobiographical fiction novel—and is not to be confused with a memoir. Although much of the story is based on true events, too many things have been changed to consider it anything other than a work of fiction. The names of characters and places have been changed, and many events and circumstances have been greatly manipulated.

It's a story about how Cassie Hunter Thomas, an ordinary country woman, thinks back on the ups and downs and changes within her lifetime. It's a story of thoughts, emotions, and timeless issues to which many women can relate.

CHAPTER ONE

I wasn't exactly emotionally and time-management prepared to relinquish my full-time roles of Mother and Employee, and when the time came for me to reluctantly surrender those positions, an abundance of previously wished-for time quickly became overwhelming.

Without my former titles and routine of operating within a busy but organized time- and pressure-filled schedule, I lost important parts of my identity, my sense of purpose, and any semblance of motivation to make decisions.

The previous two years had taken quite an emotional toll on my life. My son pursued a job opportunity far from home, moved to another state, married, and became a father. My daughter earned her nursing degree, married, and also moved to another state.

Having a job to head out to each morning helped to alleviate the sense of loss in my empty nest, and a dim glimmer of hope existed that my income would exclusively be used to build a nest egg for my husband

Jacob and me. Our flight to financial freedom looked promising—until I assumed my new role of Downsizing Statistic.

The dispiriting chain of events that led to downsizing also led me to feel like some sort of failure, but I hated to openly admit it and literally ached inside. I wondered: *"Why? What have I done wrong? I was conscientious, worked hard, cared about my job, and never took it for granted. I tried to prove my worth and to be a valuable asset to the operations. Why was it necessary to sell the properties where I worked? I wish I were still there."* I wanted to cry.

Of course, my best options were simply to snap out of it and not to allow myself to take the blame for things over which I had no control. Rationality finally brought me to the conclusion that I was hired at a time when my family desperately needed it, and my employer, quite frankly, hadn't promised me a permanent position until I chose to retire.

Depression wasn't an option that would change my status, so I made a concentrated effort to review my life and, upon reflection, it became clear that many initially perceived negative occurrences ultimately proved to be stepping-stones that led to positive experiences. When previously faced with inexperience and adversity, an almost unbelievable spiritual strength had always carried me ahead, and perseverance helped me to emerge somewhat stronger and wiser. I'd survived those inconvenient times with gratitude, strength, pride, and a feeling of relief that I *had* survived.

While considering my quieter and less bustling household, I recalled a time when I'd told my grandfather I was so happy with my roles of wife and mother that I wished my children could stay young forever.

My grandfather exuded wisdom when he smiled and softly said: "Oh, Cassie honey, you don't really wish that. I believe you were born to be a wife and mother—those roles come so easily and so naturally for you—but just think of all the children in the world with physical and mental issues that don't allow them to truly grow up. Think of the parent who worries for her child's well-being because he'll never achieve physical- or mental-maturity. Remember how pleased you were when you thought you were all grown-up? Remember how happy you were when you married Jacob and how fulfilled you were when you became a mother? You surely want your children to experience those same wonderful gifts of life. You won't be ready; but it'll happen, and you'll adjust. Until that time comes, appreciate every minute of life, and when your children are grown and you become a grandmother, you'll think about how much you and I loved each other, and you'll understand what I've said." He was right. I do.

My grandfather impressed upon me that everything happens for a reason and in its own time, and it actually seemed to work out that way. Generations of women survived the empty-nest syndrome. Multitudes of women survived being downsized. And, I'd survive.

While sadly mourning my losses in that empty nest with a very small nest egg, and while feeling like someone had clipped my wings, my emotions were put into perspective when a dear friend, who was my age, lost her battle with cancer.

It was imperative that I find a new and vital role for myself—something that would restore my drive and self-confidence—something that would give my life new meaning and purpose.

I prayed for guidance and searched for motivation and inspiration. One day it struck me that an opportunity had arrived. For decades, I'd dreamed of having time to write—maybe a novel, maybe a column for a local newspaper, or maybe some magazine articles. It was time to come to my senses, to make the necessary adjustments, to productively use the abundance of time to my advantage, and to turn my dream into a goal.

To get my life on the right track, for peace of mind, and in order to utilize some guilt-free time and freedom to pursue my career choice, it was necessary to put things in order. My first task was to make a To-Do List that would give me a sense of direction and help to keep me on that right track. As each task was completed and a line was drawn through it, it took me one step closer to turning my goal into a reality.

I sorted through and organized storage containers, cabinets, drawers, and closets. After nearly twenty-five years of living in the same house, I actually knew where to quickly find the flashlights, batteries, tape, extension cords, extra light bulbs, and my sewing- and craft-materials.

Found tucked away in several drawers and containers were photos and snapshots I'd nearly forgotten we had. I went to the attic, grabbed a large box, carried it downstairs, and set some smaller photo-filled boxes inside. As I cleaned and sorted through every nook and cranny in my house, I gathered and tossed the additional stray pictures into that box. I didn't know it then, but that batch of photos would lead me another step closer to the fulfillment of my goal.

One evening, satisfied that every window, wall, ceiling, floor, closet, and item in my home had been cleaned and/or organized, I decided to do something with those pictures I'd tossed into my treasure-filled box and pulled it into my living room, set up a utility table, collected the albums and frames I'd purchased for my task, and I began.

Over a period of several days, after Jacob left for work, I spent many hours sorting through the log of lives represented by those pictures. As I reminisced, those vivid reminders of my loves and losses became indicative of how the years too quickly became the past, and I became quite emotional with the thought of how persistently and impartially the family statistics fluctuated in accordance with births, marriages, and deaths.

I found pictures that ran the gamut of our lives, from our great-grandparents to our grandparents, from our parents to us, and from us to our children and grandchild. There were pictures of generations of family members I could only slightly recall, and some handed-down photos of folks I didn't know, but who'd apparently been important to somebody else in our extended family. From other pictures, happily smiling faces of our friends looked back at me, and photos from work-related functions warmly reminded me of those people with whom I'd worked.

Each picture evoked a memory that made me even more acutely aware of the importance of time with family and friends. They were reminders of childhood and friendships, of falling in love and rearing my children. They reminded me of struggles, milestones, and triumphs. I thought of things I hadn't thought of for years.

With each picture and its accompanying memory, I smiled, laughed, or cried. The memories stirred up by that box of pictures took me on an emotional and cathartic roller coaster ride that opened my mind and touched my heart, and I relived nearly every day of my life, until—almost as if looking through a stranger's eyes—I was forced to see it from a new perspective and to come to a conclusive understanding. My life had been riddled with some inconveniences, but it had also been tremendously blessed. My existence served—and continues to serve—several purposes, and I'm exactly where I'm supposed to be. I'm moving from one accomplishment to the next challenge—and knowing *that* gives me a sense of cleansing, a sense of healing, and a surprising sense of peace.

The initial plan was to organize the photos in some sort of sequence—probably in chronological order—but with the mixture of families, the pictures of people and places I didn't remember or recognize, and being nearly overwhelmed by the sheer magnitude of it all, I decided that as long as those pictures were placed into those albums and frames, another task would be accomplished.

~~I picked up a black-and-white snapshot that showed my pregnant mother, my father, my twin brothers, and me. Without even looking for a date, I knew the picture was taken when I was still two years old. At first glance, we looked like the picture-perfect family, but as the five images incongruously smiled back at me, I was certain that fear and sadness lay deep within at least one of those souls. It was just an old black-and-white picture with shades of gray, and the year 1953 was printed along the white, scalloped border.

CHAPTER TWO

Even though some people say that children can't remember things from such an early age, I remember my mother who died as the result of an automobile accident shortly before I turned three. Ruth Robinson Hunter was a passenger in her friend's car, and she and Betty were killed instantly one rainy day when, on their way home from grocery shopping, the car hydroplaned, slid off the road, careened down an embankment, and crashed into a huge oak tree. At the age of twenty-five, my mother's life on earth was suddenly ended, and when she was so suddenly gone from my life, I began to miss her and have never stopped.

Memories of the layout, colors, shapes, and textures of the house in which we lived remain vivid in my mind. Perhaps because we were not to have much time together, I was allowed to absorb some beautiful memories of my mother and of our surroundings of home, for my many future references.

My mother was a petite woman whose beauty was nearly breathtaking. She was about 5'2" tall and usually weighed around 100 pounds. I don't exactly remember those statistics from being with her, but I was told about her so many times and have looked at so many pictures of her, that it almost seems like a memory. I definitely remember the feel of her—the presence of her—and the feeling of her absence.

A favorite memory: My mother sat with one leg crossed under the other on our gray-and-red vinyl sofa in a room where the windows cast light streaks and shadows through wide-slatted wooden Venetian blinds.

Her nose slightly tilted up at the end, and her large round hazel eyes were accented by the long curly chestnut-brown hair that framed her beautiful and eternally ageless round face. Her rich full lips were usually painted red to match the enamel on her fingernails, but the red didn't seem flashy; it was just an early 1950's fashion trend.

My mother looked especially pretty in her orchid maternity dress and matching orchid shoes. Often when we sat together, she lifted her maternity top and revealed the skirt's round, cut-out and open section, with a drawstring that tied just above the tiny growing mound inside her. We made eye contact and smiled when she reached out, took my hand, covered it with hers, and guided it across the silkiness of her exposed slip's blue-white fabric. I was filled with wonder each time my tiny hand slid over the kicking baby who lived right on the other side.

The sound of my mother's laughter and her easy smile filled me with a sense of genuine love.

Everything wasn't beautiful and picture-perfect, though. Many of my memories also include my father's ever-present and repulsive smell of liquor that was usually accompanied by his loud voice and some form of violence. My father physically and verbally abused my mother, my older twin brothers Anthony and Levi, and me. His sort of violent behavior, however, seemed to be a somewhat common and accepted—but hushed—part of society in the 1950s.

At the time of our mother's death, Anthony and Levi were six; I was less than three; and Samantha, whom we dubbed Sammie, was six weeks old. Daddy was a young man, barely more than a child himself, when my mother's death suddenly left him with four young children for whom he was totally and solely responsible. Of course, it was particularly difficult for my father to deal with that reality, but no matter how hard he tried to escape, no amount of anger, booze, or violence could change the fact that, at the age of twenty-five, he *must* find a way to deal with that tremendous amount of responsibility for which he was totally unprepared. He surely was terrified to look into his uncertain future, especially since his life so unexpectedly had taken such a dramatic and tragic turn from the one he'd anticipated.

Somehow, it turned out that we all moved in with my paternal grandparents, Kate and Isaac Hunter, whom we children affectionately called Granny and Pappy. Given Daddy's circumstances, coupled with his understandable lack of parenting skills and his sporadic periods of employment and unemployment, it seemed we were all financially and emotionally better off living with Granny and Pappy Hunter. Unfortunately, Daddy was at odds with whomever he made his home.

Pappy earned what could be considered a middle-income salary at a locally based utility company, but his position often kept him on the road and away from home much of the workweek, and by the time the five of us moved into their home on the farm, Granny was committed to an already established and quite time-consuming general store business.

For the first three years following my mother's death, our primary home was with Granny and Pappy Hunter. During those summer months when my brothers didn't attend school, however, if things didn't go as our usually volatile father wanted, and even though we didn't understand why, he headed us kids toward his old beat-up and rusty truck and drove us off to the home of our maternal grandmother "The Widow Maddie Robinson." Then, when things didn't go Daddy's way at Grandma Maddie's, he loaded us kids back into his old beat-up and rusty truck, drove us away, and we all went back to live with Granny and Pappy Hunter.

Our grandparents were concerned for our well-being and eager to help, so our swinging-door relocations were treated as unobtrusive, even though our moves definitely meant major lifestyle changes for everyone who unexpectedly and without question became involved—and the frequent and irrational anger-spurred moves definitely exacted an emotional toll.

After my mother's death, I developed a strong bond with Grandma Maddie and believed that, if given the choice, I'd prefer to live with her. But, when faced with the actuality of that situation shortly before I turned six, my decision turned out much differently than I would have predicted.

~~I placed the old black-and-white photo in my album, reached into my box of pictures, and pulled out one that had been taken in Grandma Maddie's backyard, where I stood with one leg lifted and bent at the knee, and with my right arm proudly wrapped around a shiny dimpled baton. My siblings and I had spent that entire summer with Daddy at Grandma

Maddie's because he'd found a reason to be extremely angry with Granny and Pappy Hunter, and his retaliation was to yank us from their presence. Our lengthy stay at Grandma Maddie's led me to believe we'd made a permanent move, but I was wrong. That summer, I found it necessary to make one of the most difficult decisions of my life.

CHAPTER THREE

It was the year I was slated to start first grade, and it was also one of those days when we were still at Grandma Maddie's. It seemed that Grandma Maddie, who looked like an only slightly older version of my mother, had been delegated on that late summer's day to have a chat with us children. She gathered us near her in the coziness of her neat-as-a-pin living room where rays of sun easily found their way through the sparkling glass of the windows and bounced off the linoleum's pattern of red-and-pink flowers on a light gray background. The sunshine made the room seem even more glistening and clean, but our arrival caused a few dust particles to dare to dance in the beams of light.

Grandma Maddie sat on the gray-and-red vinyl sofa that had come from what we'd known as our home with Mommy, and in the center of a soft and fuzzy gray throw rug was the little gray enamel-painted coffee table that also had been passed along from our mother's living room three years earlier. Sammie leaned against the sofa and clung with one hand to

Grandma Maddie's knee, and we three older children sat on the floor, with our crossed legs partially resting on the soft rug that covered a small section of the shiny linoleum, and our bottoms rested on the coolness of the floor.

When she saw that we were finally settled, Grandma Maddie slowly and very carefully began her explanation, and it looked like she was trying not to cry. "I want you kids to know that I love you all very much, and nothing will ever change that, but this situation in which you're sporadically moved from one place to another must stop. Along with your daddy, your other grandparents and I have discussed this situation at great length. Cassie is to be enrolled in the first grade soon, so it's time for us to make some necessary decisions. The main thing right now is to determine with whom you kids prefer to live so you can be enrolled in the proper school."

The presence of the sunshine suddenly seemed out of place, and I squinted in response to the defiantly bright light. My stomach slowly tightened into a knot. The necessity for a decision seemed to be relevant to the beginning of the new school year, and because it was I who was starting to school for the first time, I somehow felt responsible for what was about to happen.

My brothers had already attended school for a few years, and we hadn't been questioned about our living preferences during those previous years, so I didn't understand why my entrance into first grade warranted giving us a voice in where we settled. As much as I loved the sound of Grandma Maddie's voice, I didn't want her to continue, but she did.

"Anthony and Levi, you attended first grade in Maple Grove. After your mother passed away, you moved in with your other grandparents and transferred to second grade in Bookerton. You might remember some of the kids with whom you attended first grade here in Maple Grove, but we adults understand that it might be difficult for you to leave the friends with whom you've attended school for the past three years. I've been asked to explain to you that if you decide to stay with me, you will all be enrolled in school at Maple Grove. If you prefer to move back to your other grandparents' home, then arrangements must be made to enroll Cassie in school at Bookerton. We agree the decision should be yours, and you must know that—whatever you decide—it will be all right. We'll always love you, and we want you to believe that none of us will be hurt by your decision. We want what's best for you. We want you to be happy and to feel secure." Her lips trembled as she forced a smile.

I sat still, kept as quiet as possible, and silently hoped that a unanimous decision would be reached to stay with Grandma Maddie. Over the years, I'd overheard several loudly whispered and often heated family discussions that included my father, so I knew finances were a concern, and it was the consensus that a widowed grandmother couldn't financially compete with grandparents who had two incomes. An almost ten-year-old Anthony began. "I love you, Grandma Maddie, but you know I love Granny and Pappy Hunter, too." He stopped talking and looked at Levi, who nodded and took the lead.

"Me and Anthony have already talked about this stuff, Grandma Maddie. It's like Anthony said. We do love you, but, well, we'd really like to go back to Bookerton." In an effort not to hurt her, he was determined to give her a plausible excuse, but at the age of ten he wasn't proficient with his reasoning. "Well, shoot, we have buddies there—and, anyway, most of our stuff is still at Granny and Pappy Hunter's. You know Daddy takes us from one place to the other so fast that we don't ever have time to get all our stuff."

A tear spilled from Grandma Maddie's eye, and she tilted her head and looked away.

My heart ached when Sammie, who'd recently turned three, spoke with as much decisiveness as she could muster, and she made no excuses. "I wanna go home. I miss Gwanny and Pappy Hunnew. I miss my bed an' aw my stuff. Pweeze. I wanna go home."

Her tiny body slowly slumped, almost as if it were suddenly punctured and developed a slow leak. Her quivering chin dropped to her chest, and after a slight whimpering sound that resembled that of a puppy that'd recently been weaned and taken from its mother, she lifted her eyelids, looked over at us three siblings, and added her final plea. "Pweeze, pweeze, I weally wanna go back home," she begged. It nearly broke my heart.

I looked at Anthony and Levi's little round, slightly smudged and freckled faces with their outlines of chestnut-brown curls that reminded me of our mother's hair. Anthony's glossy black cowboy hat came to a stop somewhere around the middle of his ears and was held tightly in place with a black twine rope. A black wooden cylinder that encased the ends of the rope was pressed snuggly under his chin. Levi's matching cowboy hat hung around his neck by its twine rope and rested on his back, between his shoulders. Their matching blue-and-white plaid shirts were neatly buttoned, and their shirttails were shoved down inside their slightly oversize jeans. The stiff legs of their indigo pants were rolled up twice, and the boys' fake-leather holster belts that each held a pair of fake-pearl-handled silver-colored six-shooters, gathered the waists of their jeans all around their middles and held them up a little too high above the boys' waistlines.

Their black-and-red cowboy boots were covered with the brown dust they'd stirred up outside while they played the parts of carefree cowboys who rode their wild mop- and broom-stallions, just shortly before they were called in to make one of the most important decisions of their young lives. They tried to look grown-up, but they looked exactly like the ten-year-olds they were, and it was clear that my brothers desperately wanted to settle comfortably where they were most familiar and had close friends.

I glanced over at Sammie. She wore a yellow flowered sun suit with rows of ruffles that covered her bottom. Her white cotton panties peeked out from beneath one side of her sun suit's elasticized leg hole. The tender skin on the tip of her pug nose, cheeks, and shoulders was bright pink from a little too much exposure to the sun, and freckles seemed to sprout from those pink areas. She was barefoot and stood just a little pigeon-toed. Against her face, she held her white blankie, which had been washed and bleached so often and finger-rubbed and dragged around for so long, that it had taken on the appearance of being totally constructed of thousands of tiny, white fuzz-balls. Her thumb lay comfortably inside the warm confines of her mouth, where Sammie seemed determined to powerfully suck the juices from it, and when she chose to remove it, her wrinkled thumb nearly always looked like a long bleached prune. Her index finger wrapped across the freckles on her shiny pink sunburned nose. The finger's pressure slightly pulled her eyebrows downward and caused her eyes to be forced out of their normally rounded shape. She'd recently awakened from a nap, and one side of her nearly white, fine, and wispy baby hair floated in all directions, almost as if someone had rubbed her head with a balloon and the static electricity had taken over. Her pouty lips surrounded her thumb, and she made subtle sucking sounds. Her huge tear-filled eyes held the unmistakable hope to return to the only mother she'd ever known. She was truly vulnerable.

I loved my brothers and sister and knew we couldn't be separated. We'd already suffered too much loss and uncertainty, and the one constant we needed was that we could depend on each other. At the age of less than six, I needed to believe we would always be together and that nothing would ever change that. As much as I loved Grandma Maddie and wanted to stay with her, I also loved Granny and Pappy Hunter and shared Grandma Maddie's wish that my siblings would be happy.

The ache in my heart at the point of leaving Grandma Maddie couldn't compare with the resulting devastation to my soul if I weren't with my brothers and sister. My own desire couldn't override the desires of my siblings. Deep within my being, I also knew the ultimate decision wasn't mine. Regardless of whether or not I was outnumbered, I wouldn't expect any one of those three to sacrifice for me. At that precise moment, I realized the true meaning of self-sacrifice.

In my young mind I knew what must be done and heard my own decisive voice. "I'll go back to Bookerton." I didn't say it was what I wanted to do; I just said I'd do it. My little-girl heart almost stopped beating at the very thought of leaving Grandma Maddie, and my body literally trembled and wrenched inside. Too soon after we arrived at our decision, and just shortly before the time I was to enter first grade, Daddy loaded us back into his old beat-up and rusty truck and moved us back to Granny and Pappy Hunter's.

~~I placed the majorette-wannabe picture in the album and rummaged around in the box until I found a picture of Pappy and Granny Hunter. In that picture, they wore gardening clothes. His head was covered with an old familiar felt hat. Granny's head was protected by a wide-brimmed straw hat with a ribbon that tied under her chin. Pappy's left arm was lovingly wrapped around Granny's shoulders, and her right arm wrapped around the back of his waist. They looked content, but I didn't need a picture to remind me of how much I knew they'd loved each other, or of how much I'd truly loved them.

CHAPTER FOUR

Pappy's job took him away on frequent business trips, and Granny was committed to her business for several years prior to our first temporary live-in arrangement. It was a plus that The Bookerton General Store was situated on the property directly across the road from her house, but Granny tended the store and took care of paperwork on evenings and weekends, until long after most folks had gone to bed. Because of their busy schedules and prior commitments, each time our father arrived at their home with four youngsters, my grandparents found it necessary to immediately hire household help for those times during which we shared their home. In their efforts to protect us children and to make life easier for everyone involved, all three grandparents made whatever transitions were necessary to oblige Daddy's ever-changing moods.

In the 1950s, many local girls who'd finished high school were eager to become employed as live-in help until they married and had their own homes. For us, that meant that until their residences became more permanent, or until we children were taken from the Hunter home and moved to the Robinson home, numerous young women entered and exited our lives. We became emotionally attached to some of our live-in baby sitters and, when those girls or we children moved out, it was difficult to say good-bye.

Frequent good-byes were the norm, however, until upon our apparently more decisive and permanent move in 1956 when our grandparents hired a widowed Olivia Schultz, who left her own child with his grandmother and moved into our Hunter household. Because Granny was so busy at the store, and because Pappy's work often required that he be away from home for several days at a time, much of our schedule was supervised by Olivia, who soon became another mother figure to us.

When Pappy returned from his frequent business trips, we grandkids were absolutely delighted with his loving presence. We developed a welcome-home ritual in which we children huddled around our grandfather while he rummaged and searched through the folds of wrinkled clothing in what he called his gripsack.

We waited, with great anticipation, while he made quite expressive faces and fretted over an imaginary problem. "I surely haven't *forgotten* it. Hmm! I *thought* I had it with me. I surely didn't *misplace* it. No! I *know* I put it in here. Oh, my goodness, I hope I didn't *lose* it!"

We expectant gift recipients weren't really worried, though. We smelled cinnamon from the time Pappy started his search, but we always went along with the big dramatic production and absolutely writhed with anticipation. We decidedly amateur Thespians displayed our most dramatic and seriously worried looks, wrung our grubby hands, leaned closer and closer over Pappy's gripsack, stretched our scrawny necks in all directions, and expressed our deepest concern for Pappy's absentmindedness, until those long red pungent sticks were in our greedy and grateful hands.

"No! Here it is!" he'd announce.

Then with an exaggerated sigh of relief and, with his head thrown back, he lifted his eyes toward the heavens as he pulled out a glossy, wrinkled, almost wrapping-paper brittle and crackling brown paper sack with its tiny-notched-edge top carefully twisted around its secret contents of bright red cinnamon stick candy for each of us. We knew he hadn't forgotten. We knew he'd never forget.

Because of that memory: Cinnamon often simmers in my potpourri pot and cinnamon-scented candles burn throughout my home, because the aroma provides me with a gentle comfort in its constant and subtle reminder of a special time with my beloved grandfather, Isaac Hunter, a man I truly adored.

Our usual routine, whether Pappy had worked away that week or not, was that most Friday nights he drove Olivia to her mother's home and drove us kids to Grandma Maddie's. Pappy returned home and spent weekend time with Granny. On Sunday nights Pappy picked up us kids and Olivia, and we returned to Bookerton to start the next week of school and business, but I always looked forward to my upcoming Friday nights and weekends with Grandma Maddie, and I relished the time we spent together.

During the summer months when there was no school, we helped at Granny's general store, but when business was a little slow, we were allowed to have friends visit, or we were allowed to visit friends. We had a one-hour per week time limit with each other, and even though our contact was minimal, I had playmates with whom I'd eventually attend first grade in 1956. Barring the occasional spat, we usually had quality playtime for that tremendously appreciated one hour during the week.

When I played with my friends, I was impressed with any doll that still had her original hair and had somehow escaped the child-mother/amateur-beautician's wrath of the scissors that made less fortunate dolls have endless bad hair days. I was also amazed with my own doll that wet her diaper, and was even more amazed when I found some of her clothes that weren't mildewed as a result. I was delighted to have access to my household's perpetual rag bag, where I retrieved old pieces of cloth that I folded into scarves and diapers for my fuzzy-headed, pants-wetting doll, and I was proud to share the contents of that rag bag with my friends for their dolls. We used our imaginations, talked to those little molded chunks of rubber and plastic, and pretended that they responded.

When we played, we squealed and screamed, ran and jumped, and laughed and cried. We had times when we quarreled and just as many times that we reconciled.

We weren't accused of being hyperactive or pumped full of prescription drugs, and we weren't taken to psychiatrists. Of course, there were a few exceptions to the rule, but most of our parents and grandparents taught—and we children were expected to learn and practice—the differences between acceptable and unacceptable behavior. We also learned the limitations and possible consequences of our actions. Adults cared about us, took time to act as authority figures, and made every effort to instill in each of us: good moral values, a sense of responsibility, and a sense of direction. But, even with all that support and guidance, I was still a little apprehensive about my entrance into first grade.

~~I placed the picture of my grandparents in the album, and because I was reminded of my first school year, I searched through the pictures in my box until I found one that was taken at the bus stop on my first day of school. Even though the bus-stop picture was a lovely historical marker for that day, it was also a reminder of one of my most embarrassing moments.

CHAPTER FIVE

When my first day of school arrived, I had mixed feelings of excitement and fear. The excitement was caused by the fact that I was wearing new clothes and shoes. Previously, unless a major event occurred, store-bought clothes were reserved for Easter Sunday, my birthday, and Christmas. That morning, I wore a brand-new pair of white cotton panties, a brand-new shiny cotton petticoat with a ruffled skirt and a tiny pink bow stitched right in the middle of the upper chest, a brand-new red dress with white trim, brand-new white anklets with a red lace ruffle, and a brand-new pair of black patent-leather shoes.

Before I was allowed to step outside, Granny stood behind me for what seemed like hours, rubbed a small dab of petroleum jelly into my white-blond hair until it glistened, built a head full of banana curls, and added a long, red, grosgrain ribbon to my hair. It was a chilly September morning, so Granny made sure I wore my new red cardigan with its shiny red plastic buttons, and she pulled the white collar of my dress to the outside of the sweater's neckline. I stared into the mirror and thought I looked beautiful.

Granny insisted that my brothers wait for me, but as soon as I got near them Anthony and Levi bolted through the kitchen's screen door like a couple of race horses that had just heard the starting bell at the Kentucky Derby. I held out a hand and caught the door a mere millisecond before its spring snapped it back and smacked me in the face, and when I opened my eyes, it was evident I'd have to high-tail it if I hoped to catch the other Derby contenders. My shoes had slick soles, and Grandma shouted out dire warnings about not ruining my fancy banana-curled hair, so I saw little chance of my racing at a rate of speed to close the gap between the galloping steeds and myself. It was also quite evident that my brothers intended to stay far in the lead. Much to my dismay, Sammie and Granny followed me out of the "starting gate" and across the yard toward the bus stop.

As I tried my best to narrow the distance between us, I overheard Anthony complain to Levi: "Man! I can't believe this. It looks like the Hunters are gonna hold a family reunion at the bus stop."

"We'll just act like we don't know 'em," Levi groaned. "Ignore 'em. Sammie and Granny are only comin' 'cause o' Cassie."

"Well, I hope they don't stay long, and I'm tellin' you right now, I'm gonna die if Granny brought her camera."

"Don't make any threats you don't wanna keep," warned Levi, " 'cause she has it with her."

Even though I was embarrassed nearly beyond belief, I think it was much worse for Anthony and Levi. At the age of ten, they most certainly were totally humiliated even at the prospect of the upcoming fiasco.

As if the looming threat of Granny's camera action weren't bad enough, Sammie added to the spectacle.

She sucked her thumb, rubbed the bridge of her nose, clung to her ratty old blankie, cried, tried to talk with her mouth full of thumb, ran along, and tried to close that gap I struggled to keep between us.

"I don't want Cassie to weave me! I wanna go to school wif Cassie!"

With each step I took, it sounded to me like Sammie's cries became shriller and louder. She sounded almost as if she were operating a police car's siren and was hot on my heels. There was absolutely no chance of ignoring her pleas.

I finally made it to the bus stop and stepped to the end of the line of kids who'd already gathered for the bus. Just as Anthony had predicted, it looked like a Hunter family reunion. But, it also looked as if our reunion group had invaded some sort of an anti-reunion group of protesters. The other kids at the bus stop were not impressed with our invasion and gave us their severest sourpuss looks of displeasure.

I couldn't stop what was coming and thought that being more embarrassed was impossible, but Granny quickly changed that thought when she took each anti-reunion protester by the shoulders and moved and repositioned the kid around in line to where she thought was that particular kid's right spot for the makings of a perfect picture. She blared out instructions, just as if she were everyone's grandmother.

"Now, Freddie Junior, don't make faces. You stand up straight."

She took a reluctant Susie by the hand and repositioned her. "Susie, you smile really pretty, now." Susie instantly obeyed the command to smile, but it wasn't pretty. In snotty retaliation, she exhibited her fakest smile—more of a sneer.

Benny was put in his right spot and was actually scolded. "Here, here, Benny! Don't you put your fingers up behind Kathie's head! You behave yourself!" Benny knew he'd better put those fingers back down, and he did, but he didn't look very happy about it.

After Granny had us all perfectly positioned, she began her picture-taking process. She fumbled with the square box and couldn't seem to decide whether or not she needed a flashbulb. She mumbled and asked herself all sorts of sky-condition and photography-technique questions. We kids, who faced through the light fog and toward the morning sun, squinted our eyes, wrinkled our noses, glared, fumed, and grumbled. Granny focused, voiced a few more instructions on being patient, and re-checked the sun's position, almost as if she actually expected that it might give up on us and move to another bus stop. She snapped shots with an installed flashbulb, removed the hot, gray-bubbled bulb, juggled it around between her hand and the air, and just in case the use of a flashbulb had been a wrong choice, she then insisted that we all wait while she snapped shots without the flashbulb. It was my strongest desire to be as inconspicuous as possible, but it was a rather difficult task, especially because I'd been followed to the bus stop by a thumb-sucking, whining sister, and a flashbulb-flashing granny who boisterously and several times commanded: "Everyone say cheese!"

The last thing I wanted was for my pedal pusher and tennis shoe wearing, unprofessional photographer grandmother to be snapping pictures as she announced to every school-aged kid who lived within my bus-stop area, "This is Cassie's first day of school, you know!"

Those kids whom Granny had forcefully lined up already knew I was new at the bus stop, and they didn't care. Even though we lived in a small town and those kids were my neighbors and playmates, I noticed that, at the bus stop that morning, most of them were definitely upperclassmen who had little time and patience for all the hoopla. Everyone, except the photographer and the photographer's thumb-sucking and blankie-dragging assistant, was relieved when the bus finally arrived. I was on my way to school!

I felt a little guilty when I didn't respond to Granny and Sammie, who stood at the edge of the road throwing kisses and waving their arms in all directions until the bus was out of sight.

I didn't know what to expect when I stepped on the school bus, and I surely didn't know what to expect when it was time to step off. As a passenger in our family's car, I'd ridden past the schoolhouse several times and was familiar with its formidable red brick structure, but until I stepped off the bus and onto the wide concrete walkway that was filled with scores of people from several age groups, I didn't realize just how intimidating entering that formidable structure actually was.

I stood in a sort of daze. My eyes moved up-and-down and from side-to-side as I tried to take in the whole picture. I had no idea where I was supposed to go, so I just stood there. People walked around me as if I were a tree. I was ready to cry, and was probably about ready to wet my pants, when Anthony and Levi came to my rescue. I'm not sure whether they wanted to help, or if they just didn't want my navigational ignorance to embarrass them in front of their friends, but without a word, they motioned for me to follow and led me inside the building.

Stepping into the building from the sunlight temporarily blinded me, and my sense of smell took over while my pupils dilated. My nostrils were immediately filled with dry stale air and an unforgettable odor of stagnant oil. Eventually, my eyes adjusted to the change of light, and I saw that the walls were painted, or had acquired, a sort of beige color. In sharp contrast to the beige walls and ceiling were dark oiled wooden floors, wide dark baseboards and door trim, and stairs with matching dark wooden railings and banisters. Huge dark wooden doors with tarnished-brass number plates identified each classroom. Anthony and Levi silently led me to the first-grade classroom and sort of shoved me through the door with the tarnished plate that clearly identified it as #1.

In contrast to the darkness of the hallway, the light was nearly overpowering in the classroom. Two walls were covered with enormous windows that nearly reached the ceiling. Tan, brittle looking paper blinds were pulled down to the center rail of each window. Some blinds were marked with unattractive water stains, and some were even torn. A few windows were open to allow for air circulation, so the classroom air was somewhat less stuffy than the hallway air. Several large white light globes hung low into the room, and although they were attached to long black pipes that were fastened to the high ceiling, the globes looked almost like white balloons suspended in midair. Blackboards with chalk- and eraser-filled troughs covered most of the area on a third wall. The fourth wall had two openings that provided an entrance and an exit on each end of what I later discovered was the cloakroom.

The room contained the teacher's wooden desk and chair that were placed in a cater-cornered position. Three long wooden tables, each with ten little wooden chairs around it, filled the majority of the floor space. I hesitated when I stepped into the room, and Mrs. Millie Smith noticed my hesitancy.

"Come in, dear, and have a seat anywhere there's an empty chair. I'll assign seats later."

My first day of school turned out to be a great disappointment. The day tediously wore on. Something was wrong. Had my brothers led me to the wrong classroom? If not, I'd surely been assigned to the wrong teacher. As far as I was concerned, Miss Millie, as we were instructed to address her, wasn't doing her job. She wasn't teaching me how to read, and I was confused about that. Learning to read was the only reason I even wanted to attend school.

I loved to touch books, to look at the pictures, and to invent my own stories. I loved it when someone read to me and allowed me to escape into those books. I was a friend to those main characters and knew their families and friends. I was in those homes and dreamed of owning those magical toys. I knew those animals and recognized those trains and automobiles. I remembered and learned from those morals and lessons. I even liked to smell my books. So when I started to first grade, I expected to learn to read! I just didn't know it was going to take so long.

On that first day of school, I was fully aware and somewhat disappointed that Miss Millie didn't even ask whether or not I'd learned how to say and recognize the letters of the alphabet, whether or not I'd learned to print my very own name, or whether or not I'd learned how to count fairly well for a kid who'd just shown up for her first day of school. She didn't even *ask* if I *wanted* to learn to read. She seemed more interested in seating us students in alphabetical order and having us introduce ourselves. In my opinion, too much time was wasted on the explanation of classroom rules and expectations, and with the explanation of recess rules and expectations. That wasn't why I was there. I had my own expectations.

When it was time for us to go out for recess, I nearly dreaded it. I was afraid I might be overlooked as a playmate. I was afraid everyone else might ignore my presence on the playground, and I'd be left to face it all alone—whatever "it" was. Time spent on the playground, however, wasn't as bad as I'd anticipated, and playtime quickly ended.

When we returned from recess, I was sure that Miss Millie would get down to the business of teaching me how to read, but she didn't. She just filled the time with a bunch of talk, and she read us a couple stories. I'd already figured Miss Millie knew how to read, and I wondered why she wanted to keep the magic and the mystery of reading all to herself. That afternoon, I resigned myself to the idea that it might be awhile until Miss Millie discovered she had a teaching job ahead of her.

Fueled by disappointment, I realized how truly lost I felt without the embarrassing duo from the bus stop and would have given almost anything to be home with them. In my lonesome, frightened, and homesick heart, they were forgiven for their early morning behavior.

After a few more days at school, we started printing our names on wide-ruled tablets, using bright yellow #2 lead pencils. It was important to Miss Millie that we were able to write our first, middle, and last names. I didn't have a middle name, so I assigned myself made-up names. From time to time, I borrowed the name of a family member or a friend, because, between writing sessions, I forgot what name I'd previously used. I probably invented names that were misspelled and invalid, too, but Miss Millie didn't say anything to me about it, so I supposed she thought it was all right—or maybe she just thought I was a little strange.

Miss Millie became obsessed with teaching us how to print the letters of the alphabet, how to form and spell words, and how to write numbers. She failed to notice, however, that I wanted her to teach me how to read. I wondered if Miss Millie even knew her students couldn't read, because when she finally discovered that some of us could already write our names when we arrived at school, she might have thought we already knew how to read, too. I didn't have the nerve to ask her about it, though.

Eventually, after what seemed like an eternity of that printing business and putting those printed letters into little formed words, and after going over and over and over them, Miss Millie finally issued each of us a book about a couple of kids named Dick and Jane, and their dog named Spot, but it seemed that all they did was run. There surely was more to reading than reading about a boy who ran, a girl who ran, a dog that ran, and those kids who ran after the dog as the dog ran. Another odd thing was the author's insistence that everyone *see* them run. I hoped there was more to reading than that!

I wasn't spending much time on learning to read anything of much significance, so I concentrated on developing my friendships. Even though our contact had been minimal and some of us were friends even before we entered first grade, during school class periods we made eye contact, exchanged shy smiles, and shared hushed whispers. We developed friendships at a time when it was all right to hug, to hold hands, and to put our arms around each other as we spent precious time together during recess and lunch periods. It was a time when brand names of clothes didn't impress us. Most of us wore clothes that were homemade, hand-me-downs, or homemade-hand-me-downs. We were impressed, however, with books, sharpened #2 lead pencils, new tablets with our names boldly printed on the front covers, thick coloring books, and boxes of crayons with two sections that held more colors than we'd ever imagined. My friends and I had our own little world of friendship, and we looked forward to our time together.

~~I smiled as I positioned the bus-stop photo in the album and reached into my treasure-filled box. I pulled out a picture that happened to show me sitting on my daddy's lap, but I don't remember that ever happening. That's sad.

CHAPTER SIX

Some of my memories are filled with confusion, disbelief, and wonder. They're muddled memories of events from a child's point of view and could be accurate assessments, or they could be assessments clouded by fear and misunderstanding. As I remember it, though, my father stayed with us in the home of my grandparents until I was about seven or eight years old. I don't remember what set him off, but one afternoon Daddy lost his temper, grabbed me by the arm, and literally beat me into a merciful unconsciousness. It might have been worse, but as I later learned, Anthony and Levi acted as a team and jumped to my defense. They bit and pulled at our father until he came to his senses and stopped his rampage.

When I eventually awoke to the downstairs sound of loud voices and to an almost unbearable pain, I realized that my grandmother apparently had been summoned for help and attended to my needs. I lay in bed on my tummy, looked over my shoulder, and saw the bruises and bumps that covered my unclothed back, bottom, and legs. I wondered what I'd done to cause such a commotion. I knew people wouldn't do such horrendous things to those whom they loved, and I wondered why my daddy hated me so much. I felt guilty for causing his outrage and thought that if I knew what I'd done wrong, I'd never do it again. Sadly, I didn't know what it was.

Literally within hours after that incident, Daddy moved out of his parents' home, and I'd guess Granny and Pappy must have insisted that their hotheaded son leave before a more serious tragedy occurred, especially because his numerous tirades seemed to worsen with each occurrence. I didn't ask where he was, and nobody discussed it with me. Somehow, though, without understanding why, I felt guilty—and responsible for his disappearance.

Once or twice a year after Daddy's relocation, he dropped by our home for short uncomfortable periods of time. During those visits, he didn't associate much with us kids, but I don't think he really knew how to talk with us. Daddy may have wondered whether his presence would be accepted, whether anyone remembered things he wasn't proud of having done, and whether Granny and Pappy Hunter would welcome him. He needn't have wondered.

Even though his actions were often less than admirable, and in spite of the fact that he never showed up without smelling like the contents of a whiskey bottle, Granny and Pappy were glad to see him and welcomed him with open arms—arms that he avoided like the plague.

Anthony, Levi, Sammie, and I always hoped he was glad to see us, and I think we all shared an unspoken hope that, during the time since his last visit with us, Daddy had somehow seen the light. Then as suddenly and as mysteriously as to why he had come, he was gone. What remained were a miserable silence, an almost unbearable disappointment that was filled with questioning glances, a longing for his acceptance and love, and the hope that Daddy's next visit would be sober, loving, forgiving, and filled with laughter.

Several times between each of my father's visits, I adjusted the three-way vanity mirror in my bedroom, stood in front of it, and looked at myself to see what it was about me that, as many folks had said, looked like my mother. My hair color wasn't like my mother's; my own hair was almost white, rather than dark brown. But, I had inherited my mother's genes for curls and round hazel eyes. If I really looked like my mother, shouldn't my daddy be pleased to see me? What did I look like to him? Did he even see me? What were his thoughts about me and my siblings?

While standing in front of the mirror, I self-consciously practiced smiling and saying, "Hi, Daddy." What did it sound like to him when he heard the word Daddy? Because of its seldom use, the word sounded almost foreign to me. With childhood vulnerability and innocence, I believed that if I tried hard enough—even with our adverse circumstances—I could eventually please and be loved by my father. I think it almost happened once—not so much that I pleased him—but that maybe he at least *wanted* to love me.

At some point, our grandparents took us kids to a carnival in a city about thirty miles from home. We were all surprised when we ran into Daddy, but probably not nearly as surprised as he was. At Granny and Pappy's insistence, Daddy was either shamed or forced into joining our little family for the exciting carnival experience. We eventually decided to split up and head in different directions. Pappy took the boys; Granny took Sammie; and Daddy ended up with me. It's the only time I remember that my father spent any time alone with me. As we walked around together over the trampled and ankle-twisting ground, I wondered how many people who saw us realized I was his little girl. I hoped he was as proud as I was.

We stopped to look at some junky stuff at a booth, and the man inside suddenly leaped forward and startled me when he thrust a long stick toward Daddy's face and shouted: "Step right up! Step right up!" The barker, whom I thought of as Carnival Man waved the stick around in the air, and the red-and-white striped sleeve of his jacket fanned around in the wind he stirred with his rapid arm movement. His white straw hat sported a red band that matched his huge red bow tie. His white pants and shoes were almost totally covered with beige dust and grit. His voice was so loud, and his actions were so exaggerated, that I actually was frightened by his flamboyant behavior. Carnival Man continued to yell: "Step right up! Step right up!" He boldly waved and thrust the offending stick toward my father's face and repeated his chant.

Daddy didn't flinch, and he didn't seem the least bit surprised by Carnival Man's flamboyant behavior, but I was. I jumped back and to the side and landed almost directly behind my father. When I collected my wits and was able to focus, I leaned to the side, and while holding onto his belt loops, I peeked around Daddy's waist and saw that on the end of the offending stick was a top-knotted doll with a little round tummy.

It sounded to me like Carnival Man was positive that Daddy would want one of those dolls on a stick, and in a voice that had more highs and lows and more reverberations than I had ever heard, he forcefully insisted that Daddy try to win one. He was definitely persistent in his pursuit of that proverbial sucker who's born every minute.

My daddy just bravely laughed at Carnival Man's persistence, looked down at me, and his eyes met mine. I was confused by a trace of something I saw. For a split-second, I thought I recognized and captured a look of unmistakable sorrow and regret. I like to think of that as the time I also might have glimpsed a look of love. Daddy's normally uncaring behavior was betrayed by that fleeting look in his eyes, and that obviously uncomfortable and fleeting look made me think that he, too, wished our lives had turned out differently. Our eyes didn't move. They didn't blink. I smiled. I think he knew what I thought I'd seen, and he actually returned my smile. In that tiny amount of time it took for me to savor the unexpected experience, the carnival disappeared, and I felt like my daddy and I were the only two people on earth. It didn't last long. The spell was broken when Daddy turned his head in response to Carnival Man's annoying banter.

Daddy looked back up at Carnival Man, reached behind himself, pulled me back around, and held me close against his side. He kept a protective arm around my shoulders, and I was warmed by his words. "I don't need to win a Kewpie doll. This is my little Kewpie doll."

Even though I had no idea what a Kewpie doll was, I thought I should be proud that my father had said I was one—especially because Carnival Man seemed so convinced that a Kewpie doll was such a wonderful and sought-after prize. It's strange, but our eye contact and smiles, combined with my father's remark to a total stranger at a carnival, made my little-girl heart warm and formed the only good memory I have of being with my father—but, it's something.

At some point, probably when I was about ten or eleven years old, Granny and Pappy called my siblings and me in from outdoors and requested that we sit at the kitchen table. We knew there must be something serious to discuss, because it wasn't time to eat. As we scrambled around and scooted out chairs, Granny had an unfamiliar look on her face, and in spite of the racket we made, she said, "Pappy and I have some news for you."

Granny's look told me her news was serious, but her voice was soft and slightly broken. "Kids, settle down, now. We have something important to discuss with you. We just received a call from your father. He told us that he recently remarried."

We sat in silence for a few seconds, until Anthony boldly asked The Big Question. "Does this mean we're going to live with Daddy and his new wife?"

Granny and Pappy looked at each other, and I couldn't exactly interpret the strange looks in their eyes. Then Pappy took the monkey off Granny's back. "Well, I'll tell you what, dear: We don't know. If we did know, we wouldn't try to hide anything from you. I'm sorry, but I can't tell you what will happen. We really just don't know. We'll have to take this as we take everything else—one day at a time."

"When your dad called and told us he'd remarried," added Granny, "I invited him and his new bride to the house for dinner on Saturday night, and he accepted the invitation." She looked pleased that he'd agreed to come.

Just having our father at the house for dinner would seem strange enough. Since he'd moved from the house, he never sat down to another meal with us, but I thought that having him there with his new bride would be exciting and romantic. Granny talked right over my thoughts, and I didn't know what I'd missed, but when my attention returned to reality, I heard: "Now when your father and Barbara arrive, we want you kids to be on your best behavior. We've never met Barbara, and we want to make a favorable impression. Your daddy and Barbara will be nervous, and we want to make them feel at home." We nodded our understanding—what there was of it.

The following days of the week were filled with anticipation as we planned and prepared for our special dinner guests. We planned the menu. We planned what we'd wear. We planned what we'd say, even though we knew we'd never actually say it. And, we counted the days. Olivia scrubbed and scoured, waxed and buffed, and made sure the house sparkled before she left on Friday night for her weekend off.

Saturday finally arrived, and Granny didn't even work at the store. She spent the entire day at the house. She supervised and organized the family in the preparation of the dining room. It was almost as if President and Mrs. Eisenhower were coming. We laid out our clothes and counted the hours.

When the projected dinner hour was nearly upon us—the simmering pot roast with an abundance of potatoes and carrots, bacon-seasoned home-grown half-runner beans, homemade cloverleaf rolls, and homemade cinnamon-apple pies released warm aromas of what we knew represented a future explosion of taste-bud delights.

We dressed and made the final preparations. The hand-crocheted lace tablecloth that, many years earlier, had been crafted with skill and love by Granny's stepmother Effie, was carefully centered and spread over the mahogany gate-leg table. Earlier in the day, I'd been assigned to iron, fold, and crease the white linen napkins into triangular shapes, and when the tablecloth was in place, I carried those crisp napkins from the ironing board and carefully stacked them on the corner of the table, until Granny told me exactly where to place them.

We all worked diligently together and set the table with the good dishes that had been treasured and lovingly handed down through generations of Granny's family. That set of dishes was exclusively reserved for very special occasions. Each plate was covered with hundreds of painted miniature red roses that almost looked as if they'd recently been kissed with early morning dew, and each rose literally glistened against its ivory background.

Pappy swung open the seldom-used doors on the bottom of the dining room's built-in mahogany corner hutch. He lifted a cherry-wood chest from the middle shelf and opened the lid. We "oohed" and "aahed" over the brilliant contents that lay upon the burgundy velvet lining. Then, we removed the polished ornate silverware from its special hiding place and buffed it with a soft white cloth, to its most spectacular brilliance. As each completed, almost mirror-like, piece was placed beside a rose-covered plate, it caught and reflected the light from the chandelier that hung high over the middle of the dining- room table.

Granny added highly polished, spot-free glasses to each place setting. The crystal was so clear that, except for the twinkling light reflections, it was nearly invisible to the naked eye. We children clumsily stood back and watched as she added the finishing touch—a beautifully arranged centerpiece of baby's breath and aromatic red roses. We weren't rich by any stretch of the imagination, but with Granny's heirlooms and her knack for making things beautiful, on that night I felt like we ranked right up there with President and Mrs. Eisenhower.

Amid the sparkle and shine, and even in our excitement, however, I had conflicting thoughts. Although our grandparents' house had become my home, and I hardly ever saw Daddy, I still hoped he loved us kids and that he wanted us. It was bad enough that I thought I wasn't important to him, but I could hardly stand the thought that Daddy might not consider Levi, Anthony, and Sammie to be significant enough to love and to want. I wondered if he and his new wife would come in with open arms, scoop us up, and go off with us as one big happy family.

The actual and immediate possibility of that happening, however, then made me wonder if I really wanted to be taken away from what I had come to know as a comfortable and loving home with my grandparents. I worried that my siblings and I might actually be taken from our loving grandparents and familiar surroundings, from our friends, from our school, and more importantly to me—taken farther away from Grandma Maddie. The idea that our father and his new wife might openly express a desire to take us, and the idea that we might have an option to consider, would have been nice.

I needn't have worried that our father would take us from anything, however. The thrill of the evening eventually waned. The clock ticked away the hours. Supper remained in a warming mode. We waited, with empty and growling bellies, until nearly bedtime. There was no sign of Daddy and Barbara, and I wondered if Barbara even knew they'd been invited. The hope for a phone call with an explanation or an apology for their absence was eventually replaced by reality, and at last we sat down in our Sunday best to what would have been a wonderful and most appreciated meal—under other circumstances.

While we ate, the room held an unmistakable tension. It wasn't a mean tension, though. It was the kind of tension that occurs when people are trying to act like nothing's really wrong, but everybody knows there is. Nobody wanted anyone else to feel ignored, slighted, insignificant, unloved, or forgotten. It was one of those tensions in which everyone tried to make everybody else feel better. It was one of those tensions in which everyone was a little too eager to please. Everyone was a little too courteous. Nobody even fussed about whose turn it was to wash the dishes.

Nobody wanted anyone else to express disappointment. I thought it was sort of like my unrealistic expectations in anticipation of Christmas when I expected something great, but I didn't get it, and then it was just over.

~~A strange feeling came over me as I pressed that picture of my daddy and me into the album. It's too bad I can't remember ever sitting on his lap, but the picture is proof that I did. Thinking about that no-show night made me search through the box for a picture of Daddy and Barbara. I found it. That picture was taken on the first night I eventually saw Barbara and Daddy together. They stood beside each other in front of Granny and Pappy's fireplace, and they didn't look pleased that their picture was being taken. Strangely, even though the picture of Daddy and Barbara was not printed in color, I remembered every colorful detail of their appearances.

CHAPTER SEVEN

Several months had passed since our night of "Guess Who's Not Coming to Dinner," when Daddy eventually, and quite unexpectedly, brought Barbara around to meet the family. They were definitely an attractive couple. Daddy was tall and ruggedly handsome. His dark hair glistened, and his face was clean-shaven and sort of shiny. His beet-red shirt had been ironed with great care and was fresh, crisp, and neat. His shirtsleeves, with their creases pressed to perfection, were neatly rolled halfway up his muscular and tanned forearms. His black trousers looked as if they'd recently been lifted from a dry-cleaner's hanger. His shoes were spit-shined. He smelled good—not like liquor—but, like cologne. In contrast to his outward look of perfection, however, his brown-black eyes constantly shifted and scanned the perimeter, and they held a sort of wild and fearful look—almost like the eyes of a trapped animal. It was apparent that he was uncomfortable.

Barbara, who looked several years younger than my father, was absolutely gorgeous and looked quite sophisticated. Her short black hair was styled in the latest fashion, and her makeup had been applied with a skilled artistic hand. Her stunning hourglass figure was accented by the tailored fit of her classic black dress. As Barbara walked past me, I noticed that the seams of her nylons were perfectly centered, and her spiked heels set off her long shapely legs. While she stood beside my father in front of the fireplace in Granny and Pappy's living room, each piece of Barbara's tastefully combined gold, pearl, and diamond jewelry glistened and sparkled in the light of the living room chandelier. She wore a perfume that smelled expensive, and she looked like a movie star.

Barbara smiled uncertainly, and her eyes held a sort of uncertainty that matched her smile. She self-consciously glanced at each of us and was probably wondering just exactly where we all fit within her life with our father. She could have been considering any number of possibilities and was probably waiting for the proverbial other shoe to drop.

It seemed that no matter how hard we all tried, the situation was very awkward and uncomfortable. There wasn't any real and open conversation. The biggest memory of that evening for me is that the newlyweds looked beautiful. They didn't stay long, and as apparently difficult as it was for them to spend time with us, they survived the evening.

Daddy and Barbara came to the house a couple more times over the next few months, but they remained in the car while Granny, Pappy, and we four kids, who tried to please, to be noticed, and to be loved, stood in the driveway and made every effort to persuade them to come in the house. Our efforts proved to be a silly waste of time, and I invariably wondered why they'd even bothered to stop.

Eventually, we learned we had a new half-sister Rachel, and one evening Granny and Pappy took us kids to see her. We went to Barbara and Daddy's apartment, and without any amenities we immediately were led to where Rachel lay in her bassinet. I looked at the baby girl and longed for the chance to get to know her. I wanted to love her, to let her know I loved her, and to be loved by her. I wanted her to know that we shared a father and that, no matter what happened, I would always be her sister. I knew, however, that I probably would never have the chance to express or fulfill my desire. The people who would be most instrumental in Rachel's life wouldn't care whether we ever knew each other.

Engrossed in my own thoughts, I'd heard no responses to my grandparents' complimentary and "grandparenty" comments about Rachel. All I heard were a couple of masculine grunts. I felt very awkward and uncomfortable and had no doubt that our presence in my father's home was nothing more than a tolerated inconvenience. We weren't asked, so we didn't stay long.

~~The picture of Daddy and Barbara was the last one I placed on the first page of the album, and I wondered why I bothered to keep it. After giving deliberate consideration to that question, though, I knew the answer: No matter what, they were a part of my fractured family. I reached into the box and happened to pull out a picture of Granny Hunter standing behind the counter at The Bookerton General Store. If only I'd known what was about to happen... No; it's better that I didn't know.

CHAPTER EIGHT

We had little choice, so Levi, Anthony, Sammie, and I got on with our lives. We attended school, became involved in school functions, and with Olivia's assistance did our homework. We helped with Granny's general store in the evenings and on those few weekends when we didn't go to Grandma Maddie's.

During the summer months when school was out, we helped Olivia with chores around the house. We helped with the gardening, where we grew much of the produce for the store and for our own household use. We fed the horses and cattle, slopped the hogs, tended to the chickens and gathered their eggs, and we dealt with the flogging roosters. We marveled at the size of the eggs produced by our geese. We tended our pet rabbits, cats, and dogs. We helped put up hay and rolled in the bases of the haystacks while the taller adults threw hay over our heads to heighten the stacks.

At the store, we stocked shelves, cleaned, ran the cash register, and helped keep tabs on charge accounts. We were young, but the customers knew we were trained to know what we were doing, and although they trusted us, a few checked their register slips and the charges on their tab books just to be sure we hadn't made an honest mistake, and we weren't offended.

We played in our spare time, and—even though my siblings and I discussed the possibility more than a few times—we weren't exactly unpaid labor. It was certain that we didn't have much spare time to get into too much trouble, and if we'd known what the future held, we would have treasured helping Granny at The Bookerton General Store more than anything else in the world.

I had other things on my mind, though. A major change was about to take place at school. My small community's school accommodated grades one through twelve, and near the end of my fifth-grade year, an announcement was made regarding a change in the school system, as we knew it. Our community would lose its high school students to another community's school, and it would accept that school's grade and junior high school students. As I faced the impending doom of a consolidated school system, I believed I could never like those future intruders as much as my established group of friends.

I entered the sixth grade just as unsure of myself as I was each new school year. I scanned the group for my friends and saw unfamiliar faces whose eyes were not so much unlike my own, and I understood those looks of fear and uncertainty. We shared a definite feeling of apprehension, but eventually things melded together, and we consolidated our friendships along with the consolidation of the schools.

Then, on a cold and dreary January day, Granny's friend Sarah Hill came to school and requested to take me home. I was scared and knew something terrible must have happened for Mrs. Hill to take me out of school.

Had something happened to Sammie, who'd been sick that morning and had stayed home? Had something happened to Anthony or Levi at their newly consolidated high school? Their four-mile distance seemed so far away from home. Had Pappy Hunter become ill while away on his business trip? Was it Grandma Maddie? Did she die? Nothing could have happened to Granny Hunter. She was all right, because she was working at the store. Why didn't Granny Hunter come to get me? Why was Mrs. Hill taking me home? I silently walked through the halls beside a stone-faced Sarah Hill, and, on our way down the steps of the school building, I could stand her silence no longer.

I wasn't sure I wanted to hear the answer, but I shyly implored, "Mrs. Hill, please tell me what's wrong."

Sarah Hill took a deep breath and, maybe because of her own state of shock, showed no apparent sign of compassion. She didn't even put her arm around my shoulders or make eye contact as she haltingly explained. "There was a fire at your granny's store—something about the heater. Kate must have tried to put out the fire, and I was told she suffered from smoke inhalation. When Fred Stevens drove into the store's parking lot, he saw smoke escaping from the windows. He ran into the store and pulled your granny outside, but... Uh, the store's gone." Mrs. Hill didn't say anything else for a few seconds. The news that the store had burned down was bad, but I still didn't understand why I had to go home. Sarah Hill finally explained, "Cassie, I don't know any easy way to tell you this. Your granny's dead."

My knees seemed to turn to rubber, but they somehow wobbled me on down those steps and out to Sarah Hill's car. An immediate fog blurred my world. I recalled the argument Granny and I had that morning, and that I'd left the house crying because she hadn't found time to sign the report card I was already late returning to school. Guilt-ridden, I realized our final contact had been filled with anger.

Sarah Hill and I shared no more conversation, and after a short and totally silent trip in her fume-smelling car in which I felt like I was going to vomit, we arrived home. As I walked toward the two-story farmhouse, it seemed much larger—and almost scary—with the knowledge of Granny's death.

Mrs. Hill and I walked through the kitchen door. Curiously, a couple women were busying themselves in the kitchen, and Olivia was sitting on a chair in the corner. She looked as if she were in a daze and didn't even see me or make a move when I walked past her, so I went on through the room.

Even though Olivia was a very fastidious worker and the house hardly ever showed a speck of dust, it looked to me as if a battalion-sized cooking-and-cleaning crew had invaded the entire first floor of our home. The army of women seemed to have a time-honored plan and apparently came equipped with a warehouse amount of food and cleaning supplies. The troops of neighbor ladies, ladies from the church, and women from Granny's lodge hustled and bustled in all directions. Some women organized. Some women cooked. Some women cleaned. Some women just scurried around and tried to find something to do. When they finally saw me standing within their midst, they shared nods and knowing glances, and the apparently self-appointed ringleader headed in my direction. The woman walked over to me and was, as she put it, "…compelled to offer advice on how to behave at a time like this."

In a very controlled and authoritative voice, she said: "Cassie, you have to be a brave young lady. You have to be strong. You mustn't cry; if you do, you'll only upset everyone else. You have to learn to control your emotions. Your grandfather's supervisor has sent someone to locate him and to bring him home. He should be here soon. You go upstairs, now, and wait with Sammie." She cocked her head to one side, made a very stern face, raised one hand, shook her crooked index finger at me, and concluded with: "Now remember, you'll just make matters worse if you cry. Go on with you; scoot on upstairs now."

My eyes were about to be washed out of their sockets by the rush of the flood behind them, and the lump in my throat surely couldn't hold back that dam of emotion much longer, but I followed the lady's command and made sure I controlled and suppressed any emergent sign of my emotional weakness. A tremendous pressure filled my head, and another pressure pushed even more forcefully from within my heart, but I didn't say a word, and I didn't shed a tear

As I crossed the room and headed toward the oak staircase, I thought about how cruel that woman's advice was, and I wondered how she could have determined that my tears, upon hearing of the sudden and unexpected death of my grandmother—especially since, for the past nine years, she'd been like a mother to me—could possibly have made matters worse than they already were. How could everyone around me be so void of emotion? Why hadn't anybody considered that I was only a child? I needed comforting. Why had the lady thought I shouldn't be allowed to openly express my grief? That woman's attitude was very wrong, but because that was the only advice I received, and because it was from an adult, I believed it to be proper, especially because no adult with whom I'd come in contact, from the point of hearing that my grandmother was dead, had openly displayed one iota of sympathetic emotion or sensitivity.

Once again, I found myself on a stairway and was vividly aware of the strange sensation of being totally engulfed within a floating bubble. The aura of the bubble was surrounded by a dense fog that possessed a dampness which penetrated the shimmering sphere, chilled my bones, and caused me to tremble. Without any effort on my own part, it seemed that the floating object slowly transported me up and into the master bedroom from where I could hear Sammie softly crying.

The Master Bedroom... When Pappy was away on business trips, or when we weren't feeling well, Granny allowed us girls to take turns sleeping with her. When we snuggled beneath her silky, bronze-colored comforter, it was a treat that made us feel special. Sammie, who'd been sick the night before, had been allowed to sleep with Granny, and I found my little sister curled up in the corner of the big four-poster bed—the one that would never again hold our grandmother. Sammie was totally alone in that big room. I thought that was cruel, especially because there were several women downstairs—most of them mothers and grandmothers, themselves—and I wondered why nobody was offering comfort to Sammie.

Sammie's nine-year-old, skinny little body looked so small and too alone in our grandparents' bed. Her tear-filled eyes were lost in a face that expressed great disbelief and fear. As if operating in a hypnotic state, I followed the downstairs-woman's strange advice, remained controlled, fought my own emotions, and soon found myself dispensing the sort of comfort for which I, myself, so longed. In Granny's forever absence, as I sat on her bed, that silky, bronze-colored comforter was cold to my touch, and I became even more aware of the damp and chilling midday fog that surrounded me.

What seemed like an eternity later, somewhere in the far-off distance, I heard the kitchen door slam shut. Some muffled sounds of voices drifted up the stairwell, and I knew my brothers were home. At the age of sixteen, their voices sounded like the voices of grown men. I didn't clearly hear what Levi said, but I thought I recognized the voice of the lady who'd just instructed me on how to behave. Then, all of a sudden Levi's voice wailed from the dining room. "What? What do you mean? What are you talking about? How in the world can you say something like that? You leave us alone! We have every right to grieve! I can't believe you'd even *say* something like that!"

I understood the lady's desire to help in some way, and I knew she must have given my brothers the same advice she'd given to me, but I thought her efforts would be better spent in consoling four children who were absolutely shocked and devastated by yet another tragic loss.

I heard that self-appointed ringleader's voice rise to a higher pitch than before, as she admonished my brother. "Now, Levi, that's no way to behave! I'm your grandmother's friend, and I'm here to help." (I wasn't even sure who the woman was, but she apparently thought she'd been instrumental in my grandmother's life.) "Your grandfather's on his way home. It'll only upset him more if he comes home to find that you're acting rude, and I'd hate to be the one who had to tell him about your behavior. You boys are young men now, and you're going to have to be strong for the rest of the family. Your grandmother would be ashamed of you for being nasty to me. She'd be very disappointed in you. You boys are going to have to control yourselves. Your sisters are upstairs. Go up there and stay with them." One of the boys apparently opened his mouth to respond, but the lady said: "No argument, now! You boys go on upstairs!"

Anthony and Levi, apparently somewhat taken aback, joined Sammie and me in our grandparents' bedroom, and nobody knew what to do or say—so we quietly and nearly tearlessly, just sat there looking at each other, almost as if trying to make consoling contact through mental telepathy.

I tried to fill my mind with reassuring thoughts. I didn't want to think about the actuality and details of Granny's death. I didn't really want to know if she'd been badly burned. I tried to think of something else—anything else—and while we waited for Pappy to come home, I wondered how he was taking the news. I wondered how he would handle Granny's death. I was afraid. I wondered how Granny's death would affect our home. I wondered if we'd be allowed to stay with Pappy. I wondered if he'd want us to stay. I knew we could always count on Grandma Maddie, but I didn't want to leave Pappy alone—I didn't think he'd be happy all by himself. I didn't think, either, that we'd found the security that Grandma Maddie had wished for us six years earlier when we'd made our last move from her home. I wondered if security even existed.

Without any adult-offered consolation, we awaited Pappy's arrival. In my effort to suppress my imaginative and emerging thoughts of Granny's charred body from my mind, I concentrated on thoughts of Pappy. I knew Pappy was strong and could handle anything. I knew he often, quietly and without question, helped friends and family members who needed financial and emotional support, so I believed his presence at home would make everything be all right.

Pappy was a giant of a man with broad shoulders and long arms and legs. He looked grandfatherly when he wore his old wrinkled, weather-beaten full-brimmed felt hat that had some stains on it and some holes through it. His casual shirtsleeves and trouser legs were usually a little too short for his long arms and legs, but I thought he carried it off pretty well. I preferred to see him casually dressed, because I knew his casual clothes were an indication that he'd be home with us for a while.

On the day of Granny's death, however, I knew Pappy would arrive home in a neatly pressed business suit, a white shirt, and a tie. That's what he always wore to work. No matter what Pappy wore, he was a man who exuded extreme intelligence and a quiet confidence, but with no hint of pretentiousness.

I wondered how he'd physically look when he arrived home and thought of two looks I knew very well. He had a look that could melt my heart, but when he deemed it necessary, he had another look, accompanied by the snap of his fingers, that could stop me in my tracks. He could be my staunchest supporter, or he could be my strictest adversary. I much preferred the former, but usually understood the reasoning behind the latter. My thoughts were interrupted by the sound of Pappy's voice coming from downstairs.

It seemed like another eternity until I saw him climb to the head of the stairs and cross the hall. On that day, a frighteningly unfamiliar side of Isaac Hunter arrived at the head of those stairs. I almost wished for the familiar look that could stop me in my tracks. The look I saw at that moment was terrifying. It was as if each step and each breath Pappy took would be his last. When he entered the room, I saw that his broad-shouldered frame was reduced to something that made him look almost like a stranger to me. His body reminded me of the empty locusts' shells I'd seen, and it seemed that his life's light had been removed. I thought if I looked hard enough, I'd see completely through him. He looked as if all the strength had been sucked from his limp body. His gray hair was ruffled, and much more than his usually defiant cowlick stood out of place. The whites of his faded blue eyes were red with deeper red-streaked veins and looked as if they floated in a sea of saltwater. Weakness bent his knees, but he slowly and methodically dragged his feet toward us. He was so slumped that his huge gentle hands nearly touched the hardwood floor. His chin quivered. When our eyes connected, a barely audible—but heart-wrenching—sound emitted from his soul, and I was instantly reminded of the whimpering sound Sammie had made six years earlier at Grandma Maddie's, on the day she'd begged to go home. As that picture of my grandfather etched itself into my mind to create an unforgettable memory—at last, he reached us.

His comforting arms found us terrified children, and the room was immediately and completely satiated with mournful wails. Ten arms wrapped around each other and tried to shield their owners from the sadness of the world. Later, the uncertainty of our future without Granny would fully impact our lives. It was time, again, to prepare for another good-bye.

The afternoon and evening wore on, and the house was eventually filled with family members. Daddy and Barbara came. My father's sister Winnie and her husband later arrived with their five children who were all under the age of eight. My grandmother's brothers and sisters brought their families to the house. My grandfather's brothers and sisters came with their families. Grandma Maddie and my mother's siblings were there with their families. It was strange to have all those family members in a group and not be able to enjoy the experience. Somehow, we consoled each other enough to make it through the night.

The next day Pappy, Daddy, and Aunt Winnie disappeared for a while, and we kids were left at home. The house was filled with those other family members and well-meaning friends and neighbors who, without the presence of the cruel lady from the day before, seemed more at ease, and they were much more comforting toward us children—maybe because, by that time, the initial shock had worn off.

As if eating were some sort of consolation, the ladies made a determined effort to see that we ate, even though we explained we weren't hungry. They repeatedly asked if there were anything they could do for my siblings and me. Personally, I was glad the cruel lady hadn't come back, even though I was pretty sure she'd attribute her absence to Levi's behavior from the previous day.

Later in the evening, Pappy, Aunt Winnie, Daddy, and Barbara gathered us kids near them. Pappy said: "Kids, we were at the funeral home today where we made arrangements for your granny's service. Tomorrow night, Granny's body will be ready for viewing. The funeral will be held the day after tomorrow."

I had a general idea of what viewing meant from overhearing discussions between Granny and Pappy when they'd previously prepared to attend the viewing of others, but Pappy wanted to make sure we all understood, so he explained.

"Viewing is a practice in which we, as Granny's immediate family members, will go to the funeral home and sit through the evening. Others who cared about your granny, and who care about us, will come to pay their respects and to offer their condolences.

"We think you kids are old enough to make your own decisions about whether or not you want to attend viewing tomorrow evening and the funeral service the next day." He paused. "This is difficult to discuss, and I don't want to upset you kids any more than you already are, but, well, your grandmother wasn't burned. She was overcome by smoke inhalation, and thanks to Fred Stevens, she was removed from the building before.... Well, I've seen her, and I want you to know that if you decide to go to the viewing, my dear sweet Katie just looks like she's sleeping." He took a hard breath, held it a couple seconds, and valiantly fought back a sob. "We'll understand, though, if you want to stay home. I want you to know that you aren't obligated to attend the viewing or the funeral, but if you choose to attend that's fine. We don't want you to feel pressured in any way. There's really no right or wrong choice here. It's just a matter of what you think you'd rather do."

Sammie blurted out: "I don't wanna go. I don't care what Granny looks like. She's dead. I don't wanna see Granny all dead and stuff. I'd be scared."

Pappy reached over, pulled Sammie close to his chest, and said: "That's all right, baby girl; you don't have to go. I didn't really expect that you would, and we all understand. You can stay home. Of course you know that we consider Olivia to be an important part of our family, and she'll go to the funeral home with us, but the neighbor ladies have offered to take turns staying at the house, so someone will be here all the time. You won't be alone."

Anthony thought about it for a while and said: "I'll go with you, Pappy. I don't want you to go alone. Well, I know Aunt Winnie and Dad will be there, but I think you'll need me with you, too."

"I agree with Anthony," said Levi. "I think we should be with you, Pappy."

"I appreciate how you boys feel, but you really don't have to worry about me; I'll be all right. I just want you to be sure this is something with which you'll be comfortable—well, as comfortable as you can be in this sort of situation."

Anthony confirmed his position. "I want to be with you, Pappy."

"If we didn't want to be with you, we would have said so. You can count on us," Levi affirmed.

I wanted to be with Pappy, too, if that were what he needed, but I also agreed with Sammie, and the thought of going to see my dead grandmother's body was scary. I knew I had to say something, so I said, "I'll go to the viewing with you, Pappy, but I'll have to wait and decide, later, whether I'll go to the funeral."

Pappy smiled the best smile he could, wiped the tears from his cheeks, and said, "I appreciate how you feel, dear." His eyes moved from one of us kids to the other. "I want you kids to know that if you change your minds at any time, that's fine. Don't be afraid to tell one of us if you decide to stay home."

I asked, "Pappy, how long will we have to stay at the funeral home tomorrow night?"

"Only for as long as you want to stay, dear. When you're ready to leave, Anthony or Levi can drive you home. If you all decide to leave together, that's okay, too. It's going to be emotionally difficult, and you might not want to stay for more than a few minutes. If that happens, like I've said before, it's all right."

Eventually, we discussed the matter of what we'd wear to the funeral home. Anthony and Levi both were licensed to drive, so they decided to go somewhere together to shop for their suits. Barbara, the stepmother I hardly knew, graciously offered to take me and help with my clothing needs, and I was grateful.

Barbara arrived at the house the next morning, ready to take me shopping for clothes and shoes to wear to Granny's viewing. It was such a confusing and scary time for me. I'd never been alone with Barbara, and I'm sure she was as uncomfortable as I, but she was very kind and tried to put me at ease. We drove about fifteen miles to our county seat, which was where most folks in our county did their shopping, and where Barbara was familiar with all the small local shops. She exhibited exquisite taste and style in clothing choices, and it wasn't long until she'd skillfully helped me choose a proper dress for Granny's viewing.

We headed for the little family-owned shoe store where Granny usually took us kids to buy our shoes. It was one of those places where generations of owners and their family members did all the work. They knew every customer and her specific needs. It didn't matter how seldom or how often the customer visited, her last visit was always remembered and mentioned, and she felt like she was more than just a customer when she was whole-heartedly and cheerily welcomed into the store and asked about her family.

As we forced the swollen door open, its little brass bell rang and immediately summoned the tiny gray-haired saleslady. Miss Myrtle Brooks was dressed in a blue-and-lavender floral-print dress that was trimmed with a wide cotton-lace collar. She clunked along toward us wearing black orthopedic shoes that looked as if they'd squeezed the fluid from her feet and had forced it up and into her swollen, inner tube-looking ankles. Her not quite flesh-colored stockings were so heavy that they almost looked like socks. Her sort of orchid-tinted gray hair was so tightly curled that it looked like Miss Brooks had recently removed several bobby pins and simply left the ringlets in place. Her pale opaque cheeks were each spotted with three not-so-smoothly-blended dots of red rouge that had been strategically placed on the skin below the blue frames of her glasses. Her skin looked like it had been stretched as far as it would stretch and then had been let go like a rubber band, and it seemed to have snapped back and clung, precariously, to thousands of cracks and crevices. Except for the scattered brown spots, her skin was nearly transparent, and I could actually see the blue veins running beneath it. I thought the blue glasses blended well with her veins and faded blue eyes.

As she neared us, Miss Brooks reached a certain point at which her face developed a strange prunish look—even prunier than I'd always thought it already was. It seemed to me that her prune-faced juices were going to be squeezed out in the form of pity tears. I didn't think I could stand it. I knew Miss Brooks recognized us, and I knew she was aware of exactly what circumstances brought us to her establishment.

She was so flustered that it was difficult for me to comprehend much of what she said, but I understood that she'd heard of Granny's death and was paying some sort of condolences. She sang Granny's praises. Then she almost acted as if she were unaware of my presence when she looked at Barbara and said: "Oh, my, my, my! Mrs. Hunter was such a wonderful woman. She always brought the children in here to buy their shoes, you know. One time I told her that I didn't know how she coped with all those children— especially at her age—and what with running the store and all. Well, anyway, I told her I thought they must be such a burden for her. But she said: 'Oh, no, Miss Brooks. These children aren't a burden to me. In fact, I think they help keep me young.' Can you imagine her saying that? Now, I just wonder what's to become of those children. What will poor Mr. Hunter do without Mrs. Hunter? Poor Mr. Hunter surely won't be able to keep all those children now that Mrs. Hunter's gone. Oh, my, my, my! Her death is such a tragedy!"

I just stood there and listened to Barbara respond as well as she could, and I wondered, too, if poor Mr. Hunter could cope with all us children.

Barbara tactfully brought that part of the conversation to a close with: "Thank you for your concern, Miss Brooks. I'll be sure to convey your condolences to Mr. Hunter. Now, if you don't mind, Cassie is going to need some dress shoes to wear to the funeral home." She looked over at me and asked,

"Cassie, honey, do you think you know what size shoes you'll need?"

"Yes. I think I need size eight."

Miss Brooks and Barbara, apparently surprised by my response, looked at my feet, which wore my winter shoes that had been purchased the previous winter. I wasn't embarrassed about wearing old shoes, because just about everyone I knew, including me, wore each season's clothes and shoes until they were entirely too small and were passed along to somebody else, or we wore them until they were completely worn-out. No matter what the size and condition, though, our shoes were always kept highly polished.

"Oh, Cassie, are you sure about that?" asked Barbara. "You surely don't need size eight."

Before I had a chance to respond, little Miss Brooks, an experienced saleslady who definitely took her job quite seriously, said: "Oh, my goodness! No, dear! You can't possibly think you need size eight shoes!"

I was persistent. "Yes, I think I do. I really think I need size eight shoes."

Miss Brooks bustled off to get the shoe sizing gauge and brought it back to where Barbara and I had seated ourselves on a couple of the oxblood vinyl-covered, wood-framed chairs that lined a small section of the dark and dreary little shelf-covered, shoe box filled store. Little Miss Brooks was quite accomplished in her profession, and as soon as she came back to us, she professionally and comfortably straddled the shoe salesman's bench that was strategically placed directly in front of my chair. She pulled up her dress to about her mid-thigh and revealed knees that looked like the faces of two Shar-Pei dogs with their eyes closed. The tops of her heavy stockings were rolled down and held in place by a pair of thick round garters, just below her sagging, wrinkled knee skin. She reached between her thighs, grasped the center of her floral-print dress and, with some semblance of modesty, shoved her handful of dress under her rump and sat down on it. She placed the shoe sizing gauge on the sloping side of the shoe salesman's bench and instructed me to remove my right shoe.

As I removed my shoe, Miss Brooks extended her right arm and hand and held them impatiently in midair. As soon as my old shoe hit the floor, she bent forward, grasped my ankle and firmly planted my socked foot down on the measuring tool. She determinedly shoved my heel toward the lower end of the numbered device, as far as it would go. She pushed on the top of my foot, pressed against my toe area, examined the numbers, and almost as if she'd won a $50 bet, she proudly exclaimed: "Just as I thought! I knew it; I knew it! Cassie, honey, you wear size four. What in the world made you think you needed a size eight?"

I didn't understand the concept of a rhetorical question, so I gave her an answer. I wasn't a sassy kid; I'd been taught to be polite and to use proper manners. So, I spoke in a polite tone. "I know I wear size four, Miss Brooks, but that's not what I was asked. I was asked what size shoe I think I need, and like I told you, I think I need size eight."

Miss Brooks and Barbara shared looks of bewilderment and slight disgust, and those looks didn't get past me. I knew I had to give some sort of explanation, so I said: "Last summer, when I was getting ready to go to church camp, Granny took me shopping for summer clothes and shoes, and while we were on our little shopping spree, Granny said: 'I'm absolutely astounded at the growth spurt you're experiencing. On our stop at the shoe store, I'm going to run in and buy you a pair of nice white open-toed dress sandals for church services at the camp, and I'm determined to make sure your new shoes are big enough that you won't outgrow them by the end of summer.' So, Granny picked out that pair of nice white open-toed dress sandals in size eight."

Miss Brooks said: "Oh, Cassie dear, I remember that your grandmother came in here and bought a pair of sandals, but I thought they were for her. Are you sure you aren't a little confused?"

"No, Miss Brooks. I'm not confused about that. Those sandals were for me." Barbara and the little saleslady exchanged strange looks, again, so I said: "It made sense to me, because that's the way it works with my winter coats. The first year I wear a new winter coat, the ends of the arms hang nearly to my knees, and the hem hangs nearly to my ankles. The next year the coat fits better, but it's starting to look bad. Then, the third year I wear my winter coat, it fits pretty well, but it looks like I need a new winter coat. So I figured we were going to start the same stuff with my summer shoes."

Even though I'd reasoned out the problem for them, Barbara and Miss Brooks sat absolutely speechless. While I had their full attention, I continued my story. "Well, I did feel pretty bad about the sandals, though. I didn't have a chance to try them on before I left for church camp. We went home from shopping; Granny shoved the bag with the shoes into my suitcase; and I left for camp early the next morning. On the day I was supposed to wear those shoes to church services, I slid my feet into those brand-new nice white open-toed dress sandals, in size eight, and my toes didn't even show beyond that wide piece of leather that crossed over the top of my foot."

Miss Brooks quickly blinked a couple of times, jerked her head back until I thought she was going to reel off her shoe salesman's bench, and she finally nodded as if she understood why I couldn't see my toes—after all, dealing with shoes was her life's profession. I thought she and Barbara were starting to get the picture, so I explained: "If it weren't for the straps that buckled around my ankles, I never would have been able to keep those flapping-and-flopping sandals on my feet." The ladies nodded. "I tried to convince another girl at the camp to trade shoes with me before we attended church services, but she wouldn't do it. I was so embarrassed. When I wore those shoes, I thought I looked like a clown who wears great big, floppy, white shoes, so I told the girls at church camp that I didn't think I'd ever wear another pair of white shoes. When I got home, I didn't say anything about it to Granny, but I hid the shoes and hoped she wouldn't ask me why I hadn't been wearing my new sandals.

"But, anyway, this is the first pair of shoes I'll be getting since I got those size eight sandals, and because Granny decided I needed size eight, I know she'd want me to get size eight shoes to attend her viewing, and then I can wear them to school all winter and not have to worry about outgrowing them. I know that's what Granny would want, so please let me get size eight shoes."

It didn't take much for a grieving twelve-year-old to wear down a frazzled stepmother and an elderly orchid-haired maiden lady. Miss Brooks and Barbara looked at me, looked at each other, and suddenly—almost as if she'd received an epiphany—Miss Brooks proclaimed, "Oh, my goodness! I remember! When Mrs. Hunter came in that day, she explained that she was running a little late and was in a bit of a hurry to get back to the general store. She held up our usual size five display sandal, said she didn't want to take our display shoe, and asked if I had another pair like those in the back. I thought she didn't want that particular size, but she must have meant she didn't want to disturb our display.

I pride myself in knowing my customers' needs, you know, but I misunderstood her meaning and thought she was buying the sandals for herself—she was alone, after all, and I automatically went to the ware room and got a box of size eights—her size—and bagged her purchase. Oh, my goodness—she wanted the display size five for you, Cassie! I should have asked! Oh, dear. Cassie, honey, I think your grandmother meant for you to have those sandals—but not in size eight. That was my mistake. I'm so sorry." So, with that explanation, we moved on.

When a possibly (but not *obviously*) frazzled Barbara and I returned home from shopping, we discovered the kitchen and dining room held enough food to feed our family for several weeks. What a difference a day makes.

Someone had brought sourdough cookies to the house and, of all the food available, those were the only things I could get past the lump in my throat—that lump which still held back a dam of emotion. Somehow, I knew as I ate those cookies that I'd probably always think of that day and have a nagging sense of sorrow every time I saw a sourdough cookie. They were like some sort of a connection to that day.

It was almost time for Granny's viewing, so I dressed to go to the funeral home, and we eventually left the house.

I stood back from the casket and looked at Granny. I think it was her mouth that bothered me most. Her mouth looked cold, strangely peach-colored, stretched, and permanently glued shut. She looked almost unfamiliar with her pasty complexion and with her hair styled in a way I'd never seen it. Her glasses, strangely enough, had been placed over her closed eyes. I thought that was really odd. She'd been dressed as if she were going to attend church, but then she'd been covered with a silky-looking cover that, in my opinion, made her look as if she should have been dressed for bed. Her hands, which were the same pasty color as her face, were folded and crossed over her midriff and lay on top of the silky, ivory-colored coverlet. Her fingernails were tinted with light pink enamel. I focused on her narrow, scratched and worn silver wedding band. I didn't attend her funeral.

For a long time, I remembered Granny as my dead grandmother with that putty-like face—not as a viable living being. I found that my memory of her dead body was my prevalent memory until the night she crossed the dining room, leaned against the archway to the living room, looked at me, and smiled the smile that opened her lips and left me with a more familiar look. In that dream, I was granted forgiveness for the argument we'd had on the morning of her death, and I felt a miraculous sense of peace and closure.

The next few months were lonely for everyone in our household. We'd lost much of our feeling of home. Everything seemed odd and out of place. Even though Olivia did her best to keep things running normally, Granny's presence was truly missed. Pappy worked away from home more frequently and was usually home only on weekends. He chose not to rebuild the store and sold the property to another family who built their own general store on the site, because following the destruction of Granny's building and stock, the small community definitely missed the convenience of having that service.

I wasn't helping in the store, so my weeks seemed longer, and eventually even our family's regular weekend routine changed. Anthony and Levi, and Sammie and I continued to ride along with our grandfather when he took Olivia to her mother's home on Friday nights, but Pappy didn't want to be alone in our own big empty and lonely house, so he requested that we children alternate weekends between him and Grandma Maddie.

~~The picture that showed Granny Hunter standing behind the store's counter went into my album. I searched around in my box and was disappointed to discover that I had very few pictures of Grandma Maddie. My favorite one was one we'd taken at her house on Christmas Eve. The one thing I could always count on was that I'd spend Christmas Eve at Grandma Maddie's. Except for our first Christmas after we married which we spent in South Carolina, my husband Jacob and I continued the tradition with our children, and we spent every Christmas Eve with Grandma Maddie for as long as she lived.

CHAPTER NINE

I loved my grandfather but hated to relinquish any time with Grandma Maddie. Grandma Maddie was my link to my mother. She was my comfort, my contentment, and my closest thing to a sense of security. She was my one constant. She talked with me and listened to me. She shared my thoughts and was my confidant. She knew the names of my best friends and my most intimate secrets. Grandma Maddie taught me how to quilt and covered me with our homemade quilts when I napped. Those quilts that initially felt so cool on my little-girl body soon captured my warmth and held it close around me, as if Grandma Maddie were holding me swaddled in her loving arms.

Her back porch was where we spent most of our summertime weekends swaying on the old squeaky porch swing that had at least one layer of green paint for each year it had hung there. We carefully swung back-and-forth in our extreme effort to prevent spilling Grandma Maddie's hot creamed coffee, and I occasionally took a sip of that liquid that I thought definitely smelled better than it tasted. On a regular basis, the neighbor ladies congregated on Grandma Maddie's porch, because they knew, too, how special Grandma Maddie was. She gave nearly everyone who came in contact with her a sense of comfort.

How could I give up my weekends with Grandma Maddie? How could I give up the time with my head on my grandmother's lap and the feeling of my grandmother's gentle touch as she stroked my hair? How could I give up the inviting freshly laundered and starched smells of her apron on which I lay my head? How could I give up hearing Grandma Maddie's kind and gentle words? How could I endure an even more limited time with the woman I loved so much? How could I give up time with the woman who lovingly called me Little Apple Dumpling?

Nothing in my life seemed fair! Then something happened that, again, made me know the need for self-sacrifice, and I decided that my brothers, my sister, and I must alternate weekends between our widowed grandparents. One Friday night, after literally begging to go to Grandma Maddie's, I lay sulking in bed because my begging had gone unrewarded. I was totally exhausted and felt tremendously uncomfortable in that bed.

After Granny died, Sammie and I were relocated into the master bedroom, and I never felt that we belonged there. Pappy moved into the smallest of all the bedrooms, which previously had been Sammie's. I felt like everybody was out of place and disoriented and absolutely hated being without Granny in what I formerly had known as my grandparents' bedroom. Sammie and I occupied the room that had formerly, but certainly no longer, held such meaning of being pampered and special. We occupied that double bed and lay beneath that silky, bronze-colored comforter, which no longer had the same pampering quality. The comforter's outside surface was cold and served as a constant reminder of my loss.

I looked at the closet door and knew that our little short dresses hung where my grandmother's suits, lodge gowns, and dress coats had formerly hung. That closet had been home to my grandfather's business suits, dress shirts, and his highly polished shoes. It was the closet that previously held the secrets of Christmas. Sammie's and my little-girl clothes and little-girl shoes were simply displaced intruders. I pictured my dead grandmother's donated clothes crumpled in a Goodwill bin, and I imagined them being worn on strangers' bodies.

We, and our things, were so out of place, and in that dark and quiet loneliness of the night I put the edge of that silky, bronze-colored comforter in my mouth and stifled my sobs. Shortly afterward, I heard similar heart-wrenching sounds coming from my grandfather's newly assigned bedroom. For as long as I could, I held my breath. I didn't want to make another sound. I didn't want Pappy to hear me, and I didn't want him to know I'd heard him.

When I could hold it no longer and had to breathe, I took short, shallow breaths and felt warm tears run down the sides of my head and dampen the hair at my temples. It felt like the warm tears immediately turned to ice water as they saturated my hair, and I nearly froze. I pictured my grandfather's huge frame, probably lying in a fetal position and crowded in Sammie's little twin bed. I imagined Pappy facing the tiny closet door knowing that his business suits and dress shirts were all shoved tightly into that compact space and hung on the rod that had been lowered for Sammie's convenience. I visualized my grandfather's shoes placed in a neat row on that tiny closet floor. I thought he might be looking through his nearly lifeless eyes at the closet that previously held Sammie's clothes, toys, coloring books, and other little-girl treasures. I wondered if he felt as intrusive in that room as I felt in the one I occupied.

My thoughts were brought back to reality by those sounds that had become all too familiar coming from Sammie's old bedroom. I knew, without a doubt, that my grandfather's mouth was tightly clenched over the corner of the Little Dutch Girl quilt that had been Grandma Maddie's and my homemade gift to Sammie.

The quilt that was too small to fully cover Pappy's body was also too small to fully cover the sounds of his sobs. I knew then, without question, that we must alternate weekends with Grandma Maddie and Pappy, and that we must make our grandfather know we loved him and wanted to be with him. I knew Grandma Maddie would miss me, but I also knew she'd understand my sense of responsibility for Pappy's need. With that decision made, I rolled to my side, made a spoon with Sammie, and wrapped my left arm protectively around her. I knew time would pass and hoped that, as several people had told me, it would also heal. I eventually drifted off to sleep.

Time did pass, but the gloomy winter dragged and spring's arrival was somewhat less exciting and brilliant than usual, so I was glad when school was eventually out for the summer. For several months I'd managed to go through the motions of life after Granny's death. I'd thought that when school was out I'd be able to find things to occupy my time, but I wasn't spending as much time with Grandma Maddie, and I wasn't spending time working in the store, so it wasn't as easy as I'd thought it would be.

~~Grandma Maddie's Christmas-Eve picture looked fine beside Granny Hunter's general-store picture. When I dug down into my picture box, I discovered there was a period of time in which no pictures were taken at Pappy Hunter's and realized that Granny Hunter must have been the only photographer in our family. I didn't need a picture to remind me, though, of the summer after her death. That summer was a bad one. It was a summer of discovery. It was a summer of true revelation. It was a summer of great disappointment and sorrow. It was the summer I almost wished I were deaf.

CHAPTER TEN

On sort of a hot and lazy Saturday afternoon, I walked past Pappy, who'd nodded off on the patio glider, and went inside where it almost felt like I'd stepped into the coolness of air-conditioned space, but it smelled fresher.

The day before, we girls had helped Olivia give the house its thorough weekly cleaning, right down to polishing the windows, so everything was neat and nice and smelled fresh and clean. The sparkling windows were open, and the screens allowed the gentle breezes to infiltrate the house with a fresh, almost sweet aroma that followed me through the house and up the stairs.

When I entered the bedroom, the bronze-colored curtains gently lifted, ballooned, and fell with the touch of the wind. They would have appeared ghostlike if it weren't so light within the room, and if I'd gone in there at dusk, those flowing curtains probably would have spooked me to the point that I'd have hurried to close the windows.

I'd originally planned to grab the book I'd been reading but changed my mind and decided to try on summer clothes. It wasn't long until my drawers were nearly emptied, and my bed was piled with shorts and sleeveless tops. It was quiet in the house, and I heard the sound of a vehicle as it pulled into the driveway. I left my bedroom, crossed the hall, walked down the first three steps onto the landing, and looked out the window. I saw my daddy's car. As usual, I couldn't help myself; I was excited and glad for the chance to see him, and I hoped even more that he would be glad to see me. I waited a while to give Pappy and Daddy a chance to talk, and I hoped Daddy would eventually call out for us kids, but I knew he wouldn't.

Sammie had gone to spend an hour at a friend's house, and the boys were riding horses in the field. I thought that because it was so quiet around the place, Pappy and Daddy thought I was out and about, too. So I decided to pick out my prettiest shorts and top, to put them on, to go out on the patio, and to make my presence known. Just as I was about to exit the kitchen door, I overheard the beginning of a conversation that stopped me in my tracks. That was the day I almost wished I were deaf.

I heard my granddad address my father in a slow and questioning voice. He said, "Hank, now that you and Barbara have been married a while and have a child, I wonder if you've considered having your other kids live with you."

I couldn't believe it. I was scared. I couldn't stand the thought of being moved away from Pappy. I'd thought he needed us. I'd thought he wanted us. I thought life must be so much simpler for people who were in secure homes with secure families, and I wondered if I'd ever be in a place where I felt secure.

Although my thoughts ran rampant, I realized that silence was my father's only response to Pappy's question.

Pappy continued. "Now that your mother's gone, and because I'm away so much, it might be a more normal life for the kids if they were with you and Barbara. It might seem more like a normal family situation. Barbara's young and could have a positive influence on the girls, and the girls would be so good to Rachel. I know the boys—well, they're hardly boys, anymore—would be a big help to you, as far as keeping up with the chores goes."

More silence followed—except for the pounding of my heart. My knees were weak, and I could have sworn my heart imploded.

Pappy made an offer. "I've been thinking a lot about this. Since you're renting and don't have your own house, maybe you and Barbara would like to bring Rachel and move in here."

Well, I thought that if any changes were made like that, it might not be as bad as I'd anticipated.

My father's silence was deafening, but I knew he was still there.

Pappy then suggested, "Olivia could probably be persuaded to stay on."

My father's silence, once again, was his only response.

So Pappy forged ahead: "I'd be willing to give you the house and move a trailer out back. I could stay there on weekends and when I don't have to work away from home. That way the kids and I could still spend time together."

Nothing.

"Hank, I know this is a lot for you to digest right now, but maybe you can give it some thought. Discuss it with Barbara and let me know what you decide."

I wasn't exactly paralyzed, but I don't think I could have moved if someone yelled "Fire!" I was weak, and the only reason I knew I was still alive was because I heard my imploded heart pumping itself back into shape. The wait for my father's answer, however, was not long.

He immediately, and without a hint of doubt in his voice, answered his father with: "Dad, I don't need to talk to Barbara about this. I don't want to move in here, and I don't want to take the kids. If they're too much of a burden for you now that Mom's gone, then even if it means separating them, I'll see that they're put into homes."

I'd caught that burden word, again, almost as if it were emphasized. I wondered if everyone, except my grandparents, thought of us children as burdens. I wondered who we were burdening, if not our grandparents. I didn't want to believe what I'd heard, but I'd heard it. I was definitely disheartened by the fact that my own father couldn't be convinced to take his own children, even if a live-in housekeeper/babysitter and a pretty decent house and farm were thrown in for good measure.

Then, with a very pained and almost apologetic voice, Pappy replied, "Oh, Hank." And I felt the impact of the pause that allowed him to regain his composure before he continued. "These children aren't a burden to me. I love them dearly, and I need them as much as they need me. I just thought now that you and Barbara are married, and because your mother's gone, that you might want to have your children with you. I thought maybe you didn't want to upset your mother and me by asking for them when you first remarried. Then I thought that maybe you didn't want to upset me by asking me for the kids after your mother died. I thought if you wanted to have them with you, it might be easier if I brought up the subject. I didn't want you to think I was trying to keep them from you, but now that I know how you feel, I won't mention it again. I only want what's best for those children—and, Hank, they must never know we had this conversation."

I quietly crept back upstairs, where in the sanctuary of my room I relived the sound of disappointment I'd heard in Pappy's voice when he heard Daddy's response. I knew my grandfather wasn't disappointed that we children wouldn't be leaving him. I knew he was disappointed in Daddy's failure to understand that he considered us to be wonderful treasures that he was willing to sacrifice and to return to his son. I was glad Sammie and the boys weren't around to hear that conversation. I stayed in the bedroom until I heard Daddy's vehicle leave.

Even though I was only twelve years old, I kept my knowledge of that conversation to myself for several years, until one afternoon—long after I'd reached adulthood—when my grandfather was discussing the complexities and unknown outcomes of parenting, that he had a slip of the tongue and referred to that discussion between him and his son. He immediately apologized, but I explained there was no need for an apology and admitted I'd overheard their conversation. We had a real heart-to-heart discussion in which I quoted the conversation, nearly verbatim, and he reluctantly admitted that I hadn't misunderstood a word. As he'd done so many times in the past, my grandfather pulled me close to his chest, held me, and we cried. We both regretted what had been said, and we both regretted that I'd heard it. We agreed that we were grateful for the relationship we'd built with each other over the years, though, and we expressed our sorrow for my father's losses. Then, we just let the old father-son conversation go. It no longer held any significance.

During the weeks when he didn't have to be on the road and away from home, some of our favorite times were spent in the living room where Pappy and we kids made every effort to entertain each other. Pappy, who had a sponge-like thirst for knowledge, relaxed in his easy chair that was strategically placed beside the bookcase filled with encyclopedia that encased his favorite type of reading materials, and sometimes he read to us from them.

Some evenings Anthony played his guitar, and he and Levi sang. At least one night a week, Anthony and Levi took turns playing chess with Pappy. He'd taught them well. As they sat and schemed and planned their every move, I often wondered whether my dad ever played chess with Pappy, and I wondered if they'd ever had a bond.

Even though I wasn't sure whether my father played chess, I thought that, in his effort to control our early childhood situations, and in his desire to be rid of us children, he acted as a skilled chess player who moved us kids as pawns to capture his parents' emotions. I thought he probably always had a plan that eventually fell into place, and he got what he really wanted. By strategically planning and using cunning moves, he actually set up his chessboard in a way that looked as if he lost the game. I believed, however, that when he was rid of us children, Daddy secretly thought he'd stealthily and actually Checkmated. But I also thought that without knowing we were pawns in his game, we kids were the ones who'd actually won.

Sammie and I didn't participate in the game of chess; we had other things to do. I was nearly thirteen years old, but I didn't think I was too old to take turns with Sammie as we spent many evening hours combing and styling Pappy's hair with the little black plastic comb we found waiting for us in his shirt pocket. Pappy always had a neat haircut, so the only hair we had to work with was the hair on the center top of his head, but we made the most of it. Pappy patiently endured the pulling out of his hair tangles that we inevitably created and flinched and jerked as little as possible when his tender scalp was cracked with the snap of misdirected rubber bands. He quite forcefully agreed with our necessity for the use of clip-on barrettes and deserved an academy award for his display of false modesty as he admired himself in the ornate, heavy, silver-plated, hand-held mirror we provided for his preening purposes. He seemed to bask in the constant sounds of our jabber and giggles.

Some evenings, Pappy simply relaxed and cut and cored homegrown bright red apples that he lifted from the old scouring-pad scratched and cleaned aluminum pie pan that lay on his lap. He quartered the apples, and as he held the crisp and juicy white meats down toward the four of us who sat on the floor around his chair and almost on his feet, four hands shot up and clawed toward each piece until we'd all captured and devoured our fill. While Pappy peeled and offered apples, he listened to whatever we had to say, even when we all talked at the same time in our efforts to vie for his undivided attention. Then, when we finally exhausted our entertainment skills, we begged Pappy to tell us his stories. He was quite the storyteller and held us spellbound for unforgettable hours with his spin of a tale. In addition to loving him, dearly, we absolutely adored him.

Pappy gave us his love and attention, but it wasn't easy to deal with the loss of my grandmother, and it was especially difficult to watch the effects of her loss on my grandfather. Even though I was glad we were with Pappy, it wasn't easy to accept the idea that my father didn't want his own children. It hurt deeply, and although I didn't mean to think about it so much, I couldn't push it out of my mind. I was in a daze through much of the time that passed, and without the reassurance of Granny Hunter's guidance, I was concerned about my future. I had a lot on my mind; and without my grandmother's presence, I depended more and more on my relationships with my friends.

My friends and I kept in touch over the summer months, and we agreed that we would adjust and enter junior high school with a little more self-confidence. We somehow felt older with the loss of the high school students, and we easily moved into the seventh grade. We giggled about boys; we played kissing games at parties when boys attended, and we felt the exhilaration and guilt of young passion. We experienced puppy love and had small crushes on any number of unknowing classmates.

Even though we occasionally fantasized about future dating, our friendship was more important, so each girl was willing to surrender her unspoken crush if a friend expressed interest in the same boy of her own dreams. We attended school dances and ball games. We entered talent shows and acted in school plays. We spent our lunch money in a small local restaurant where we drank sodas, ate Sloppy Joes, savored lollipops, and listened to our favorite songs on the jukebox. Long before we ever heard of bonding, we had bonded, and even as children, we recognized the significance of our relationships. We shared our thoughts and ideas, our fears and fantasies. We wondered about life in general, and we wondered whether we'd ever find the balance that would bring us feelings of maturity and security.

~~Time marched on, just as if Granny Hunter were still alive, but it apparently had marched on without pictures. The summer passed without pictures, and only professional school photos showed up in my box for that autumn. Christmas passed without pictures. During our process of making adjustments, I guess nobody thought about taking over Granny Hunter's job of capturing our family's precious moments. The absence of pictures for that period of more than a year made me sadder than if I had them to remind me of those times. Even without pictures to help serve as reminders, though, I recall the events that took place the second spring after Granny Hunter's death.

CHAPTER ELEVEN

My friends and I had our own fantasies, but we found it rather funny when we discovered that my grandfather—even in his ancient fifties—had a few fantasies of his own. Pappy started what I thought was his new fantasy life when he began spending a little time with widowed friends and neighbor ladies. After several dates with one particular lady who'd been a family friend for many years, it seemed to me that Pappy was seeing her in a somewhat different light. My friends, my siblings, and I held discussions in which we agreed it was apparent that Mrs. Powers had become more than just a friend to Pappy.

We were all impressed when Mrs. Powers said, right to my brothers' faces: "Levi and Anthony, you are absolutely charming! I believe you could charm the birds from the trees." Mrs. Powers was always kind to us, and we agreed that she was very attractive—even though she was an older lady in Pappy's ancient age range.

One beautiful spring day when Mrs. Powers visited the house, we all enjoyed some lemonade and conversation as we sat on the patio's old metal glider and chairs that made soft squeaking noises when we glided back-and-forth. The squeaking made it nearly impossible to catch all the words of the conversation, but if we timed it right and moved back-and-forth in unison, we managed to catch most of the words.

After a little time was spent chatting with us children that day, Pappy said, "Kids, I know you enjoy Mrs. Powers' company, but I think it's time for you to go in and clean your rooms." We knew something was up; Pappy had never sent us off so abruptly, and I thought he'd acted a little odd ever since Mrs. Powers had arrived. He was a little too quiet and actually seemed a little nervous.

We took the hint, politely said our good-byes to Mrs. Powers, and headed toward the kitchen door, but I think we were sure that none of us was going to clean a bedroom. We went inside, walked up the stairs, and huddled on the upstairs landing, which happened to be the greatest place to listen to patio conversations. The words drifted up and through the open window and almost forced us to listen to them. Nothing very interesting happened for a while.

Then he did it. Pappy summoned his courage and broached the subject of marriage. "Evelyn, your friendship is very dear to me, and I wouldn't want to lose it. Kate and I knew you and Harvey for too many years to sacrifice that. I don't know if I might be overstepping my boundary, here, and if I'm out of line just say so. I promise I won't be offended. I'll understand."

"My goodness, Isaac, what is it?" Mrs. Powers sounded genuinely concerned. "I can't imagine that you could say anything that would destroy our friendship."

"Well, Evelyn, we've been seeing each other for a few months, now, and I don't know if we feel the same, but I wonder if you've ever considered remarrying."

"Yes, Isaac. I have considered it, but there are so many things to be taken into that consideration."

"I agree. I suppose I'm not going at this in a very good way. I'm a little nervous. What I'm really trying to ask you, Evelyn, is if you would consider marrying me?" Pappy sounded apprehensive, but I couldn't understand why. He was such a wonderful man that I was sure his proposal would be accepted without hesitation.

"Isaac, as you said, we've been friends for a long time, and I think the world of you. Back when Harvey and Kate were alive, we all had a great respect for each other. Harvey and I admired you and Kate for the kind of people you were. We appreciated your sense of obligation and responsibility. We even marveled at how you and Kate somehow found the strength, the time, and the energy to rear your grandchildren, not to mention the expenses that certainly go along with that responsibility. Unfortunately, although I respected you and Kate for doing it, it isn't something I think I could do.

"I'll be frank, and I'm almost ashamed to admit it, but if you were alone I might at least consider your proposal. Please don't think unkindly of me, but as sorry as I am, I couldn't possibly face the next few years knowing that I'd have to help rear your grandchildren, even though I think they're absolutely charming. I've been away from child rearing for too long—and I'm not getting any younger, you know. I'm afraid such an undertaking would be too much for me. I'm so sorry, Isaac; I truly wish things were different." She gave a nervous laugh. "It's ironic, isn't it, that one of the reasons I have such great respect for you, is also one of the reasons I couldn't possibly consider marrying you."

We nosy kids froze on the landing, and I had an intense feeling of sadness for Pappy. I was afraid that, once again, we'd disrupted his life. I wished we hadn't been so nosy but we were sure, at the onset of the conversation, that it would turn out quite differently.

"I honestly understand, Evelyn." Pappy, once again, was kind and selfless. "I appreciate your candor. As you know, I'm totally committed to those children. They come first with me, and I've never made any secret of that. I hope you understand, too, that I wouldn't sacrifice them for another marriage."

"I know, Isaac; and as I've said, that's one of the things I respect most about you. It's one of the things, too, which makes me so fond of you, but I have to be honest with you—and with myself—about my own capabilities. I've enjoyed our time together—the companionship—and have considered that we might come to this proposal and have searched deep within myself. As difficult as it is to admit, I simply don't believe I have it in me to take on such a household. I hope you understand."

"Of course I do, Evelyn."

"You know, Isaac, I'll be even more candid with you. Please hear me out. We've been such good and comfortable friends over the years and have been open with each other from long before our first official date, so I'll be blunt. I don't think I'm the woman you're really interested in, anyway. You've been honest with me from the beginning about seeing another woman— a woman for whom I believe you care a great deal more than you do for me. I could hear it in your voice the very first time you mentioned her name. Is it possible that you asked me to marry you with the thought that I'd be the best 'fit' for the kids because they're familiar with me—that maybe a transition involving me would be simpler than one with Rose? If that plays into it, you know that wouldn't be fair to anyone. You need to follow your heart, and you know where it will lead you, Isaac. You need to consider your own feelings, trust your own judgment, and know that those grandchildren will love the woman you love. Please think about that. I hope, like you, that we will remain friends—but I don't think you and I could ever be more than that. You know Rose is the right one for you."

"Evelyn, you're a wise woman and a very dear friend. I would never intentionally hurt you, but I'll admit: You're right in your assessment. I do love Rose, but she lives hours away, and she and the kids have never met. Even though Rose knows I love her, could she see it as selfish and unfair of me to ask her to leave her family and familiar surroundings to come here and help me take care of my own family? *Would* it be selfish and unfair of me? I'm afraid it might be too difficult to work out everything that would be involved if I were to ask Rose to marry me—and I don't want to put her in a difficult position. I feel so torn."

We four eavesdroppers looked at each other and mouthed: "Rose? Who's Rose?" Nobody on that stairway landing had a clue.

"Isaac, you have to do whatever it takes to make it work. You'll think of something. If Rose feels the same way about you, she'll *help* you figure it all out, and those children will make whatever adjustments are necessary on their part. Now, listen; promise me you'll do the right thing for yourself. Nothing will ever destroy our friendship, and even if we never see each other, again, we'll know we parted with a great mutual admiration and respect—and we'll also know we loved each other but were never in love with each other." They both laughed and moved on to a comfortable exchange of small talk.

Eventually, we heard Evelyn Powers drive away. Pappy remained true to his commitment to us absolutely charming grandchildren, and a few days later, he explained: "I know you kids really think a lot of Mrs. Powers, and I hope you won't be disappointed when I tell you this, but we might not be seeing her quite as often as we have been for the past few months. She's a very nice lady, and we'll always be dear friends, but we've decided to spend less time together. After all, we do have other commitments." That was that. I don't remember, however, seeing or hearing from Mrs. Powers after that day's good-byes on the patio.

Weeks passed with thoughts of the mysterious Rose never far from the minds of us children, and we nearly gave up on Pappy ever doing what Mrs. Powers suggested was the right thing to do—until near the end of that summer.

We kids were invited to spend a week with our father's sister. On our way to Aunt Winnie's house, our grandfather stopped in a little town that he apparently had frequented on his many business trips, and he asked a friend to go along for the ride. He made formal introductions and insinuated upon us children that we were to be on our very best behavior. Rose was no longer a mystery woman.

~~I remembered a picture from that summer. I dumped out several pictures from the box and scrambled them around on my table until I found the one I needed. It was Pappy and Rose, and I was glad I remembered having that photo. Rose's picture deserved a place right up front on the album's pages. She definitely—and lovingly—belonged with my other grandmothers.

CHAPTER TWELVE

When Rose Johnson rode along with us on our way to Aunt Winnie's, I discovered that she was very personable, and she showed a genuine interest in what we kids had to say. She earnestly listened and responded to our remarks, and she gave us an extreme amount of attention. We wondered, however, just how close she really was to our grandfather.

We rode in the backseat of the car and sneaked peeks at Rose. We sneaked peeks at each other from the corners of our eyes. From his rearview mirror, Pappy sneaked threatening glares and pleading looks at us, which just made us behave even more atrociously. We knew we had him at a point where he didn't want to make a scene and, as far as we were concerned, any impending retribution was worth the immediate thrill of pushing our behavior to the limit. At that point, I don't think any of us *burdens* thought we'd ever see Rose Johnson again, anyway, so we must have believed we couldn't get ourselves into too much trouble. I actually thought our trip would end as a big joke where we'd once again tease Pappy about having a girlfriend.

We older kids forcefully convinced Sammie to climb over the seat and ride up front between Pappy and Rose Johnson, and Sammie was mad. She didn't want to miss what was going on in the backseat. Anthony and Levi were nearly eighteen years old, but that day they acted as if they were about nine. The boys made mock-kissing gestures and noises. They rolled their eyes toward the backs of their heads, batted their eyelashes, and made lovey-dovey faces. Eleven-year-old Sammie twisted in the seat, craned her neck around toward us, giggled, and fidgeted. The boys pulled her hair and shoved her head back around toward the front. Sammie whined and fidgeted even more. We all punched and poked at each other, made goofy faces, and shoved our knees and feet against whatever we could reach.

We held our hands over our mouths in unsuccessful attempts to keep from being heard as we giggled, but that effort produced even stranger and more unexpected noises. "Giggle tears" streamed down our faces. We figuratively, if not literally, embarrassed the dickens out of our grandfather. We were definitely much too old to behave in that manner, but Rose Johnson seemed totally oblivious to our weird, although somewhat typical, childish behavior and frequently smiled while mentioning her own grandchildren who were about our ages.

Upon our arrival at Aunt Winnie's home, it was obvious she was as confused as we were and shared in our wonder concerning just how close Rose Johnson was to Pappy. After a little awkward conversation and an awkward lunch, Pappy and his surprise-guest Rose Johnson left for the drive home.

At the end of our week's visit, Rose miraculously came along with Pappy to reclaim us charming grandchildren. She seemed to genuinely understand everyone's feeling of discomfort and made every effort to put us at ease. She sweetly smiled and did her very best to be cordial. She was a real trooper.

During dinner, Pappy forthrightly made an announcement. "I want you all to know that Rose and I plan to be married." He might as well have dropped a bomb.

For probably the first time in our lives, we four charming grandchildren sat speechless and as still as if we were set in stone. The only things that moved were our eyeballs, but we didn't look at each other. We just looked from one end of the table to the other and waited to see or hear what was going to happen. It was almost like watching a tennis match, but the ball was invisible. First there was a period of dead silence in which Pappy's face turned red, and in which Aunt Winnie's face turned white. Total silence. Aunt Winnie looked as if Pappy had unexpectedly and forcefully shoved a sword through her heart, and she looked like she was going to croak.

I was so shocked that I don't even remember whether or not Pappy and Aunt Winnie said anything. I do remember, though, that after what seemed like another one of those eternities, Pappy and Rose headed us kids toward the quiet sanctuary of the car, where our behavior was much more subdued than on our trip in the other direction, only a week before.

Rose rode all the way back to Bookerton with Pappy and us charming grandchildren following our trip to Aunt Winnie's. Shortly after our arrival at home, Pappy called to give Daddy his good news. It was apparent from the look on Pappy's face that Daddy was about as shocked at the prospect of the union between Pappy and Rose Johnson as everyone else in the family was.

From a child's perspective, it seemed to me that because Aunt Winnie and Daddy had established their own homes and families, they probably weren't against

Pappy's decision to remarry—but, the unexpected news was just surprising, maybe even overwhelming. I thought the idea of Pappy remarrying sounded like a pretty good one and knew that if Daddy and Aunt Winnie knew what life as a widower was really like for Pappy, they'd want him to do whatever he *could* do to bring the happiness of having a wife back into his life. I thought of how he lay in bed at night and couldn't fully hide the sounds of his lonesome sobs. I thought of all the times when he didn't want to eat alone and asked for someone to sit at the table with him, even when nobody else was hungry.

I was sure Aunt Winnie loved Pappy and wished they could spend more time together, and it was easy to understand why she didn't have a chance to visit more often. For one thing, it was difficult to coordinate visitation dates with a man who worked away from home on a fairly regular basis. Also, Aunt Winnie had five young children, so a four-hour long non-air-conditioned drive over winding and narrow country roads wouldn't exactly be a pleasurable experience. In addition to the old standby road games of counting horses and cows, they'd have food stops, pee stops, referee-the-fight stops, puke stops, and some threaten-to-spank-your-rump stops.

As if that weren't enough, with five young children in tow, and with only one income, a lack of money was probably a major contributing factor to Aunt Winnie's limited visits. Her position was easily understood.

Daddy and Barbara, however, lived within an hour's drive from our house, and to the best of my knowledge, my father and stepmother invited us for only one visit to their home. After repeated invitations for them to come and visit us were ignored, however, Pappy occasionally called Daddy and Barbara and took it upon himself to warn them that, unless they voiced objections, we were all coming to visit the Hank

Hunter household. Whoever answered the phone was at least respectful enough not to make excuses and object to our dreaded upcoming arrival, and they weren't disrespectful enough to leave and let us show up at an empty house, but our receptions were definitely less than cordial.

It was always the same. Upon our intrusive arrival, and after finally gaining what felt like an almost forced breaking and entering entrance to the dwelling, we stood and waited for a brief time. Daddy never invited us to be seated, so we silently followed Pappy's lead, and we invaders found ourselves a seat. Pappy, Sammie, and I stood closely beside each other in front of the couch, formed a segmented caterpillar shape, and performed a synchronized sitting motion. Our upper torsos simultaneously leaned forward, and our rumps lowered until they hit the seat cushions of the couch. Then we leaned back. Levi and Anthony sat on the floor and leaned back against the bottom front of the couch. And, we waited out the tense silence.

When Daddy found it apparent that we actually intended to "sit a spell," he rudely—and without the slightest hint of hesitation—turned the back of his swivel chair toward us and watched television. Barbara stayed in the kitchen. We couldn't possibly blame her for the awkward situation—she was young, hardly knew us, and might reasonably have thought it was up to Daddy to take the lead in how to deal with his side of the family, and for all we knew, maybe he'd told her not to get involved with us. When we asked about the baby, Daddy always said that Rachel was going to sleep or was already asleep, and in any case, she wasn't to be disturbed.

During television commercials, Pappy made feeble attempts to strike up some sort of response from Daddy, but he was met with anything other than stimulating conversation. Daddy wasn't easily impressed with our report-card grades. He didn't seem to care with whom we were friends. It didn't matter to him that we were involved in some sort of school activity. He obviously didn't care that we had come to share our experiences with him. With his back toward us, Daddy's chair apparently swiveled—at least temporarily—in only one direction, so his reluctant and nearly inaudible, low-pitched and garbled responses to Pappy's feeble attempts merely wafted from the other side of the fortress he'd built with the back of his chair.

Those visits were so awkward and stressful, and so pointless and ridiculous, that I still smile and shake my head when I think of how Pappy took such extraneous and heroic measures in his effort to spark some life into a situation that would make his son acknowledge his own children. But most of all, I wonder why he persisted. I do remember, however, my own unyielding desire to say or do just the right thing that would change the lack of a relationship we had with our father. All these years later, I realize that Pappy and I shared that sense of responsibility to be the ones who turned on Daddy's light—that light we always hoped he would see. That light, however, remained elusive.

Actually, though, regardless of how Aunt Winnie and Daddy viewed their father's upcoming marriage to Rose Johnson, I thought it would be rather nice to have a grandmother around the house again. I thought it would be nice for Pappy to have a loving companion. I certainly understood why he was attracted to Rose. She was an independent businesswoman with a good head on her shoulders—one who'd proven herself to be an excellent financial manager. On the other side of that coin, she was a petite, feminine, raven-haired beauty who dressed in the latest fashions, wore a tasteful amount of makeup and just enough jewelry, had a knockout smile, and softly spoke with a southern

West Virginia accent. Most of all, though, her heart was as warm as her smile.

On her first evening in our home, when Rose was introduced to Olivia, it was obvious that Olivia was another one who was shocked by the news of the impending marriage. Over the next few days, Rose was introduced to Pappy's friends and neighbors who were cordial, but some were also curious and appeared to be somewhat shocked by Pappy's decision to marry an "outsider." Poor dear Rose!

Rose planned to stay with us for a week, during which time she'd have a chance to see our family in action and decide whether or not she'd be interested in moving in and taking on the brood. If she found the prospect promising, she and Pappy would definitely marry. Olivia tentatively agreed to stay and to continue business as usual. Other than a few antics on the part of us charming grandchildren, all went well, and because Pappy and Rose Johnson truly loved each other, and because Rose Johnson had such a loving and giving heart that she willingly accepted joint child-rearing duties, they eloped at the end of that week.

The day after their wedding, the new Mr. & Mrs. Hunter called home from an undisclosed location to check on us and to make sure everything was all right. We all took turns talking with Pappy and Granny Rose, as we'd decided to call her, and as Sammie was winding down her end of the conversation Olivia said, "I'd like to talk to Mr. Hunter."

She took the black receiver from Sammie's hand and stretched its twisted fabric-covered cord until it reached her ear. She stood up as tall as she could, with her shoulders thrown back in a sort of determination and her chin lifted in a sort of defiance. She took a deep breath. She stared into the corner where two walls met behind the telephone table. A couple seconds of silence passed before she spoke into the mouthpiece.

Her broken voice betrayed her stance as she said: "Mr. Hunter, I hate to ruin your honeymoon, but you'd better start home. I've decided not to stay on. I'd like to move back home with my son and my mother. By the time you arrive, I'll be packed and ready to leave."

I wondered what was said on the other end of that phone line, and I was sure that, whatever it was, it had been said with some of that shock and disbelief that recently accompanied so many of our conversations.

For probably the second time in our lives, we four charming grandchildren were speechless and as still as if we were set in stone. When I looked up at Olivia, I felt tears sting my eyes. I didn't want her to leave us.

I thought I was probably experiencing the same feelings Aunt Winnie had when Pappy dropped the bomb. This time, it was I who just about croaked. I wanted to blurt out my own obvious disbelief with, *"OLIVIA, HOW COULD YOU DO THIS TO US?"* But I just stood there and accepted it; there was nothing I could do about it. Without saying a word, I wiped the tears from my cheeks. Mine weren't the only tears in that room.

Olivia placed the receiver on its cradle and turned to look at us. "Anthony, Levi, would you boys please go across the street and get some boxes from the store?" she asked. "I'll need them when I pack my things."

We girls stood in total silence and disbelief until the boys returned with a few cartons. We followed Olivia upstairs to her bedroom and solemnly watched as she filled those boxes and packed her suitcase with her personal belongings. The boys stood in the doorway, and Sammie and I knelt on the floor and leaned against the bed. We watched as Olivia carefully and methodically removed her starched and neatly ironed housedresses from the metal hangers in the cedar-lined closet. She spread each item flat on the bed and folded it to a size that would fit each box or suitcase in which it was to be packed. She emptied each drawer and silently continued to fill her boxes. I don't remember that anybody said a word.

I prepared for another good-bye to a lady who had been my almost constant companion for many years. For me, it was almost as if I were watching somebody die, because I knew I probably wouldn't see Olivia again. My other mother-figure losses hadn't been by choice, and I couldn't understand why Olivia actually chose to desert us. I hoped the only reasons she chose to leave were because she wanted to be with her own son and because she thought that, with another woman in the house, she wasn't leaving us stranded. I wondered how long she'd stayed with us only because she felt a sense of obligation. I wondered if she'd been unhappy with the tremendous amount of responsibility that fell upon her after Granny Kate had died, especially because Pappy had been away so much. I mostly hoped Olivia wasn't leaving because we kids had done something wrong, or because with all our excitement over a new grandmother that we'd made her feel unwanted, unneeded, or unloved.

We helped carry her familiar things downstairs, and the only sounds were footsteps, bottles of rattling toiletries, little sniffles, and swallowed sobs. When Pappy and Granny Rose arrived home, Olivia was ready to leave, and Pappy drove her home. We charming grandchildren didn't go along on that ride. It would have seemed like we were riding in Olivia's hearse. Pappy returned without her, and we truly missed her. My greatest consolation was that I knew she'd be happy being at home with her own son and her mother, and I knew they were blessed to have her with them.

When Granny Rose moved into the house there were many welcomed changes—one of my favorites was that we kids were allowed to spend more time with Grandma Maddie—because Pappy had Granny Rose for companionship.

We moved back into our former bedrooms. I had my old closet back and put my treasured possessions in their old homes on the built-in closet shelves. I looked out the windows at the old familiar sights and heard the sounds of cars as they traveled along our little country highway. I heard the distant sounds of the trains' whistles from my old post.

I thought of my old planned emergency escape route from my window, out onto the stoop roof, and down the rose trellis. I heard soft whispers and laughter from the master bedroom, and the warm feeling it gave me made me glad to be back in my own room. Finally in my own bed, I rolled to my side, fluffed the pillow under my head, smiled, and drifted off to a peaceful sleep.

Along with Granny Rose came a whole new family. Her grown children and grandchildren were about the same ages as Pappy's clan. Granny Rose's family was initially more receptive to the inclusion of Pappy's family than Pappy's family was to the inclusion of Granny Rose's. That seemed odd, especially because it was she who moved from her home, moved farther from her own family, gave up her business, remarried in her fifties, and accepted the tremendous responsibility of helping to rear four kids whom she hardly knew. Granny Rose soon enamored everyone, however, and quickly endeared herself to us all.

A few months after their marriage, Pappy retired from his job, stayed home with Granny Rose and us kids, and we created some very happy times in that home. Granny Rose was a definite blessing.

I was absolutely delighted with the union between Pappy and Granny Rose. Granny Rose—being an attractive and fashion-conscious lady—was a woman who recognized the fashion needs and desires of a young girl. That attribute served to my advantage, too, because it would soon be time for me to enter high school.

~~High school was where Jacob and I met. I reached back into my box and pulled out my favorite picture of Jacob, which happened to be a military photo. He was so handsome in his honor-guard uniform.

CHAPTER THIRTEEN

I was as ready as I'd ever be to take another huge step toward becoming an adult. In 1964 my friends and I entered high school and immediately lost our upperclassmen status. We also lost some spunk and attitude but remained confident in the power and strength of our friendship. None of us wanted to walk alone through those unfamiliar halls, sit alone at lunch, or stand alone between class periods.

Once again, new faces were seen, and as with the consolidation of friendships in the sixth grade when our schools became consolidated, we incorporated new friends into our group. We were inundated with homework, but we participated in school functions, and our schedules became even more rigorous when some of us became cheerleaders, majorettes, and/or band members. We made that extra effort, though, and our friendships remained intact. Again, we had silent crushes on boys but considered the actual possibility of dating and were somewhat more reluctant to give up our own dream of a relationship with a certain boy—

only because an unknowing friend declared her interest in the same guy.

Even though it was decades ago, I still remember the first time I saw Jacob Thomas. I was a freshman; Jacob was a junior.

Near the end of that school year, early one morning in the locker hall, Jacob's cousin, Mary Lee, approached me and said: "My cousin Jacob is interested in you. He's pretty shy, so he doesn't know how to approach you, and if he knew I'm telling you this he'd probably kill me. He doesn't even know I know about it, but in study hall, his friend Mike told me that Jacob has a crush on you. I want you to meet me at the Coke machine in the school basement during today's lunch period. We'll watch for Jacob, and I'll show you who he is. After you've seen him, if you think you'd like to talk to him, I'll tell Mike this afternoon in study hall, and he'll make sure Jacob finds out."

I thought I had nothing to lose, so I said: "Okay, I'll meet you at the Coke machine, but don't you let anyone know we're watching for Jacob. I'd be so embarrassed." I thought our covert operation would give me the opportunity to check out Jacob, without Jacob knowing he was being checked out.

I could hardly concentrate on my morning classes. Even though I had absolutely no idea who Jacob Thomas was, I was interested in finding out. He was, after all, an upperclassman who also was a definite prospect, especially because he'd already expressed his interest in me. At last lunch break arrived, and I walked down to the school basement, happily foregoing lunch to meet with Mary Lee. We tried to look inconspicuous and as if we were supposed to spend the entire lunch period standing beside the Coke machine. We waited for an unsuspecting Jacob to make some sort of an appearance. As soon as Mary Lee saw him, she grabbed my arm, pulled on my dress sleeve as if she were fanning a tiny fire, and she excitedly said: "There he is! That's Jacob! There he goes up the stairs!"

I saw only the back of Jacob Thomas. With his books shoved under one arm, he skipped the steps, two at a time. He had the cutest butt I'd ever seen on a guy, and I realized that was the first time I'd consciously noticed such a thing. Something about Jacob Thomas, even though it was only the backside of him, caused me to experience strange but wonderful feelings—possibly my first real physically-attracted-to-someone feelings. The sides of his hair were combed back, and his loose natural curls actually glistened in the light from the windows at the top of the stairs. He wore a dark teal-colored shirt and black pegged-legged jeans. He wore black socks, shiny black loafers, and a patterned sweater that was white, black, and teal. And—he wore a class ring that I knew he'd eventually ask me to wear.

I'd seen Jacob from a distance of about fifty feet and didn't even know what his face looked like, but at that very moment, I knew I loved him, and I knew I'd marry him. As simple as it sounds, that's the truth. I never could explain it. I just knew it. It was that old love-at-first-sight thing about which I'd heard. It wasn't puppy love; I'd experienced that. When I was about eleven years old, I was introduced to the thirteen-year-old son of some family friends, and even though it was obvious the older boy didn't care that I existed—for the following few weeks, puppy love hit me hard. I was hardly able to eat or sleep, could hardly think clearly, and every time I closed my eyes all I could see was that thirteen-year-old boy's face. The feeling I had for Jacob Thomas wasn't like that. I knew, without a doubt, that I belonged with him and that someday it would happen. I just had to be patient.

Once in a while after school, I went to visit Grandma Maddie, who lived within walking distance of the high school building. One particular afternoon I crossed a bridge on my way to Grandma Maddie's and came to a little section of the highway where a guardrail along the road doubled as a seat for some of the high school boys who seemed to think they were too cool to ride the school bus, and who opted to hitchhike home, which at that time was a pretty safe thing to do in the area. That afternoon, Jacob Thomas was one of the cool guys on the guardrail. He was too shy to make contact with me when he was alone, but when he was with a few other cool guys, he went along with their whistles and catcalls which, at that time, was also a pretty safe thing to do in the area.

I gratefully and sort of guiltily felt a little like a budding sex object, but proper behavior dictated that I prove myself to be a lady and to ignore those old cool boys. So, I reluctantly but quite deliberately, made a conscious effort to make myself appear to be making a conscious effort to ignore those whistles and catcalls and to make absolutely sure not to make eye contact with any of those cool guys. I just sauntered right past them, in a way to make sure they knew I was just sauntering right past them. I acted just as if they weren't perched on the rusty guardrail. If Jacob Thomas wanted to know he'd gotten my attention, I decided, he was going to have to do better than that.

Several weeks passed, and Jacob made no attempt to approach me. Based upon what I'd been taught, it was the boy's responsibility to make the first move, so, I, of course, made no attempt to approach him. While I patiently waited in the hope that Jacob would make his move, I double-dated a few times with other couples and just bided my time.

Then one night while attending a prom with Dale Webster, that son of family friends who'd previously evoked my first puppy-love experience and who'd evolved into being a friend who needed a date, I found myself seated at a two-couple table in the high school gymnasium.

To my immediate left sat Dale Webster; to my immediate right sat the stunningly beautiful Alice Maxwell; and directly across from me sat Alice's neighborhood friend, Jacob Thomas. Because I'd only previously clearly seen his backside, and because it had been weeks since I'd seen even that, and because I'd only seen him in my peripheral vision when he sat on the guardrail, I don't know how I knew he was Jacob—but I knew—even before anyone made introductions.

That was the first chance I had to closely inspect Jacob. Although I hardly saw two of those people at the two-couple table, I certainly did take advantage of my chance to soak in every bit of Jacob Thomas, with his glistening black hair, his slightly freckled face, and his beautiful hazel eyes. Most of all, though, I noticed his sexy crooked smile, and that happened to be the clincher. I couldn't help but wonder what it would feel like—another strange feeling—to have Jacob Thomas's thick full lips pressed against mine. As it turned out, a substantial amount of time would pass before I'd find out.

Poor Dale and Alice might just as well have come to the prom with each other. We were all too shy and awkward to hold intelligent conversations, but nobody who sat there needed a degree in electrodynamics to know that definite sparks flew across the little table with the romantic and quickly dripping candle in its center, and with the decades of bubble gum stuck to its underside.

About two weeks after the prom, Sammie and I were playing badminton in the yard when a warm summer shower fell and drenched us; but that warm summer rain was so refreshing that we decided to continue our game. Shortly after the rain subsided, a shiny pickup truck pulled into the grocery store parking lot across the highway. I recognized Jacob Thomas as the driver. Two women, who turned out to be his mother and grandmother, exited the truck and went into the store. I watched from the corner of my eye—a pretty difficult thing to do while playing badminton—as Jacob slid across the truck seat to the passenger side and watched us girls bat the shuttlecock back-and-forth.

Before his mother and grandmother returned to the truck and he ran out of time, Jacob waited for one of my sideways I-see-you-watching-me glances and motioned for me to walk over toward him.

I looked at Sammie and through clenched teeth, almost as if I were a ventriloquist so Jacob wouldn't see that I had noticed and was talking about him, I said: "That's Jacob Thomas. He wants me to come over there." Then I asked the rhetorical question: "What should I do?" As if I expected to pay any attention to Sammie's advice!

"I wouldn't do it if I were you," she quickly responded.

"Oh, there's nothing wrong with going over there."

Sammie looked pretty serious, and with one of those I'm-warning-you looks on her face, added, "I'm telling you—you don't want to go over there..."

Without giving her a chance to finish, I interrupted her little lecture. I quickly decided that she was just a kid, and I didn't have to pay any attention to whatever she had to say, so I gave her an "Oh, quit being so bossy; I'm going," and I defiantly walked away from her.

She called after me: "Okay! Don't pay any attention to me! Go ahead and go! But, you'll be sorry."

I thought, as I supposed Sammie did, that Pappy wouldn't like it if he knew I even considered being bold enough to walk over and talk to Jacob, but I really didn't think it was so terribly improper and couldn't understand why Sammie was so against the prospect. She was usually the one who over-stepped the boundaries, and it was odd that she'd try to stop me from doing something a little out of the ordinary, so I closed my ears to her continuing protests and walked out of the yard.

My heart pounded so loudly that I was afraid Jacob might hear it. My legs were actually weak as I walked toward him, and I didn't even bother to look along the road for oncoming traffic. I concentrated on looking as disinterested as possible and made a feeble effort to appear inconvenienced by Jacob's request.

I made my way to where he was, and when I got close enough to get a good look at him, I realized in the full bright sunlight that Jacob was as cute as a button, and I wondered if he realized just how good-looking he really was. I also noticed that he eyed me in a pretty strange way and egotistically wondered if he was having similar thoughts about me. I stood by his dad's truck and looked in through the window. I saw that Jacob wore only swimming trunks and tennis shoes. His skin was as bronze as was possible, and his teeth were as white as snow. He grinned that sexy crooked grin and just point-blank asked, "Uh, Cassie, would you like to go to a movie with me Saturday night?"

My heart pounded!, pounded!, and pounded!, but I said as quietly, and as slowly, and with as much false disinterest as I could: "Oh, I don't know. I'll have to check with my grandparents and ask if it's all right."

Jacob said, "Uh, I'll call you later. Okay?"

And I responded with my very own brilliant, "Okay."

I stood beside the shiny green pickup truck for about ten awkwardly silent seconds, but for what seemed like about ten awkwardly silent hours, and because Jacob couldn't seem to keep his eyes off me, I was thrilled by what I thought was his intense and quite obvious attraction to me. I sweetly smiled and lowered my eyelids. I looked back up at Jacob, and we made definite eye contact. He literally could not keep his eyes off me. As thrilled as I was to have such an ardent admirer, it eventually became somewhat embarrassing. I'd never had anyone actually stare at me, and it was obvious that Jacob was fighting to hold back a full-blown burst of laughter from behind his smile. I thought he must be ready to explode from the sheer happiness at just being in my presence and with the hope that we might actually have a date for Saturday night. I was sure that if I stood beside him much longer, my own excitement would pop right out of me, and because I didn't really know what else to say, I just said, "I'd better go."

That was that; the most important thing had been discussed, anyway. I walked back to the badminton net and nonchalantly continued the game with my know-it-all grinning-from-ear-to-ear sister, who for once followed my lead, just as if we had nothing better to do, and just as if we had nothing important to discuss.

As soon as Jacob drove his family from the parking lot, Sammie and I ran toward each other and reached across the net! We grabbed each other's arms, squealed, got all wide-eyed, and jumped up-and-down. It was difficult to contain my excitement; jumping up-and-down seemed to help.

Sammie looked at me, and in a high-pitched voice she cried, "Oh, aren't you excited?" My head quickly nodded up-and-down. "Did he ask you for a date?" I quickly nodded, continued jumping up-and-down, and was totally speechless. "This is what you've been waiting for!" Sammie burst out laughing and finished with: "Well, Old Miss Priss, I tried to stop you, but you wouldn't listen. Oh, man! You should see yourself!"

I immediately stopped all motion. My shoulders drooped, and I stood frozen in place. Sammie and I released our arm-clutch. Sammie leaned forward and folded her arms tightly across the area immediately below her rib cage, and she laughed until she could hardly catch her breath.

I made a mad dash for the house and ran through the back door, through the kitchen, through the dining room, across the living room, up the stairs, hit the landing, and looked in the mirror that hung over the hall table. I thought I would die. I absolutely thought I would die!

The summer rain had felt good, but it had been very cruel to me. My blond hair, which had been teased into the latest rounded bouffant fashion, was soaked and looked like a bunch of wet matted straw. Part of it was plastered to my head; clumps of it sort of looked like they were about to slide off my head; and all of it was generally in one sweet mess. Rain had mixed with my hair spray to form various shaped white droplets and clumps that decorated my ratted masses like small glistening icicles. My hazel eyes, with their long, naturally dark lashes that many people told me were among my best features had been betrayed by the mascara that I thought was necessary for added accent. The summer rain had mixed with the black non-waterproof mascara, and my face was smeared and streaked entirely to my neckline with that diluted mixture. I absolutely thought I would die! I thought about how handsome I'd just been thinking Jacob was as I'd stood so closely to him just minutes earlier. Then I thought of how strange I must have looked to him and realized why he hadn't been able to take his eyes off me. I'd thought I was so coy and cute, and even a little bit sexy. My gosh! I looked like a human-cannonball clown who'd returned from being shot into a lake from the end of an exploded cannon. I thought I might not be able to face Jacob on Saturday night, but I got over it.

I requested and was granted permission to go to a movie with Jacob, maybe because Pappy thought the boy couldn't be all bad—after all, he'd asked me out even when I'd looked like a clown gone bad..

For the big first date, I borrowed a lime-green sleeveless A-line dress from one of my best friends, Pattie, who'd made the dress herself. I tried to get as much sun as I could that day and hoped my lobster shade would turn brown by evening, but it didn't. No matter what color my skin was, though, when Jacob Thomas pulled into the driveway, I was ready for Saturday night.

I looked out from the upstairs landing window, saw the required other couple in the car, noticed that Jacob's parents' car was as shiny as his shoes and his hair, and I knew Jacob was ready for Saturday night, too. I hoped Jacob wouldn't honk the horn for me or Pappy would tell him all about how a gentleman does not honk for a lady, but Jacob's dad must already have given him the "Never Honk" speech, and I watched as he walked across the patio and politely acknowledged Pappy's presence on the glider. Jacob lifted one foot up behind the calf of his other leg, rubbed the top of his shoe against the back of his jeans, added a little shine to the top of that shoe, repeated the process with the other foot, and knocked on the door.

I walked downstairs thinking that, accented by my few pieces of jewelry, my red skin and borrowed lime-green A-line dress made me look like a psychedelic Christmas tree, but as embarrassed as I was, I forced myself to exit the door. I simply said, "Hello." Pappy watched with the critical eye of the gentleman he was, so as I walked beside Jacob toward the car I hoped he'd open the car door for me, or Pappy might give him that whole "Door Opening" speech, but Jacob's dad had covered that one, too.

Pappy issued a warning. "By the way, Jacob, have her home by midnight."

Jacob politely and quite respectfully answered, "Yes, sir, Mr. Hunter. I will." Pappy really loved the *sir* word, and I guessed Jacob had easily scored a few points with it. He walked around the car, got in, and as we drove away, Jacob offered the other couple and me some spearmint gum. We all accepted, chewed the gum and sniffed the spearmint aroma as it filled the spotless interior of the car—and even today when I smell spearmint gum, I have a warm memory of my first date with Jacob Thomas.

We went to a drive-in movie, which was the only way to attend a movie in our area at the time. Jacob and I probably said about ten words to each other the whole time we were there, but it was an absolutely electrifying experience. Jacob also had a midnight curfew, and he had to drop off the other couple, so I was home about a half-hour ahead of my curfew. Pappy was happily impressed with Jacob's schedule.

Nice girls were required to follow the three-dates-before-the-first-kiss rule, so when Jacob walked me back to the door from which he'd originally picked me up, we simply and politely thanked each other and said we'd had a nice time.

"I'll, uh, call you. I mean, uh, if you'd like that, Cassie."

"Okay. I mean—if you want to call—it's okay," I responded. Jacob smiled, nodded, turned, and walked to his car. I went inside, ran up the stairs, and watched from my bedroom window as he backed out of the driveway, pulled out onto the highway, and drove away. I watched until his car lights were out of sight.

The next day when Jacob called, even though I was embarrassed and dreaded doing it, I said: "I have to tell you something. I have a time limit on the phone. I'm only allowed one call."

At that time, people in our small community shared party lines, and during each call, a buzzer sounded shortly prior to a three-minute automatic cutoff, and at the three-minute point the line automatically went dead. I explained to Jacob that I was to exercise courtesy and certainly was not to tie-up the line for the other folks who shared our party line.

Initially Jacob understood, but as our relationship blossomed, he discovered a way around our telephone dilemma. If he called my home number with the assistance of an operator, there was no automatic cutoff. Using that method, depending on whether or not Pappy was around to keep an eye on whomever answered the phone and to notice how long I was on there after I answered it, one call often allowed Jacob and me an unlimited amount of phone time. I knew I was pressing it, but technically it was only *one* phone call. When we heard a click on our party lines and knew that someone else needed access, we quickly finished our conversations and hung up. I didn't want to risk someone complaining to Pappy about my long-term phone use.

Jacob and I held fairly decent conversations on the telephone, but when Saturday night arrived—the only night I was allowed to date—and when Jacob and I were in actual contact with each other, it seemed we'd already covered, over the telephone, every bit of information either one of us knew. Still, as far as I was concerned, our quiet time together was absolutely electrifying!

About a month after our first date, I attended an afternoon stock car race with Jacob and his parents. After leaving the race, we all stopped off at Jacob's parents' house, and I was a nervous wreck. I looked at his parents and said, "Thank you for taking me with you; I had a good time." I smiled and hoped the grit and dust I felt imbedded between my teeth didn't look as bad as it felt.

Jacob's mother, who went by her childhood nickname of Bitsy, said: "Well, we're glad you were able to go with us. Maybe we can all go again, sometime." I didn't know what to say, so I just nodded and smiled.

Jacob asked, "Dad, can I borrow the truck to take Cassie home?"

Bob said, "Sure, Jacob, go ahead and take it." Then he looked at me and said, "Well, Cassie, I hope you don't mind riding in the truck, because Jacob would rather drive it than the car."

"I don't mind," I replied and wished I could think of something to add.

We all exited the car and said our good-byes. Jacob and I walked over to the truck. He opened the door for me, and I struggled to climb up into that monster. I hadn't had a lot of experience climbing into trucks, and I'm sure I wasn't very graceful-looking as I vaulted myself up and into that contraption.

I lifted and placed one foot up to the cab floor, which seemed to strike me at about chest level. I reached around for whatever I could find—door frame, window frame, handles, seat covers, just anything to hold onto—with which I could possibly pull myself up. I bounced up-and-down on one foot until I had enough momentum and spring to catapult my body up to the seat and only bumped my head slightly as I did so. I was determined to get in there on my own steam, without Jacob having to shove me up and in.

Jacob politely acted as if he hadn't noticed my lack of truck-entering skill. I almost felt like he should congratulate me on conquering my task, but he just shut the door and ran around to the driver's side of the truck, easily hopped in, and hit the ignition. He slowly drove me home in absolute silence, and I realized the obviously extended drive that lasted for about thirty minutes was our first time alone in a vehicle. When we reached my home, I said, "Jacob, you don't have to get out with me." And in some kind of struggle to have more than a one-liner conversation, I nervously laughed and added a less than clever, "It's broad daylight, and I don't think a wild animal will get me before I cross the patio."

"Okay." Jacob was as fluent as I.

I hadn't considered a technique for my descent from the truck, however, and when I opened the truck door, it looked like a long way down to the concrete driveway. I'd already spoken, though, and had even tried to make a little joke, so I was determined to get out of that truck without falling flat on my face. I turned sideways on the seat, faced out, and grabbed the doorframe. I placed both feet together and stiffened my legs. I aimed my body like a rocket heading toward the ground, let go of the door frame, and as I slid off the side of that seat, just like sliding down a short sliding board, I felt the back of my clothes rise up around my neck. I don't know how my departure must have looked to Jacob, but he didn't laugh. Once I'd slid out of the truck and shut the door, Jacob scooted across the seat to the passenger side, faced me as I tried to rearrange my clothing, and he leaned against the space of the open window.

After a little small talk, from somewhere out of the blue, he shyly and almost inaudibly mumbled, "Do you care if I kiss you?"

I knew Pappy was probably watching out the window, and I also knew that if he saw me actually step toward that truck window, lean toward that boy, and allow that boy to kiss me in broad daylight, right there in front of God and all the neighbors, I'd be in big trouble. So, I just stood there. My mind and heart raced. I really didn't know what to say, so I didn't say a word. I just stood there. After what seemed like hours, but surely were only seconds, a silently and seemingly rejected and totally dejected Jacob lowered his eyes and quietly scooted back across the seat to the driver's side, started the truck, backed out onto our little country highway, and drove away—*probably*, I thought, *forever.*

He was so shy, and I knew he'd had to work hard to summon the nerve to ask me whether I cared if he kissed me. I knew he'd waited a whole month to even get up enough nerve to ask, because he was probably afraid I'd say no. I knew he probably felt humiliated and embarrassed, and I knew he must have felt that I'd shot him down. I knew he thought I was a lady, and he didn't want to offend me. And I knew he was wonderful.

I walked into the house, sat down right beside the telephone and waited. A few minutes later the telephone rang, and I almost didn't hear it over the pounding of my heart. I picked up the receiver after about three rings, because I didn't want him to think I was just sitting around waiting for his call, and of course it was Jacob.

He said: "Hi. I just called to tell you I'm sorry I asked if I could kiss you. I didn't mean to offend you in any way. Aw, Cassie, I hope you're not mad at me."

Silence was my immediate response. I couldn't tell him what was on my mind, and especially not what was in my heart, and I couldn't tell him that from the very first time I saw his sexy crooked smile that I wondered what his thick, full lips would feel like against mine, so I just said: "Oh, that's all right, Jacob. I'm not mad." With that topic covered, we had a nice discussion about the race we'd attended. But the prospect of a future kiss lingered in the deepest recess of my mind.

I told Sammie and Granny Rose all about the little episode, and of course they told Pappy and my brothers, and before long it was like some sort of a joke around our house. Jacob was bound and determined not to offend the lady he thought I was, so for the next several weeks, every time I came home after an evening out with Jacob, people from every bedroom in the house yelled out, "Well, did he kiss you, yet?"

In response to my silence, they all laughed. I didn't think it was funny and thought I was never going to find out what those thick, full lips of Jacob Thomas's would feel like against mine, but I was sure I just couldn't blurt out to him that I was ready to find out.

Then one December night after a dance at our high school, Jacob dropped off the other couple with whom we'd attended the dance. The usual method of operation was to drop off the girl whose house was located first along our route, and after the boy walked his date to the door, he returned to the car and rode or drove to the next girl's house with her and her boyfriend. The plan the boys devised that night, though, was that the other boy would leave Jacob's car and wait at his girlfriend's house, and Jacob would pick him up on his way back, after having dropped me off. That round trip would take about fifteen minutes. When Jacob and I arrived at my house, he walked me to the door. As usual, I said, "I had a really nice time."

Jacob shuffled his shiny shoes around on the patio. His shoes were still shiny because, even though we'd attended a dance, we hadn't danced. I didn't know how to dance and was too self-conscious to try. We only attended school dances for the chance to be together and so we could occasionally hold hands.

Jacob examined his shoes with much concentration, and after a couple minutes he said, "I'm glad you had a nice time; so did I." He kept his head down and shoved his hands in the pockets of his black overcoat. He lifted his shoulders and allowed the collar of his coat to protect the back of his neck by warding off some of the December cold. Then he said: "Well, I guess I'd better be going. I have to pick up Bill at Mandy's house. He'll be wondering where I am."

"Yeah. Well, thanks for taking me to the dance. Like I said, I had a good time." Much to my disappointment, Jacob turned and started across the patio toward the car.

To my surprise, he stopped, turned, faced toward me, and nearly inaudibly said, "Oh, I forgot to tell you something." After a long pause filled with my wonder and anticipation, and almost as if Jacob had to draw from every bit of strength within him, he almost choked out: "You looked nice tonight."

I was thrilled! He'd never complimented me, but I couldn't let him know I was thrilled, so I simply smiled and modestly said, "Thank you."

As an afterthought, and possibly in an effort to relieve his embarrassment, Jacob lost a point when he added, "Well, my mom told me to tell you that." I could have done without that bit of revelation, but I didn't care why he'd told me; I was just glad he had. I was certain that in the telling of our evening's events, I would be sure to expound upon the compliment, making it sound like it came from his heart, and without mentioning the part about it being a direct order from his mother.

Jacob stood there for a few seconds, like he wasn't sure what to do; then he made his move. To my utter surprise, he headed back toward me, walked directly over to me, looked into my eyes, pulled his hands out of his pockets, put them on my upper arms, squeezed ever so slightly, and without saying a word, he leaned forward and kissed me on the cheek.

On the cheek? We'd dated for over six months, and he kissed me on the cheek?

Mission accomplished! He turned away, left me standing in a weak-kneed stupor, and drove away in the car. I thought about it. Well, it was a kiss, even though it landed on my cheek. I was elated!

Of course when I went inside, I got the same old question from every room that held an occupant. "Hey, Cassie, did he kiss you?"

That night I proudly called out from the dimly lit hallway: "Yes, he did! He kissed me on the cheek!"

After a momentary silence, during which time I realized they were only prepared for my usual answer, they whooped, clapped their hands, and yelled "Congratulations!" It soon became apparent, however, that they weren't satisfied with that, because they laughed and added almost in unison, "On the cheek?"

I defended his kiss. "I don't care where he kissed me. He kissed me!" I went to bed and drifted off to sweet dreams.

The routine continued for another six months. No matter where we went, or with whom we went, nobody kissed anybody until I was walked to the door, and then I got my obligatory kiss on the cheek. So one night when we returned from a drive-in movie, Jacob headed for the old cheek area and, I, being the brazen hussy I was absolutely forced to become, took matters into my own hands and turned my face. Jacob Thomas's thick full lips landed right where I wanted them to land. I thought he was probably shocked by my shameless behavior, but I was ecstatic—absolutely electrified! More than a year after our first date, when I stomped up those stairs and took my stance in that dimly lit hallway, I reached toward the switch and flipped on the overhead bright lights, because I had a real story to tell.

~~I put my favorite picture of Jacob in the album and reached down and touched it, almost as if I were touching him, and I smiled. I put my hand back into the box and searched around until I found that special picture we'd taken with the Kodak Instamatic camera that Jacob had given me for Christmas. It was a picture of my hand, and I was wearing an engagement ring.

CHAPTER FOURTEEN

Jacob and I began dating the summer before my sophomore year and his senior year in high school. During that year, Jacob walked with me to my classes, carried my books, and sat with me during lunch breaks. He walked with me to my bus and called me on the telephone as soon as we both were home. We dated every Saturday night, and once in a while, Pappy allowed The Boy (as he usually referred to Jacob) to drive me to church and attend with us—even though our church services were held on Sunday. That year passed much too quickly.

Before Jacob's 1966 high school graduation, he pre-enlisted in the Marine Corps. His reasoning was that before he was drafted, he wanted to choose his branch.

During Jacob's basic training, he wasn't permitted to call or to come home, but he wrote as often as he could. I had a feeling that Jacob loved me, but he never came right out and said he did. I hadn't told him I loved him, either, but I knew I did. It was difficult for him to verbalize his feelings for me—he was probably embarrassed and afraid of sounding corny.

When he wrote letters to me, though, he was totally uninhibited and was quite adept at expressing his love for me. His written words revealed and beautifully described the appreciation and passion he had for our relationship—and there was no doubt about what lay within his heart.

I walked to the post office every day with the hope I'd receive one of those love-filled messages, and when I did I read it on the way home, because I couldn't wait until I got there to open it. Jacob's heartfelt words were the words for which I longed, and although I knew he cared for me, I didn't know how deeply he cared. His written words made up for all those nearly non-verbal Saturday nights we'd spent together watching movies and holding hands, and where sometimes Jacob faked a yawn, which of course required a stretch that allowed his arm to extend toward the car roof and settle back down and around my shoulders. Just the touch of his hand on my upper arm was enough to make me want to melt. Those nights definitely were filled with a sort of electricity that kept our feelings for each other running on a smooth current.

During the time in which Jacob and I dated through my sophomore year in high school, many of my girlfriends also moved into serious relationships with their boyfriends which placed our friendship contact at a minimum. Our bonds, however, definitely were not broken. Many of us double-dated with each other, and we suffered through each other's courtships and lack of courtships. By the time Jacob entered the Marine Corps, several of us girls had older boyfriends who'd graduated and gone away to college or into military service. Our boyfriends' absences and the longing for their presence soon threw us back into the old routine of spending more friendship time together, where we girls, as always, depended upon each other's emotional support. We comforted each other and made tentative plans for the future.

The year of my Junior Prom, Jacob took a military leave of absence and came home to be my escort. The day before our prom day, Jacob surprised me with a visit at the house. I was out on the driveway washing Pappy's car when Jacob drove up behind it. I was wearing an old pair of wet shorts and a ratty old dark-colored tee shirt. My hair lacked its usual teased style and was pulled back from my face. I wasn't wearing a drop of makeup, which was something that hardly ever happened in those days. I wasn't wearing shoes and was embarrassed, because I believed I had the most ugly feet and toes in the entire world. I was sure my *au naturel* appearance would be a definite turnoff. It didn't take long for me to decide my appearance mattered more to me than it did to Jacob; he didn't seem to notice at all. Then I sort of wondered why I even tried to look good. Jacob helped me finish washing and drying the car. He sprayed me a couple times with the water hose, and I worried that being drenched surely added to my lack of attractiveness, but I was wearing no makeup, and my hair wasn't teased, so I knew I wouldn't end up looking like I did the first time Jacob asked me for a date.

But after a while I thought maybe my lousy appearance *did* bother Jacob, because as the time passed, he increasingly looked and acted a little nervous, and it was obvious that he was definitely distracted. Of course I thought something was wrong. It could be any number of things. I was afraid he didn't want to take me to the prom. Maybe he'd found a different girlfriend. Worst of all, I constantly lived with the fear that he'd have to go to Vietnam. I finally found the nerve to ask, "Jacob, is everything okay?" My heart raced and my eyes held back tears, and I wasn't really sure I wanted to hear his answer.

Jacob dropped his head and looked down. He fumbled around for the right words. He reached into the pocket of his pegged-legged jeans and pulled out something. When he'd asked me to go steady with him, two years earlier, we'd exchanged class rings, and that afternoon I thought he was going to return mine and ask for his. I thought maybe his new life as a Marine made him feel too mature and sophisticated to be dating a high school junior.

He pleasantly surprised me, though, when he said: "Cassie, we've dated for a couple years, and I know you have another year of high school. Aw, Cassie, I'm not good with words, but you know how I feel about you. I just have to know—will you marry me?" He opened his hand to reveal a diamond engagement ring. I thought I would die! I absolutely thought I would die!

I was no better than Jacob at expressing how I felt. My heart flip-flopped inside my chest, and my knees were weak. I felt as if I were floating. My mind screamed: *"YES, YES, YES!!! OH MY GOSH!!! I CAN'T BELIEVE THIS!!! I THOUGHT YOU'D NEVER ASK! OH MY GOSH!!! YOU ACTUALLY BOUGHT ME A RING!!! OH MY GOSH!!! I LOVE YOU, JACOB!!! I LOVE YOU, JACOB!!! OH MY GOSH!!! OF COURSE I'LL MARRY YOU!!! THIS IS EXACTLY WHAT I'VE WANTED FROM THE FIRST TIME I SAW YOU SKIPPING STEPS IN THE SCHOOLHOUSE!!! I LOVE YOU; I LOVE YOU; I LOVE YOU!! SLIDE THAT DIAMOND RING ON MY FINGER, BOY!!! YOU JUST SNAGGED YOURSELF A WOMAN!!"* But, a single word came out of my mouth, and I heard myself softly say, "Yes." Jacob smiled that sexy crooked smile and slipped the ring on my finger. Then he gently kissed me.

"Wait right here, Jacob. I have to go get my camera." I ran upstairs to my bedroom and grabbed the little Kodak Instamatic that had been a Christmas present from Jacob. It was loaded and ready for prom night. I ran back downstairs and outside where Jacob was patiently waiting, positioned my hand on the patio table, and adjusted my ring to its most flattering position. I snapped a picture, turned around, and took a picture of that handsome dickens who'd just given me the ring. Jacob grabbed the camera and took a picture of me. That film was destined to record a little piece of our history.

We were going to have to discuss our engagement with Granny Rose and Pappy, which was a little scary, and I hoped they wouldn't tell us we were too young to become engaged and make me return the ring. I knew that regardless of their response, however, I would eventually marry Jacob Thomas.

My grandparents were just as understanding as I'd hoped they'd be. Even though Jacob and I were young, Pappy gave us his blessing, because he and Granny Rose had grown to love The Boy as if he were their own grandson, and they had no doubt that Jacob and I truly loved each other. So Jacob's transition from being almost like a grandson to becoming a future grandson-in-law seemed quite natural. My grandparents hugged us and told us they knew we loved each other, and Pappy said, "Jacob, the only thing I'll insist on is that you won't get married until after Cassie graduates." We agreed. Neither one of us was ready for an immediate marriage. I definitely wanted to finish school, and in the meantime Jacob had places to go and things to do.

I was scheduled for early the next morning to help my friends decorate the gymnasium for the prom. Jacob had stayed at my house until curfew the night before, so I didn't have a chance to call my friends and tell them the great news. Jacob picked me up to take me to the gym, and I wore the ring. We drove in a blissful silence filled with anticipation until we reached the school, where Jacob dropped me off outside with a promise to pick me up a few hours later and take me home. I watched until he drove out of sight.

I could hardly wait to show the ring to my friends and to tell them my news. I almost glided over the wide sidewalk that separated two of the school's structures and hurried toward the gym. I walked in, nearly ran to where my friends were gathered, and without a word, I extended my left arm, bent my wrist, and dropped my left hand, which placed my ring in a good position for my friends' examinations. They gathered around to share in my joy and excitement, and just as we had as youngsters, we squealed and screamed, ran and jumped, and laughed and cried.

Janie twisted my hand around to catch the shine of the ring. "Oh, wow! Wonder how much he paid for it?"

Pattie was mortified. "Oh, Janie! I can't believe you said that! It doesn't matter how much he paid for it. Whatever it was, Cassie and Jacob's love is worth much more than any amount of money." Profound. Pattie was deep.

Susie was elated. "Cassie, I'm so happy for you. You're both so lucky."

"I hope I can find someone like Jacob someday," announced Carley.

"I was so shocked," I told them. "I couldn't believe he asked me to marry him!"

Mandy demanded: "Cassie, you have to tell us everything. What did he say? What did he do? What did you say? What did you do? Oh, my gosh, what did your pappy and granny say?"

And in the excitement, Laura agreed with Mandy. "Cassie, tell us. Come on, you have to tell us. Was he romantic?"

Betsy tried to take control of the situation. "Let her talk. Let her talk."

So I did. I told them exactly what had happened.

"Oh, you'll have to show us the pictures when you get them developed," Dee Dee insisted.

Mandy laughed, looked at Dee Dee, and said: "Hey, Dee Dee, you don't have to wait for the pictures. Let Cassie show those to her grandchildren. You can look at the ring right now!"

Dee Dee said: "Oh, well, I guess I *am* looking at the ring right now. I'm just so excited; I want to share in it all—including the pictures."

Everybody spoke at the same time, and I was just able to pull bits and pieces from their excited questions, demands, and comments, but I knew those all amounted to about the same thing. They were all happy for Jacob and me.

We attended the prom that night, and I felt as if I were Cinderella when I got up enough nerve to attempt a slow dance while Jacob held me in his arms. I wore a floor-length, white, lace-covered gown with a blue satin ribbon that wrapped around the empire waistline and tied in a bow. My satin pumps had been dyed to match the color of the ribbon on my gown. Jacob's Marine Corps dress blues made him stand out but, unfortunately, there were many military uniforms in that gymnasium. It was late spring, 1967.

The time passed too quickly when Jacob was with me, and it passed too slowly when he wasn't. He returned home on leave in December 1967 and told me he could stay until the day after Christmas. I was so happy that he'd spend at least part of the holiday season with me, but shortly after his arrival, he revealed some dreaded news.

"Cassie, I have something to tell you, but it's really hard." I knew what it was even before he said, "I'm going to Vietnam."

I can't explain my feelings. I couldn't think of my life without him. I couldn't express my fear for what he most certainly would experience. I just softly wept, and we treasured our brief time together while trying to be brave.

The next day, Jacob flew to a temporary base in California, from where he'd be scheduled to fly to Vietnam. I didn't know the exact date, but I knew his departure would be soon, sometime during the first week of January 1968. With his imminent departure looming in the back of my mind, I had a lump in my throat for several days. On the night he was actually leaving for Vietnam, he called to tell me good-bye and that he loved me. That evening, I felt like the lump might choke me to death.

A few minutes after his call, I had to leave home for a baby-sitting job, but my mind of course was with Jacob. Shortly after I arrived at my job, the kids turned on the television, and as they quietly sat watching, a newsbreak invaded the screen, and I had a shock I'll never forget.

I heard that a plane loaded with a group of Marines who were on their way to Vietnam had gone down somewhere off the coast of California. It was feared there were no survivors. I sat down on the couch and was in such shock that I couldn't even walk to the telephone when I later heard it ring somewhere in the far-off distance. The little girl of the house answered the phone, walked over to me, and said the most blessed words anyone could have said at that time.

"Cassie! Cassie! Jacob wants to talk to you on the phone." I jumped up and grabbed that phone as if it were my lifeline.

I nearly screamed: "Jacob, you're all right! Oh, Jacob, I was so scared. I was afraid you were on the plane that went down. I just heard about it on the news."

The somber tone of his voice told me he obviously was shaken when he responded. "Yes, Cassie; I'm okay. I called your house, and your Granny Rose gave me the number where I could reach you. I wondered if you'd heard about the plane crash. I guess you did, and I guess it just wasn't my time to die. I was supposed to be on that plane, but at the last minute a few of us were rescheduled to leave on a later one; it'll be leaving in just a little while."

I cried. "Oh, Jacob, I'm so glad you called to tell me. I was sick when I heard about it. I love you so much, Jacob. I'm so glad you're okay. Jacob, you be careful and come home safely to me. I'll be praying for you."

"Oh, Cassie, I love you, too. I wish I could stay on here all night with you, but I don't have much time—I just wanted you to know I'm all right and that I love you. I'll see you next year." The phone clicked; the line went dead; he was gone.

~~The engagement-ring photo went right beside my favorite picture of Jacob in his honor-guard uniform. I rooted around in my box and added a few prom pictures to the album, and then I found a few of my 1968 graduation pictures. Jacob's mother had taken several of those pictures, because she'd promised Jacob she'd do it for him. We all wished he were able to attend.

CHAPTER FIFTEEN

Jacob was scheduled to be in Vietnam for at least a year from the time of his Christmas visit, so I tried to keep myself occupied with my last few months of schoolwork and activities. Along with my friends, I focused on our upcoming high-school graduation that was scheduled for the spring of 1968.

In addition to others things, graduation meant that we friends wouldn't be together nearly every day, and several adults had already warned us that some of us might never see each other again. But we were determined to remain in contact, no matter what happened, and no matter what anybody else said. We bravely expressed—only to each other—our desire "...to be out on our own where we can do whatever we want to do—without everybody else telling us what to do." Of course I verbally agreed with my friends, but I honestly felt as if I were about to be snatched from the comfort and security of my authority figures' constant, cushioning, and guiding presence.

We were actually expected to venture into the unknown armed only with embedded memories of our teachings. Right from wrong? Choices? Consequences? Responsibility? Direction? Some of us had big ideas and plans for the future, and some of us didn't have a clue. We shared the hope, however, that each of us would take her right path.

We graduated and, with great trepidation, entered an unsheltered world outside our family-oriented communities. We were pelted with a deluge of adult circumstances that forced us to draw upon our fragile web of good moral values, responsibility, and direction. As unprepared as we were, though, we made our choices—some were right and some weren't. Those were our choices, though, and we were either surprisingly pleased with the results of our decisions, or we faced a lot of that music and paid a lot of those pipers about whom we'd been warned. We each hoped to fully mature, to become somewhat independent, and to eventually become an accepted part of that overwhelming adult world.

Pappy and Granny Rose hoped I'd attend college after my high school graduation, but I had other plans. At that point, marrying Jacob Thomas and starting a family were my greatest personal and career goals in life. Pappy insisted, however, that I seek employment, because as he put it: "It'll be several more months until Jacob's tour of duty is finished, and even though none of us wants to consider it, we must face the possibility that Jacob might not return from Vietnam—and, if he does, he might not return as he was before he left. You might need to support yourself, or you might find it necessary to support your family. In addition to giving you some workplace experience, a job will help to pass the time and keep your mind busy while you wait for Jacob's return."

I did as Pappy suggested, and for the next several months, I moved from a small secretarial position to another one with a major chemical company where I earned an excellent rate of pay and received exceptional benefits. After more than a year of our being separated from each other, Jacob came home.

I'll never forget the first time I saw Jacob after his return from Vietnam. When he arrived at my house and walked through the kitchen door, his head was nearly shaved; he'd lost a tremendous amount of weight; and he shivered as if he were so cold he would freeze to death. It was still winter at home, and Jacob had recently left a climate that was hotter than my summer. His hands were shoved into the pockets of his corduroy, fleece-lined, Loden green jacket. The only things that looked familiar to me were his beautiful, although sunken, hazel eyes, and his beautiful thick full lips that trembled with the cold as they tried to form that precious sexy crooked smile.

Even though he was only slightly more than a year older than the last time I'd seen him, Jacob was different, somehow, but I would never truly know how different, or why. I just knew he'd experienced things about which I'd never know, and I was grateful that he'd survived.

During a period of adjustment, Jacob and I dated a while, became reacquainted, and decided to marry. Even though our families encouraged a church wedding, Jacob and I were both too shy to stand before a crowd during a wedding ceremony, so we convinced our immediate family members that we didn't want a formal affair. We preferred something small and with only immediate family members in attendance. My family's minister assured us that, barring some unforeseen circumstance, he'd marry us whenever we were ready; so we thought we were set.

Eventually, Jacob arranged a five-day leave of absence that would become effective in two weeks, and that time allowed me to work out a notice of resignation at work. Three days before Jacob was to arrive in West Virginia, I had a bout with kidney stones and was in the hospital until the day of his arrival. We were a little pressed for time, and we unfortunately hadn't researched the steps on how to make our marriage legal.

When we arrived at the county courthouse to apply for a marriage license, we stopped and read a message that was posted on the door. We'd arrived an hour after the noon closing for the weekend, and that meant we couldn't apply for our marriage license until Monday. We knew a three-day waiting period for the license to be approved would follow. We called our family doctor who informed us of a three-day waiting period for our blood test results, and because it was a weekend, our Dr. Ware couldn't get our blood samples to the lab until Monday. And, that meant we couldn't be married at least until Thursday, which would have been all right, but when we got home and called the minister's house, his wife apologetically informed us that the minister was unexpectedly called out of town and wouldn't return that week. Jacob's leave of absence would end before the minister's return, so we thought we'd just have to wait until Jacob could arrange for another short leave and start all over again, but at least we were aware of how far in advance we'd need to begin the process—and it seemed that the weekend wasn't a good time to start anything. Things weren't working out according to our tentative plans, and we were very disappointed.

We discussed the delay with our families, and on Monday evening Jacob and I went to visit Grandma Maddie. Shortly after our arrival, she said: "After you called this afternoon, I told my neighbor about how disappointed you are that your plans to get married this week fell through, and Esther said, 'Tell the kids that in North Carolina, they can have blood work done, be issued a marriage license, and be married—all on the same day.' So, I thought you might want to at least consider Esther's idea."

It didn't take much prodding to convince us to consider that option. Jacob said: "Well, it's up to you, Cassie. But, if we apply for our license and have our blood tests tomorrow, it'll be Friday or Saturday before we can be married here, and Rev. Masterson still won't be here to perform the ceremony, so we'd have to contact another minister to marry us. Then we have all your packing to do, and we have that fourteen-hour drive back to South Carolina, and we have to find a place to rent before I report back to base on Monday. If we go to North Carolina tomorrow, everything will be closed by the time we get there, but we can be married on Wednesday. That extra couple of days could help us out a lot. If you want to wait until later, though, I'll request another leave of absence, and I don't know when I can get it, but like I said, it's up to you."

I was nervous, but I was psyched and ready to marry Jacob. We wanted to be married that week, and it looked like it might happen after all. When we discussed the new plan with our family members, Jacob's dad said: "You know, Jacob, your cousin Jennifer and her husband Terry recently moved to a little town in Tennessee, just across the border from North Carolina. If you decide to go tomorrow, maybe you could give them a call and spend the night down there."

When Jennifer and Jacob were children, they lived next door to each other and had always been close and familiar, so Jacob thought his dad's idea was a good one. Jacob called his cousin and explained our situation. I could hear Jennifer's excitement coming from the receiver as she said: "Oh, Jacob, you and Cassie come down and stay with us! You know you're more than welcome. This is so exciting! When do you plan to be here?"

Jacob held his hand over the mouthpiece of the phone receiver and looked at me. "Cassie, Jennifer wants to know when we can be there. Do you think you could be ready to leave early tomorrow morning?"

"If you want to go tomorrow, I'll be ready. Tell Jennifer I said thanks."

"Well, I don't want to rush you or anything." Then he grinned.

"Tomorrow's fine with me, Jacob." I was so nervous, I could hardly think straight. I thought it was funny that only a few hours earlier my world was nearly at a standstill, and it rapidly started spinning like a top.

Jacob removed his hand from the phone receiver and held it away from his ear. He motioned for me to lean toward him and to listen to the conversation. "Jenny, would it be all right if we drive down tomorrow? We could be there sometime in the early evening."

"Oh, Jacob, I'll be looking forward to having you two lovebirds in my home tomorrow night. Now, don't you stop anywhere and eat dinner; I want to cook something special for you. Oh, I'm just so excited! I can hardly wait to tell Terry. You'll get a chance to see my boys; you won't believe how they've grown since you last saw them."

Jacob asked for directions to Jennifer's house, and after he received them, he thanked her and told her we'd see her the next evening.

Monday night, I packed a few things in my red overnight and weekender cases that were a part of the set I'd received as graduation gifts, and on Tuesday morning Jacob and I loaded up and drove to Jennifer's Tennessee home. The car was filled with an excited tension, and I wondered how surprised Jacob would be when he saw me on our wedding night, wearing my silky red lace negligee.

I was so grateful to Jennifer, who welcomed us with open arms, and I told her so as she hugged me. We had a wonderful dinner, and Jacob and Jennifer caught up on old times.

Jennifer hadn't seen Jacob since before he went to Vietnam, and he had never seen her youngest child, so there was a lot of family news to discuss. I tried to listen and tried to stay focused, but it was impossible. If there'd been a quiz following the conversation, I'd have failed it.

All that night, I lay awake and was very aware that in the next room lay that man with the sexy crooked smile. I wondered how well he slept.

~~I rooted around in my box and found a picture of me wearing my pink Easter Sunday suit, along with a horrendous hat that I could understand caused Jacob to laugh the first time he saw it. I even laughed when I looked at the picture. Back then, I was slightly offended, though, when Jacob wasn't crazy about the hat that did actually look like the huge white upside-down flowerpot he'd used as a comparison. That pink suit, *sans* the hat, also turned out to be my Wedding Day suit, but I didn't care that I wasn't wearing some fancy wedding gown. I just wanted to marry Jacob, and my attire during the event made absolutely no difference.

CHAPTER SIXTEEN

Early Wednesday morning, Jacob and I drove across the border to North Carolina and went to the courthouse in a small town where the clerk instructed us to go to the town's hospital, have blood work done, return to her with the results—and then we could apply for our marriage license.

We followed the clerk's instructions, returned to the courthouse, and were issued the proper paperwork. Almost as if reading our minds, the friendly clerk finished up with: "If y'all don't have other arrangements and would like to see a minister, y'all go on across the street to the Baptist Church and just walk on in. The minister will be in there, and he'll perform the ceremony. He does this sort of thing all the time."

Jacob and I walked across the busy intersection, stepped up onto the sidewalk, and our eyes were drawn from the steps to the steeple of the huge cut-stone structure. As our heads lifted and our eyes moved upward and widened, our chins dropped down and held our mouths agape. We came to our senses, climbed about twenty concrete steps, and walked into the quiet sanctuary of the church building. We stood inside the door for a few seconds to allow our eyes to adjust from the bright outside sunlight, to the inside light that filtered through the stained-glass windows. The church was so much larger than our little country Methodist Church building that I couldn't help wondering if every church in our county could have been placed inside that Baptist Church structure. Its splendor was quite impressive and nearly overwhelming.

We cautiously roamed around, tentatively searched the premises, and eventually followed a faint typing sound until we found a room with a sign that designated it: The Pastor's Study. With his hands on the typewriter keys, a man looked up from behind his desk—immediately flashed an enormous, white-toothed, southern-welcome grin—and identified himself as Pastor Jennings. He motioned us in, and in a sweeter- and slower-than-molasses southern accent, he asked something that sounded like: "Nayow, whut kin Ah dew foe yew two yungins?"

I actually heard Jacob swallow before he said: "The lady across the street at the courthouse told us that if we'd come over here, you might have time to marry us. Do you have time, or are we interrupting something?"

The minister stopped short of jumping across the desk in all his excitement, hurried around it, instead, grabbed Jacob by the hand, and pumped his arm as if he expected to draw water. With his other hand, he clamped down on Jacob's shoulder just above the arm he pumped, and he talked so quickly and so happily that he almost began to look like a sort of caricature of himself. He grinned that big old friendly toothy grin, pumped away on Jacob's arm, and talked at the same time. "Noo, noo, yung fella! Y'all ain't interruptin' a thang! Ah'm neva too bizzy to brang two yung luvbuds togethah in the bow-ands of hoe-lee mat-roo-mowny!"

146

I was busy translating his lingo, but shortly after he began his explanation for why he was about to leave us, I realized he didn't intend to discourage us. "Nayow, y'all two wait rat hyeah. Ah'm goin' outsad to ray-owned us up a cup-a-la weetnesses. Ah won't be go-en but a meennit."

Jacob and I didn't say a word after the minister left the room. We didn't even look at each other. We silently waited with great expectations. When the minister returned with our witnesses, he explained: "Wayell, looky hyeah; looky hyeah! Ah was looky enuff to fand these two fan, hod-wukin' gintamin out theyah, jist a wukin' own a city sewah lan, not too fah down the straite. Ah aysked them to coom own in and weetness a may-ridge. And, nayow looky hyeah; looky hyeah! Hyeah we all ahh. Evy-buddy riddy?"

The witnesses who'd been snatched from working on the sewer line seemed nearly as nervous as Jacob and I, and we all stood sort of uncomfortably stiff in that little Pastor's Study in the basement of the Baptist Church. Even though I was having a little difficulty understanding the minister's deep-south accent, anything he said must have been with friendly intentions, because he never quit smiling. As it usually did during my most intense times, my sense of humor pushed past my nervousness, and when I realized how we all looked, I forced myself to suppress a giggle.

A newspaper account of our wedding would not have read as usual. Ours wasn't even close to the slightly more traditional affair our families had suggested. At our ceremony, the minister wore street clothes. I wore a pink-and-white striped sleeveless blouse and a pink skirt; my suit jacket was still in the car. Jacob wore white jeans and a dark blue shirt. Our attendants, of course, wore tattered and dirty work clothes—shirts, coveralls, and work boots, but they'd removed their grubby comfortable-looking hats and twisted them around in their hands. The only thing that would have made us look like a more ridiculous lot would have been the addition of my white upside-down flowerpot Easter-Sunday hat.

Jacob and I weren't two jumps behind them, but it was quite obvious that our witnesses hadn't planned to attend a wedding. Those hard-working gentlemen who'd been outside working on the sewer line—not too far down the street—respectfully held their hats in their hands and solemnly listened, along with us two young lovebirds, or luvbuds, as the smiling aren't-we-all-just-so-danged-happy-to-be-here minister began the service, and I had absolutely no idea what he said. I hoped, however, that he knew what he was doing, and I hoped that God thought it was all right.

Jacob and I repeated what we were told to repeat, or at least I hoped we did, and we answered the questions we were required to answer, and I hoped we'd answered correctly. When the minister completed the ceremony, it didn't sound to us like he said anything that even remotely sounded like Jacob could kiss the bride, so Jacob didn't. We stood in awkward silence a while, then we turned around to face our witnesses who suddenly beamed from ear to ear, and I wasn't sure whether I saw tears or twinkles in their eyes. The fellows extended their hands to Jacob and me, and one said. "Coon-grat-shoo-lay-shuns." He actually broke down the syllables for his rendition of the word. The other man was so nervous that he just blurted out, "Ah hope ye look." His was the most difficult to translate, but I guessed he meant he wished us luck.

The proud witnesses and the minister signed the marriage certificate. We politely thanked them, and Jacob paid the minister. We left The Pastor's Study and walked back out into the bright sunlight and onto that street with the still-broken sewer line. I've often wondered if those three men had any idea what a wonderful and lasting union they'd "hoped look" to, and I've often wondered if those men ever thought it would last. I am sure, though, that there has never been a more significant service.

When Jacob and I called home to let my grandparents and sister Sammie know our wedding ceremony was completed, after the usual happy and congratulatory comments, Pappy said: "We got a call from Rose's daughter, and she'd like for us to come down to her house and help with a little project. Since your wedding plans were juggled around, we didn't think you'd mind if we leave, so we told Jacqueline we'd bring Sammie and come down for a day or so. Why don't you and Jacob come back and stay at the house, gather your things together, spend tomorrow night here, and on Friday we'll be home to see you Thomases before you leave for your new home in South Carolina."

"Thanks, Pappy. That sounds like a good idea." I also thought that plan would give Jacob and me a little privacy before everyone else arrived at the house.

We spent our wedding night in a little motel somewhere in Virginia. That night's union began a whole new lifetime of warm, tender, and beautiful memories.

Our next night was spent at the Hunter house. I'd started learning to cook when I was probably about ten years old, and that night after the wedding night, I decided to throw together a spaghetti dinner for my new husband and me. For some reason, at least where I'm concerned, cooking a meal is sort of like styling my hair—when it's really important, when I really want it to turn out well, and when I really try my hardest—it flops.

Jacob still occasionally mentions the first dinner I cooked as his new wife. It was terrible, and he says that for a long time after that disaster, when I mentioned that spaghetti was my favorite dish, he wondered why, and when I mentioned that I might cook spaghetti for dinner, he hoped I wouldn't.

After several months without my favorite meal, and after we'd become somewhat more comfortable with each other as husband and wife, I broke down, didn't mention my plan, and made a pretty edible batch of spaghetti that turned Jacob into a believer.

After that first disastrous spaghetti dinner, we spent our second honeymoon night in my old bedroom, and although the house was empty except for us Thomases, the Hunter spirits lurked in every nook and cranny. It was a strange feeling to be a married woman with my husband in my grandparents' home, and especially in that little girl's bedroom that Jacob Thomas had never seen. It was at the same time fearful and embarrassing, and exciting and beautiful.

The next day the Hunters returned home, and we Thomases gathered and loaded my belongings—at least as much as would fit in Jacob's new 1969 Dodge Muscle car. When we were ready for our departure, we stood on the patio to bid my grandparents and my little sister farewell. A mixture of sadness and excitement tugged at my soul. I was saying good-bye, again, but I was also saying hello to a whole new life, the life for which I had dreamed. I stood beside Jacob, the man who had so completely and so easily become the other part of me.

I believed Pappy knew what was in my mind and what was in my heart, as I looked at the ones I'd be leaving behind. He understood my turmoil, and he wrapped his arms around my shoulders, pulled me toward him, placed one huge but gentle hand behind my head and held it close to the warm and loving heart within his oversized chest. It was exactly where, for various reasons, I'd previously found myself so many times.

As Pappy hugged me, he said the words I will always remember. He said, loud enough for Jacob, Granny Rose, and Sammie to also hear: "Dear, I've lived with you since you were a small child. I know your strengths, and I know your weaknesses. I know your temperament and your personality. I know who you are. Now that you're a married woman, I want you always to remember: If you and Jacob ever have an argument, and if you ever feel the need to come back home—forget it. I love you, but, as I've said, I know you, and I'll side with Jacob, because the argument probably will have been your fault."

We all laughed, and some of my feelings of sadness, apprehension, and premature homesickness were made less intense. We weren't really saying good-bye; we were saying: No matter where we are, no matter how long the time, no matter how far the distance, and even after death, a part of us will always be with each other.

Jacob and I drove from West Virginia to South Carolina, went to our little military town, searched the mobile home parks, and took the first furnished mobile home we found available for rent. We unloaded our car and cleaned our mobile home. We arranged and rearranged the black-and-white vinyl-covered furniture in an effort to make the impersonal things in that room reflect our decorating tastes. We sat back and grinned from ear to ear. We soon grew to love every inch of that many-times-previously-rented mobile home.

It wasn't long after we'd finished cleaning and rearranging that we hopped in the car, took the money we'd received as wedding gifts, and stopped and made our first major purchase. We bought our very own black-and-white television, complete with its own black-and-chrome metal cart on wheels, with a handy little magazine shelf on the bottom. We went to the supermarket and loaded two shopping carts with merchandise. Then we returned to our love nest and carefully placed each newly purchased item in its proper place. That little trailer quickly became our home.

Jacob had already had time to adjust to not having the comforts of his old home, so it was I who at that point was going through the greater transition. I wasn't living with my familiar structure, which meant I'd lost a lot of my at-home conveniences. From Jacob's paycheck, which he always handed over to me, we paid rent, automobile insurance, utilities, gasoline expenses, and clothing expenses. We even paid to do laundry at a Laundromat. The big challenge, though, was buying groceries.

My marriage and relocation found me living a tremendously different lifestyle from that to which I was accustomed. I'd been reared on a farm where we raised, grew, picked, dug, and canned or froze many of our own vegetables, and we butchered much of our own meat. Jacob and I didn't have the luxury of walking down to a basement where we could choose from jars of colorful, ready-to-cook vegetables, and we didn't have a huge freezer where we could simply open a door and choose from a variety of meats. We couldn't carry a bowl down to the potato bin and load it full of potatoes. Instead of natural gas with which to heat and cook, I had to adjust to the use of propane, which wasn't such a different cooking source, except that it didn't last forever.

Our sporty muscle car "ate" better than Jacob and I did, because by the time we spent so much money on our trips back-and-forth between South Carolina and West Virginia, we had very little grocery money left. It was challenging for me to adjust to the prices of groceries, and when we went to Piggly Wiggly where we could buy a variety of canned vegetables on sale for ten-cents per can, we stocked up. We often ran short of money to pay for our kitchen's propane tanks' refills, so for about three days of every month, I turned on our wedding-gift electric deep fryer and heated our canned goods in it. By the end of the month when we were out of propane, we were usually out of a lot of groceries, so we shared a ten-cent can of unseasoned lima beans for breakfast, a ten-cent can of unseasoned lima beans for lunch, and a ten-cent can of unseasoned lima beans for dinner. It didn't really seem so bad, and after a few months it became routine.

When we made our trips back to West Virginia, we filled our bellies with that good old home cooking. We were always given delicious homemade baked treats to take back to South Carolina, but we usually polished those off and had brushed the crumbs from the car seats long before we got to the state border. We weren't great food-money managers, but we had enough pride not to tell our families about our lean financial times, because we didn't think our priorities were out of order. We weren't spending our money foolishly; we were spending it on gasoline to visit our families.

Of course, Jacob and I had discussed wanting children, but we hadn't talked about when we'd like to have them, so when we suspected we might be expecting our first child, we were both surprised, but absolutely thrilled by the prospect.

I made a call to our military hospital and was informed that, as a military member's spouse, I was required to be examined by a civilian doctor, or to wait until I'd missed three consecutive menstrual periods, before I would be given an appointment at the military hospital.

I hadn't missed three consecutive periods, so I decided to wait until we went back to visit our family and arrange for my trusted family physician to confirm or disprove the pregnancy. I don't regret making that choice, because I think Dr. Ware was nearly as happy for Jacob and me as if he were one of our own family members when, after receiving the results and calling me back into his office, he said, "Yes, Cassie, we're going to have a baby."

When I was growing up, our family's Doctor Ware, who was a country General Practitioner, probably had more knowledge and experience than many who, today, call themselves specialists. He was, depending upon whom he saw—and depending upon the circumstances—patient and understanding, or short, clinical, and critical.

I was comfortable with the familiar intimacy of Dr. Ware's little country office setting. About a dozen vinyl-covered chairs were shoved back against three of the faded walls in the waiting room. Over the inside-spotless, outside-spotted windows, and on plain white metal curtain rods, hung straight beige fiberglass curtains that were so thin they nearly looked like they had only one side. An old scuffed and polished table stood in the middle of the worn but freshly mopped linoleum floor that allowed a disinfectant cleaner's scent to evaporate and permeate the room. The table held a transistor radio that, during office hours, was always tuned in to a country-music radio station, at a time when I thought all country music had a yodel, a whine, and a twang. Outdated, yellowed, tattered, and seldom glanced-at magazines were tossed beside the radio and contained articles that were absolutely of no interest to anyone in that room.

Folks sat around and chatted while they waited for Dr. Ware to throw open the thick brown leather-covered and brass-tacked door to his office, release one patient, and hurriedly call out, "Next!" Then everyone nodded toward the next patient, signaled the "We're all aware that it's actually your turn, so don't be afraid to jump up and go on in..." code, and easily incorporated any newcomers into their conversations.

When I was a child, I was also comfortable with seeing Dr. Ware in my home, because when folks were contagious, or when they were just really too sick to dress and go wait in his office, Dr. Ware made house calls with his worn leather case that I thought must be filled with all kinds of potions and cure-alls. I always felt familiar and comfortable with our doctor-patient relationship and knew I'd miss having his guidance throughout my first pregnancy.

Back in South Carolina, with confirmation of my pregnancy in hand, I eventually went for my first appointment at the base hospital and was absolutely overwhelmed by the layout—and practices. Even though I spoke with someone who handed me a gown and directed me to where I would strip off and slip into the gown—and even though she gave me some sort of garbled instructions on how to find my way around the enormous building to where I was to wait to be seen by a doctor—when I left her presence, I lost all sense of direction. The thing that helped me to find my way through those look-alike, sterile, clinical halls was that every pregnant lady had been issued a noisy, rustling, white-paper gown (and, depending upon their stages of pregnancy, many ladies should have been issued two). I followed the sounds made by the scores of noisy, rustling, white-paper gowns until I found the lumbering herd of expectant mothers, whom I then followed to our point of destination.

The first time I followed that lumbering herd of white buffaloes (with varying widths of embarrassing flesh-colored strips of naked skin down their backsides) into the hospital's waiting room, the room was eventually filled with about fifty women, who, regardless of their stages of pregnancy, were scheduled for their first visit at that particular clinic. The glare of those ultra-white walls and the ultra-white ceiling, along with the scores of super-ultra-white-paper gowns nearly blinded me for a few seconds. When my pupils returned to normal, the only colors that stood out were the ladies' various shoe colors that matched their humongous and outstandingly colorful purses. Those huge purses looked ridiculously out of place in the lumbering and rustling white buffalo herd, but they somehow struck a balance with the humongous, colorful, and highly teased bouffant hairdos of the expectant mothers.

A nurse appeared before our group of various girth-sized ladies, and in a very curt monotone military voice and manner, she instructed: "Ladies: This is your first scheduled visit to our clinic. Some of you are here to have your pregnancies confirmed. Some of you have had your pregnancies confirmed by civilian doctors. Some of you are here after transferring from other military installations. But, because this is your first visit to OUR clinic, it is our procedure to require that you bring along a urine specimen on your next visit. Be sure the container is clean before making your deposit. Deposit your FIRST morning output on the MORNING of your next scheduled appointment date. Tightly close the filled container and clearly label it with your proper name. Now: Remain seated, ladies, until your name is called, then proceed to the front of the room. Someone will escort you to—and will remain with you, during—your examination by your attending physician."

The routine began. Each mother-to-be rose when her name was called and immediately reached one hand behind her in a valiant effort to close her gown's gap. Each surely hoped that she wouldn't join the group of those humiliated ones who'd been unsuccessful in their attempts at closure—those who'd waddled away exposing flashes of their flesh and flashes of their fanny cracks. Clamping her knees together, each mother-to-be squatted down as gracefully as was possible, probably hoped she wouldn't topple over as some others nearly had done, and then reached for her own humongous and outstandingly colorful purse, which held the only key to her individuality among the herd. As comical as the actions were, I was one of those mothers-to-be whose name could be the next one called, so I sat in silence. Everybody did. I didn't crack a smile. Nobody did. I didn't say a word. Nobody did. I was glad each time another's name was called and dreaded the time when mine would be. It was comforting to know that the longer I sat, the fewer the people would be in attendance to view my own rise to possible humiliation. At some point, I was destined to reveal my own flesh-colored strip of skin, along with my own fanny crack. Ruling out the upcoming examination by a total stranger, even though he was a doctor, I thought the waiting-room routine definitely had to be the most humiliating experience a woman could endure in that place, with what seemed like hundreds of strangers' eyes watching, but I was wrong.

On my next visit to the base hospital, after donning my issued white-paper gown, I took a place in line with the other mothers-to-be, and we were soon herded off to another room. We stood against the wall, clutched our white-paper gowns' backs and our suitcase-sized purses, and listened carefully as we were instructed, again in a very curt monotone military voice and manner: "Ladies! Step forward and deposit your specimen-filled containers on the table in the center of the room. Everyone is to wait until each name has been verified and matched to a specimen, then you will all be excused at the same time to return to the waiting room for your examinations."

In an attempt at modesty, we specimen-retrievers found it necessary to release the backs of our gowns and stood back as closely to the wall as was possible, while we dug down into our humongous and outstandingly colorful purses and rummaged around through their ample contents that probably didn't include a nickel. When my turn came, with one hand I lifted and deposited my own container on the table in the center of the room. With my other hand, I held my humongous purse behind me and pinched the gap of the gown shut, while trying to make sure the purse covered any exposed fanny part. We were required to supply our own specimen containers, so our contributions varied in shapes and sizes, most of which resembled small to large aspirin bottles. Each container was tightly closed and was clearly marked with each lady's name, as per prior instruction. A nurse then read from a paper on her clipboard, and each specimen was verified. After all containers were accounted for and were matched with the proper owners, one name remained on the list.

The obviously disgusted no-nonsense nurse narrowed her eyelids until they looked like two slits, and her hard, cold, steel-gray eyes searched accusingly around the room. I could almost feel those dart-like looks stab me as they passed my direction. The nurse somehow managed to actually screech through her clenched teeth: "Mrs. Lupinsky? Is there a Mrs. Lupinsky in this room?" Terrified silence followed her nearly ear-piercing question.

Our husbands might have been used to that kind of military talk and behavior, but it looked to me as if we naïve mothers-to-be, who'd obviously come from various sheltered backgrounds, were not accustomed to being spoken to in that tone of voice, and everyone appeared, quite frankly, to be intimidated by it—even though only one of us was Mrs. Lupinsky. In fact, just thinking that I might be mistaken for Mrs. Lupinsky if she didn't hurry and speak up, made me afraid I might involuntarily produce another urine specimen right on the spot.

Finally, poor little mousy Mrs. Lupinsky, who looked hardly old enough to be married, hung her head and summoned her courage to softly answer the question. "Yes, Ma'am; I'm Mrs. Lupinsky." She looked like she was going to her own hanging, and I wasn't so sure she wasn't.

The sarcastic, crabby-assed nurse didn't appear to care that Mrs. Lupinsky was mousy and young. She walked over, scrunched her tall self down to match heads level with Mrs. Lupinsky's, cocked her own head to one side, and got right up in the little head-hanger's face, just like some kind of wannabe drill instructor.

She was absolutely merciless. "Mrs. Lupinsky, it seems that you have difficulty following instructions. We seem to have no urine specimen for you. Is there some sort of a problem you'd like to tell us about? Perhaps you'd like to come back tomorrow, just to bring your specimen, and we'll have to arrange for somebody to make a change in her schedule to run the tests on your contribution, rather than being able to take care of it on this day, which has already been designated for testing. Well, Mrs. Lupinsky? What do you have to say for yourself? Please: Enlighten us."

Poor little mousy Mrs. Lupinsky looked as if she were about to cry, and before the nurse had time to search for a rope and fashion a noose, she finally confessed. "I did bring my specimen, but…"

The nurse insensitively demanded: "But? But? But, what? Either you brought it, or you didn't bring it. There are only two answers, here, and I'm sure you understood that if you did bring it, you were expected to place it on that table. You did see the other ladies' bottles on the table, didn't you? Mrs. Lupinsky? If you did happen to bring it, then, well, please produce it, so we can get on with this. I think you've caused us all to waste enough time."

As all eyes watched, the color of Mrs. Lupinsky's face reddened and heated, until it—or maybe it was the combined fear-driven adrenalin from each of us others—almost heated the room. By that time, the possibility of showing her butt crack was the least of poor little mousy Mrs. Lupinsky's embarrassment worries. She dutifully reached into her own humongous and outstandingly colorful purse and pulled out a quart-sized mayonnaise jar that was totally filled with her early morning amber-colored liquid. It looked as if Mrs. Lupinsky had brought enough pee for all of us. Absolutely no one cracked a smile, except the nurse who seemed more than satisfied, and we got on with it.

On each subsequent visit to the base hospital, I went to the same waiting room, but was examined by a different doctor. As expected, no bonding and trusting doctor-patient relationship was formed.

Usually on payday weekends, Jacob and I left South Carolina on Friday nights and made the more than fourteen-hour drive to West Virginia. We traveled old Route 21, as crooked and as winding as it was, because there weren't many interstate highways at the time. It wasn't long until those trips became more than uncomfortable for me as I rapidly became a wider-flesh-colored-strip-down-my-back lady. In my compassion for Jacob, who'd been in Vietnam for so long, and who'd been deprived of seeing his family for that period of time, I didn't complain—well, at least not as much as I could have—about my discomfort during travel, and we continued to make those long, sleepless, bladder-pressing, and back-aching trips.

Because of our limited weekend-pass time, and because of our lengthy travel time, we made infrequent stops. The sporty muscle car, however, got only about ten-miles per gallon of gas, and even though it required so much of our money, I was glad for the gasoline fill-up stops, where I could find a restroom for those five minutes of blessed relief. Many years later, Jacob confessed to me that he hated those long drives home, but he thought I was probably homesick, and he didn't want me to think he'd taken me completely from my family. I confessed that I wished I'd known what he was thinking.

~~The picture of me in my Easter Sunday/Wedding Day suit went into the album, and I looked in my box for the picture of our first married Christmas together. It only shows the tree, and I laugh every time I look at it. That Christmas didn't turn out as we'd expected it would, but it was funny, touching, and wonderful.

CHAPTER SEVENTEEN

J acob and I decided to spend an intimate first Christmas as a married couple in South Carolina and set a December 26 departure date for our two-week visit back in West Virginia.

Our families conventionally celebrated with freshly cut green pine trees for Christmas, but that particular year I was enticed by a new fad, and Jacob and I broke from tradition. We celebrated with our very own gaudy, six-foot tall aluminum tree, and to add to the ridiculously festive look—aimed right in the tree's direction—was a spotlight with a whirling multicolored reflector that alternated green, red, and blue colors against the tree's garish shiny brightness.

In preparation for our day-after Christmas departure, I cleaned the refrigerator and its freezer, and to keep cleanup and expense at a minimum, we opted to buy two TV dinners that consisted of turkey, dressing, mashed potatoes and gravy, and some sort of cranberry delicacy for dessert. Because Christmas didn't fall on one of the last three days of the month, we had enough propane to bake the dinners, and we happily sat down to our meager meal, which seemed like a feast to us two young lovers who were spending our very first married Christmas together. No matter what we had for dinner, I was sure the company and location were better than those of the previous Christmas Jacob had spent in Vietnam.

Before we had a chance to dig a fork into the hot meals, there was a knock at the door. Our questioning looks signaled that we had no idea who would be knocking on our door—especially right at the beginning of our intimate dinner on Christmas Day. As far as I knew, we hadn't invited anyone—it was supposed to be just the two of us. We stood up and walked to the door.

When we opened it, we found Ben Parrish standing on the other side. Ben looked like he thought we should be expecting him, held up a bottle of champagne—definitely not vintage—and smiled as he said, "I hope I'm not too late for dinner." I immediately thought Jacob had forgotten to mention he'd invited Ben, but when I glanced over at him, Jacob looked as surprised to see Ben as I was.

Luckily for Ben Parrish, we lived in a blessed time of courtesy and manners, so what choice did I have? "Oh, no, Ben, you're not too late. You couldn't have timed it more perfectly. I just took dinner from the oven." Even though I was embarrassed to serve him Christmas dinner from an aluminum tray, I had no other choice. That was all we had, and no matter how embarrassed I was, it was mandatory to be polite, and I was glad I hadn't already taken a bite out of my shiny tray's contents. "Ben, please come in and join us."

When Ben walked into the kitchen and saw the chrome and fake-wood table top, complete with its two intimate dinner place settings of little aluminum sectioned trays that held our pitiful excuse for a meal that suddenly looked like rubber turkey, dog-food dressing, slimy gravy, fake mashed potatoes, and the *piece de resistance* cranberry-jam delicacy for dessert, he looked as if his choice of champagne were just the right accompaniment to our meal, and when I saw that look flash across his face, I glared at his Dime-Store champagne and instantly but silently agreed. Jacob, obviously oblivious to what Ben and I were thinking, continued to look surprised—actually a little dumbfounded—and he hadn't said a word since we opened the door and found Ben standing outside. I sort of decided that maybe I had no grounds upon which I could blame Jacob for not telling me he'd invited someone, because maybe he hadn't.

Even though it was midday, I feigned an excuse of morning sickness, and following Ben's half-hearted protest, I made an effort to assure him that what looked like my meal was actually his meal. "Ben, I've been having a little problem holding anything down, lately, and this is definitely your meal. I'll feel better if I just drink water. By the way, Ben, would you like to open the bottle you brought?" I hoped that by asking, I'd appear gracious, appreciative, and somewhat worldly, and because I wasn't sure what was actually under the colorful foil-wrapped top, I hoped Ben could open it without a corkscrew.

His response was: "Well, I know you and Jacob don't drink alcoholic beverages. I just thought I should bring something. I figured you probably wouldn't want to open it, especially because you'll be leaving tomorrow, so if you don't care, I'd like to take the bottle with me when I leave." Ben seemed to be under the assumption that he didn't live within that same blessed time of courtesy and manners in which I believed we lived—and I wondered why he'd brought the bottle and flashed it around upon entering our home. At that point, I actually was embarrassed that I'd tried to appear worldly and had asked if he wanted to open it.

I wasn't sure whether poor old twenty-one-year-old Ben was a cheap wino, whether he wanted to return the bottle and have his dollar refunded, or whether he was just plain nuts for thinking he'd give the impression of being suave and sophisticated when he carried the bottle into our home, so I said: "It was really nice of you to bring champagne, Ben. It was a lovely gesture, and it will be fine with us if you take it when you leave. You're right; we're leaving tomorrow, and you might want to share it with some of the guys who are staying at the base through the holidays." Ben looked almost relieved when I said that, so I guessed I'd said the right thing. I knew, too, that he wouldn't look like such a suave and sophisticated hotshot when he carried the bottle back outside.

So there we sat—two lovebirds, with an intruder in our nest—and I felt about as welcoming toward Ben Parrish as I did to his chintzy fake champagne. I hated his intrusion. He was a vulture-like vampire who'd shown up to rob our nest and suck us dry, and it was obvious he didn't plan to replenish our fluids.

He pillaged and plundered our intimate Christmas together! He ravaged our plans! He had no idea what evil thoughts lurked in my mind! It was lucky for Ben that I knew we were living in an age of courtesy, whether he knew it or not.

I watched that uncouth partridge dig into my pear tree and eat my pitiful excuse for a meal. Then he lied straight through his teeth and said, "Cassie, this meal was baked to perfection." He sounded absolutely honest, however, when he added, "I genuinely thank you for sharing your meal with me." His taste in champagne may have been questionable, but his look of gratitude was genuine. That was all it took to dissipate my hateful thoughts, and I remembered that his previous Christmas, like Jacob's, had been spent in Vietnam. I looked at Jacob and realized we all knew Ben hadn't actually been invited to our home by anyone other than himself, and I was deeply ashamed of that.

Ben was single, and most of the other single guys had gone home to spend the holidays with their families. Ben's family lived in New York, and as was evidenced by his choice of fake-gift beverage, he probably couldn't afford the trip home for the holidays. I realized he had nowhere else to go where he could be with friends, which was the next best thing to being with family, and I was finally struck with the understanding that Ben didn't want to spend Christmas alone, and I felt bad that we hadn't invited him. I was so ashamed for my thoughtlessness and was even more ashamed for my immediate thoughts upon his arrival. So I decided to do my best to make him feel welcome at our little shiny aluminum-tray and -tree Christmas, because I knew that Ben had hoped we would. After all, being charitable is a large part of what the Christmas spirit is about.

The day after Christmas, Jacob and I left our little town in South Carolina and made our usual first gasoline stop. When the station's owner was cleaning our windshield, he looked inside the car, smiled at me, and apparently noticed my new Christmas-gift maternity clothes—which I really didn't need, yet, but wore because I was so excited. Buck went back into the station and returned with a little 18-inch tall, stuffed Santa Claus. He motioned for me to roll down my window and handed the little Santa through the opening to me. He smiled his grandfatherly and knowing smile and said, "Merry Christmas, Mom." I smiled my appreciation, placed the little Santa doll across the unborn child in my tummy, and he rode to West Virginia with us.

I can't help but think about how that little Santa Claus became a permanent fixture under our many future Christmas trees. When our firstborn child was about sixteen years old, he went out to the garage, built a wooden sleigh, and painted it red. He stuck the nearly seventeen-year-old Santa Clause in it, brought it in to me, and said exactly what Buck had said: "Merry Christmas, Mom." Santa and his sleigh became a set, and when our adult kids come "home" for Christmas, our grandchildren always check out the Santa in his sleigh, and I tell them that old story about Buck and Santa, even though none of them is old enough to appreciate my sentimental tale. But, someday they will.

A few months after that aluminum Christmas, Jacob received word that he was eligible for an early discharge from the Marine Corps. The Vietnam veterans were given something the military people called an early out. That meant Jacob and I would be back in West Virginia for the birth of our first child. Along with his early discharge, Jacob was given medical insurance to cover the costs of future prenatal visits and the costs of delivery. Although our early discharge was a pleasant surprise, we were somewhat unprepared for it. We hadn't planned for future housing and possible job opportunities back in West Virginia. We thought we'd have plenty of time to consider major changes in our lifestyle, but we were wrong.

So when the time came, a few weeks before our first child's due date, Jacob and I bought a homemade utility trailer in which to haul our additional belongings back to West Virginia. We were amazed that we'd packed nearly everything we owned into the car for our initial after-marriage trip to South Carolina, that we'd already accumulated so much in our married life, and that we needed a utility trailer to haul our additional worldly goods when we made our move back home.

We drove away with the car windows down on that warm spring day, fully aware that we were driving toward an uncertain future in West Virginia.

After a few hours on the road, Jacob said, "There's a bad wreck up ahead."

I strained to see what he'd apparently seen but saw nothing. "Where do you see a wreck?"

"I don't see one. I smell one," he replied. I didn't know how to respond, so I didn't. I just looked over at him and was bewildered by the strange look on his face. Without my asking, he explained: "I smell blood. When you've lived closely with that smell, you never forget it."

A while later we were flagged to a stop at the scene of a terrible accident. We sat in stone silence and watched while mangled bodies were gathered from the blood-covered highway, placed onto gurneys, covered with sheets, and loaded into emergency vehicles. When that morbid task was completed, we slowly followed the line of traffic behind the ambulances with flashing lights but no sounds of sirens. We knew everyone involved in the accident was dead.

We sat quietly, alone with our thoughts. I realized I would never know the impact of the atrocities Jacob had endured in Vietnam, but I was sure that no matter what obstacles cluttered our paths, they would prove, in comparison, to be minor inconveniences. I didn't ask Jacob what he was thinking, and I couldn't imagine. I dealt with my own thoughts.

I thought about how from the beginning of our married life together, as I lived with the boy who'd too quickly become a man, I suffered with him during his nightmares about which, unless I tenderly and cautiously asked, he never talked. I learned to lie still and to remain quiet when that gentle man suddenly and

169

protectively threw his body across mine and when, with his mouth so close it barely brushed my ear, he frantically whispered: "Sh. It's okay, buddy; it's okay. Sh. Sh. Everything will be okay. I know it hurts. Sh. Sh. It's okay. No, no, buddy; I won't leave you here alone. I'll stay with you. Sh. Sh. I know, buddy. Yes, I know. I promise—I won't leave you. I won't let you die alone. Sh. Sh."

Jacob meant his buddy no harm, so I was never afraid of him during his nightmare. I was, however, afraid for him and was so sorry for the pain he suffered when he relived that nightmare within a nightmare.

Jacob had been involved in the 1968 siege at Khe Sanh. It was impossible for me to imagine what that time was like for him and his fellow servicemen. It was impossible for me to understand his fear and pain. I would never know that sense of his total devastation and the almost unbelievable events he'd witnessed and endured. It was impossible for me to imagine his thoughts and his memories, or to ever know his grief.

As the drive home that day took us back to West Virginia, I didn't know that Jacob would be affected by those events in Vietnam for many future years—but he was. Unfortunately, I came to expect that Jacob would relive those nightmares when he heard, in the subconscious of his tormented sleep, the sounds of airplanes as they flew over our home at night. Daily, Jacob exercised great control and never behaved in irrational or radical ways. He hid his scars well.

I remember that after being home for at least fifteen years after that turbulent year in Vietnam, however, one day when Jacob ran across a picture of one of his buddies who hadn't survived Vietnam, he picked it up, silently looked at it, and then silently looked through it into that past I will never know. He walked down the hall and went into the bathroom, where he cried mournfully and uncontrollably. Our children and I wiped tears from our own eyes, as we sat and waited for that honorable man—who is definitely our hero—to achieve some sense of relief.

~~I placed the picture of the aluminum Christmas tree in the album and looked for the picture of Jacob's buddy who hadn't survived Vietnam. I thought about how sorry I was that someone who'd been such an important part of Jacob's life was never a living part of mine. When I found Danny's picture, he received a place of honor in our album of family and friends. I thought about how grateful I was that Jacob had survived and had come home to start his new life with me and the family we'd have. Too much death was in my thoughts. I needed to find a promise of new beginnings. So I searched through my stash of pictures and found the picture we'd taken outside in front of our house on the day we brought our newborn Meeghan home from the hospital. Two-year-old J.R. sat in a folding lawn chair with his little arms wrapped around his swaddled two-day-old sister.

CHAPTER EIGHTEEN

Shortly after Jacob left for Vietnam, his father accepted a job promotion that required relocation, and Bob and Bitsy Thomas eventually settled in a little Ohio town just across the West Virginia border. When Jacob was awarded his quite unexpected early discharge, his parents invited us to stay with them, and upon their insistence, we gratefully accepted their invitation and agreed to stay until after our baby was born.

We temporarily settled in and eagerly awaited the baby's arrival. A few weeks passed and one day Jacob's grandmother called and asked to speak to Jacob. "Jacob," she said, "I wondered if you'd come up and help me with some chores. If you drive up this evening and spend the night here, you can get an early start in the morning."

Jacob said, "Sure, Grandma, I'll drive up this evening." Jacob was very fond of his grandmother who'd lived, for several years, across the street from the house in which Jacob had lived until he left home to join the Marine Corps, and he looked forward to spending some time with her in his old hometown. So that evening, he made the ninety-minute drive to her house and planned to do as she requested. That night, however, didn't turn out as any of us expected.

After a warm shower, where pulsating spurts of water vibrated on my aching back, I turned in for the night. Around 2:30 a.m. I awoke with an odd feeling of discomfort, suspected I might be in labor, and tried to determine how long I should wait before disturbing my in-laws.

I tried to justify the timing of my trip while tentatively creeping across the dark hallway, finally built up my nerve, and softly knocked on the door of the master bedroom. I heard grunted and muffled sounds.

"Huh?"

"What was that?"

"You hear something?"

"Hmm?"

"Oh, my, it must be Cassie!"

They were awake! All of a sudden the near-silence that followed my creeping moves was shattered. Four feet slapped down on the hardwood floor, and it sounded like a 1950's sock hop was going on in that room—except there was no music. Feet scooted and slid all over the place. In their effort to cover a nightgown and boxer shorts, those two must have looked like something straight out of a Marx Brothers' movie. They scurried around in there and raced each other to the door. They knew there surely was only one reason that would bring me knocking on their door in the middle of the night. The door opened. Bitsy was still pulling on a robe, and her eyes looked like they were bulging from the face of a wild woman. The movements of my in-laws' heads almost made them look like they were attached to large loose slinky-type springs and bobbed wildly ahead of their shoulders like they were in such a hurry that their bodies couldn't catch up with the idea that had sprung from their minds. They both talked at the same time.

A virtual duet rang out. "What is it, Cassie?"

"Is it the baby?"

Bob had pulled on his trousers and stood in his bare feet. Wisps of what was left of his gray hair stood nearly straight out all over his shiny head. He looked almost terrified. I stood in the doorway until Bob, in his effort to gain control of our emergency situation, guided Bitsy and me into the center of the hall and talked as he guided. "Well, now, we'll have to get in touch with Jacob at Mother's. Cassie, you get your bag ready, and Bitsy maybe we'd better call for an ambulance." He looked at Bitsy and explained: "I don't think we should start out on an hour-long drive with Cassie. We don't know what might happen between here and the hospital. Don't you agree? We'd better get moving." He knew exactly what to do, even though I hadn't verbalized any answers referring to the questions about my appearance being because I was in labor. I was terrified, myself, and was relieved to have someone else make the decisions.

Bitsy and I stood in the hall, looked at each other, and did our best to convey looks of assurance. Bob was thinking pretty quickly for a man who'd just been startled out of a sound sleep. Bitsy said: "Well, Bob, that's fine. You go call Jacob and tell him to meet us at the hospital. I'll help Cassie get ready."

I'd often wondered how I would know when my labor time was real. It seemed that about all anyone could tell me was that I'd just know, or they said that if I waited until my water broke, which would be a trickle sort of like wetting my pants, I'd know it was time. I supposed mine was one of those cases where I just knew—but I wasn't really so sure I just knew—and I continued to hope I hadn't rousted everyone out of bed in the middle of the night for a false alarm.

Within minutes, the ambulance pulled into the driveway and the doors were jerked open wide by the paramedics who pulled out a gurney and raced to the door. With their explanation that they had certain procedures to follow—even though I was able to walk and thought the procedure was somewhat uncalled-for—I was helped onto the gurney and carried out to the emergency vehicle. Bitsy climbed into the ambulance with me and settled in for the ride.

Bob was scheduled to work that morning, so he wasn't going to the hospital with us. He stood barefoot and shirtless on the driveway and called out: "You take care now, Cassie. I'll talk to you later. Everything's going to be all right. Bitsy, you call and keep me posted." Bob waved into the darkness of the night that was highlighted by the circular motions of the red ambulance lights.

Jacob was waiting at the hospital when Bitsy and I arrived, and when I got my first look at him, I couldn't tell whether he was nervous, excited, scared nearly to death, or a combination of the three.

After I checked in, Jacob, Bitsy, and I were led to a room where I could finally lie down and relax, or at least I thought that was going to be an option. I lay in the hospital bed with Jacob standing on one side and with Bitsy standing on the other. No matter how many times I rolled over, I found no comfortable position. I was poked and prodded and prepped by any number of professionals. Nurses repeatedly told me I probably wouldn't deliver until late that evening, and I thought the hours between 3:30 a.m. and "sometime late this evening" were sure to seem like some of the longest in my life.

The longer I lay there, the more intense the situation became. I gritted my teeth and tried to remain calm. I gritted my teeth and tried to convince myself that I could do it. I gritted my teeth and told myself this was what I had always wanted. I gritted my teeth and tried to smile. I gritted my teeth and hopefully asked, "What time is it?" I gritted my teeth and thought: Not until late this evening?????????

At 2:00 p.m., with my teeth gritted, thinking I had several more hours to endure my laborious little journey into motherhood, and with Jacob still standing on one side of the bed, and with Bitsy still standing on the other side of the bed, I heard what sounded like the burst of a water balloon.

In one swift move, Jacob jumped back against the window. Bitsy immediately ran out the door. I thought I'd exploded. That little trickle sort of like wetting my pants definitely did not apply to me.

Because of my pain-induced and nearly hallucinogenic state, it almost seemed like the rush of water had propelled Bitsy out of the room. In my goofy state of mind, her arms flailed around in all directions; she rushed through the hospital's hall and looked a little like an octopus fighting her way through a tempest-tossed sea; the tone of her voice resembled that of a dolphin's communication; and, her excited and high-pitched voice made its way to the nurses' station, announcing: "Her water broke! Her water broke! Hurry, somebody; come quickly! Her water broke!"

A nurse responded, "We heard it; I'm on my way."

A couple orderlies entered the room and quickly shoved a gurney up against my bed. The nurse said: "Okay, Mrs. Thomas. You just scoot yourself on over here. Move over onto the gurney, Mrs. Thomas! Mrs. Thomas? *Mrs. Thomas!* You move on over to the gurney. You're going to have to help, here, Mrs. Thomas."

Well, that was easy for her to say; she wasn't in the middle of a contraction. "Okay. I'm coming; just give me a second; I'll be right there. You won't have to leave without me." The nurse sort of laughed, and I glanced over toward Jacob for some sort of an eye-contact reassurance, but he was still plastered against the window and looked more frightened than I felt.

The gurney was right up against my bed, but for a very uncomfortable reason, that distance seemed much too far away. I gritted my teeth, rose up to scoot over onto the gurney, and saw the water-splattered wall at the foot of my bed. It definitely had not been a trickle, and I was fully aware that during my conversations with mothers concerning the event of water breaking, I'd never heard that pressure-induced, balloon-bursting, and water-splashing sounds might occur. With an orderly at the helm of my ride, I was whizzed down the corridor and wheeled into the delivery room, where the gurney made a sudden and almost screeching halt.

It seemed to me that the delivery-room staff spoke in louder than normal voices. Did they think I'd lost my hearing, or that I was under the influence of some sort of drug that was going to put me to sleep before I heard and responded to what they said? If those were the cases, they were wrong on all counts. Because I didn't move immediately upon command, it was possible I gave the impression that I really didn't hear them. My ears caught the words, but my body rebelled for a bit. It took some major effort on my part to catch my breath and to give the speakers a satisfactory response.

The reason for my lack of immediate verbal response should be quite obvious to the nurses who surrounded me. My entire torso was out of control. My entire huge hump of a gut rose; it fell; it was concave; it was convex; it was convexo-concave. I felt as if someone had mistaken my lump for a huge glob of bread dough—and that beast was kneading it from the inside out. My already taut skin stretched even more than I imagined was possible, and it seemed to pull every bit of my innards along with it. I wondered if it were possible for a human being to be turned inside out, and if it weren't, somebody within me was giving it his best shot to be the first to succeed.

A female voice asked just a little too loudly: "Mrs. Thomas, did you know your Dr. Ware is out of town? Mrs. Thomas? Mrs. Thomas?"

For crying out loud! The annoying chatter eventually received my response. "No, I didn't know that. Any doctor will be okay with me." I didn't give a fig who was there to catch that Herculean intruder; I just wanted somebody to point him in the right direction for his grand exit and hoped he'd become quicker and gentler about it.

The loudest toned nurse attempted to reassure me. "Dr. Letterman will be your attending physician; he's seeing Dr. Ware's patients while he's away. Dr. Letterman is another excellent doctor. I'm sure you'll be pleased with him."

At that point, I didn't care whose name was after the title, and I was more than willing to forego the amenities. It seemed like an eternity until Dr. Letterman sauntered into the room, but it couldn't have been very long, because at 2:17 p.m., I heard something that sounded like someone pulled a size 12, foot-filled rubber boot out of knee-deep mud. Then I heard a distinct thud that I knew must be the sound of two Herculean handfuls of innards being dragged, slammed, jammed, and wedged into my cervix, which that Herculean intruder had used for a door when he finally made his exit from the womb. We'd delivered a perfect and healthy baby, who was surprisingly much smaller than I'd expected.

I heard some clinical noises, and then I heard a little mewing sound, which also surprised me. I'd expected more of a roar from someone who, while inside my body, had felt so gigantic. Finally, Dr. Letterman announced, "It's a boy!"

The baby's skin was a little blue looking; he'd been pushing pretty hard to beat the expected and estimated time of arrival; and he was probably more than a little stressed. I watched—weak and satisfied, and cold and clammy—as the nurses suctioned and wiped the little blue being. I looked at the tiny life and, absolutely immediately, no longer cared that the tiny creature had so recently caused such an inner turmoil in his struggle to find his way out and into the world, but I found it amazing that he wasn't holding at least a mile of my intestines and a chunk of my liver in his little clinched fists.

It was a time when the father wasn't permitted in the delivery room, so when the nurses finished their routine and placed the naked, kicking, and mewing baby across my breast, I could hardly wait to tell Jacob we had a son and that he was perfect.

When the doctor finished his job and gave the all clear, the nurses placed the cleaned-and-swaddled baby in my arms and wheeled us out into the hall on a gurney so I could tell Jacob the gender of our child. I said, "Oh, Jacob, it's a boy!"

Jacob, who looked much more at ease than when I'd last seen him plastered to the window, said: "Aw, Cassie, I love you. I'm so proud of you. I wanted a boy!" Then he leaned over and kissed us.

Boy Thomas was soon placed in an incubator to warm his little blue-cold body, and I was placed under a blanket to warm mine. Spouses and other family members weren't allowed in the patients' rooms when the babies were with the mothers, so Jacob and Bitsy walked down the hall to the nursery, where they could both get a glimpse of our little guy. They returned and gave me a full report.

Jacob said: "Oh, Cassie! He's perfect. I think he looks like me. Mom said he looks like I did when I was a baby. It's going to be a few days before you can leave, but I can hardly wait to take him home where I can hold him. I'm gonna miss you, but I'll be here every day and stay for visiting hours. At least I can see the baby through the nursery window."

We were so excited. We called and gave the good news to my family members. And when we called Bob at work to tell him it was all over and that everything was all right he asked, "Who does the baby look like?"

"He looks just like you, Bob. He has very little hair, and he has no teeth," I teased. The new granddad laughed.

When visiting hours were over and everyone had left, the warmed little Boy Thomas was wheeled into my room for his first feeding. That was where I had my first chance to really examine him closely, and when I unwrapped the blanket from his tiny body, I was a little concerned. I'd baby-sat from the time I was twelve years old and on numerous occasions I'd been around infants who belonged to family members and to family friends. I had not, however, seen a brand-new, only-few-hours-old unswathed baby.

Even warm, Boy Thomas was some sort of a purple color. His nearly opaque skin was wrinkled and peeling. He had hardly any fingernails or toenails, but those he had were sort of thin and reddish blue. His eyes were nearly swollen shut, and when he managed to open them a little, they just sort of rolled around and didn't seem to focus on anything. Right above and between his eyes, his forehead had a red-splotched area that I soon discovered resembled the one on the back of his neck. He had lots of black hair around the back of his head, but he had hardly any hair on the top and sides of his head. He even had some black hair on the tops of his ears and on his shoulders and back. I was especially concerned that he seemed to have no muscles in his arms and legs and tried to convince myself that if anything were wrong with him, somebody surely would have broken the news to me.

I hated to admit it, even to myself, but he was one ugly little critter. I'd expected one of those cute little pink, filled-out babies—the ones everyone stood over and said how cute they were. This was going to be a stretch. I wondered how Jacob and I could have produced such a thing, but it didn't really matter. As ugly as he was, he was ours, and as I cradled him to my breast—where the poor, silly little thing didn't even act like he knew what he was supposed to do with it—I knew I truly loved him, anyway. I decided that Jacob and I would just have to help the ugly little Boy Thomas cope with his life that, because of his strange appearance, would most assuredly be filled with cruelty.

The next day, Jacob was at the hospital as soon as he was allowed into the room. He and I walked to the nursery and looked at our little Boy Thomas. We both talked about how cute and precious he was, but I wondered whether Jacob was as surprised as I was with our child's appearance. He didn't express any misgivings, though, so I didn't mention mine. We oohed and aahed over that Boy Thomas in the nursery, along with everyone who came to see him. I didn't even want to know what they really thought. I just wanted them to be kind. I was still a little worried about my baby's condition, though, because none of the family members had seen any part of him except for his little face that stuck out of his blue swaddling blanket.

Jacob made another trip to the nursery while I rested. When he returned to my room, he announced: "The nurses wanted to know what we were going to name the baby. They were filling out the birth certificate, and I was so proud that I said, 'Just name him after me!' I know we had another name picked out, but I couldn't help it." So the Boy Thomas was officially named Jacob Robert Thomas Jr., and we decided to call him J.R.

A couple weeks after J.R.'s birth, we moved into a little mobile home that Jacob's parents used on weekend trips to West Virginia when they visited their family and friends. Much to my relief, by the time we moved into our borrowed home, J.R. had miraculously metamorphosed into one of those cute little pink, filled-out babies—the ones everyone stood over and said how cute they were. He was adorable.

When J.R. was about a month old, Jacob went to work for an oil company. We stayed in the little freebie mobile home until autumn and moved into our very own brand-new, we-picked-everything-out mobile home and had it set on our very own we-picked-it-out piece of property, in the little West Virginia town where Jacob had lived when he was a child.

Jacob and I thought J.R. was such a treat that we eventually decided to have another child, and two years after J.R.'s birth, Dr. Ware delivered Meeghan Elizabeth.

After the delivery, I was wheeled out into the corridor where it was time to tell Jacob, "It's a girl."

Jacob said: "Aw, Cassie, I love you. I'm so proud of you. I wanted a girl!" He leaned over and kissed us.

I didn't have such a surprise birth or first-time sighting with my second child. Meeghan Elizabeth looked about like J.R. had upon his arrival—she was ugly, hairy, spotted, and had no muscle tone—but the second time I knew what to expect, and I knew she'd outgrow the normal newborn condition.

Nearly from the time I could remember, I not only wanted to be a wife and mother, but I wanted to be the best wife and mother I could be. When I married Jacob Thomas, I knew he'd make it easy for me to be a good wife, and when we had our tremendously wanted and so easily loved children, I knew they'd make being a good mother pretty easy for me, too—and rearing those children was a task Jacob and I took very seriously.

We hadn't even considered that I might continue to work after our marriage—the plan was that I'd quit my job and move away to be with Jacob, or there wasn't much point in being married. When we experienced some lean financial times a few years later, however, we thought that—if we deemed it absolutely necessary for me to do so—with my short-term secretarial background, and with my tucked away letter of recommendation from my former place of employment, I probably could find a job with a decent rate of pay, but it was important to Jacob and me—even though it meant a possible financial struggle—that I stay home and be with our children.

As many couples do when experiencing lean financial times, we occasionally discussed whether or not I should seek employment. Our main concern was leaving our children without at least one parent in their lives most of the time—and the thought of that made us sad. Jacob and I wanted to be the ones who were present for our children's firsts, who stressed good moral values, and who guided and influenced their decisions. Even with the possible addition of my income, we considered the additional costs of: day care, an additional vehicle and its upkeep and maintenance, travel expenses, and the initial cost of a new wardrobe. And, there would be various emotional and stress costs for all of us, too.

Jacob mentioned that he could try to find a second job in the evenings, but we knew if he did that, it would mean he'd nearly always be away from the kids and me, and he'd be worn out. Our problem wasn't that we were behind—it was that we couldn't seem to get ahead. So, we held each other close, and with tears in our eyes, we decided it would still be best just to tighten our belts. We didn't want to sacrifice our family time for "stuff."

In order for me to stay home with the kids, Jacob and I agreed that we were willing to sacrifice purchases of additional material possessions. We economized in every way we could imagine. We were careful with the electricity and turned off the lights when we left a room. We ate a lot of pasta, soup beans and cornbread. When feasible, I hung clothes on the line to dry rather than use my dryer for every load. Jacob did most of our vehicle repairs. We only shopped when it was absolutely necessary, because we had no money to waste. We budgeted and managed, because we had to do it.

My time at home with J.R. and Meeghan gave me the opportunity to fill my heart's treasure chest with their presence, and to fill my mind with wonderful memories of their early years. I actually felt guilty at times because I was so happy, and I felt bad that Jacob couldn't be with us all the time, too.

I knew, however, that if I opted to work outside the home in an effort to alleviate some of our financial strain, I'd feel guilty about not being home with my children and decided that if I were going to feel guilty about something, it would be about not having a lot of extra money.

I didn't think it was wrong for other mothers to work outside the home; I knew every woman's situation was different. Many women didn't even have a belt-tightening option, because their household incomes were less than ours, or because their household expenses were more than ours. Many women preferred to establish outside careers, and I respected their educational accomplishments that allowed them to acquire their dream jobs. I just thought that if I worked outside the home, it wouldn't be the best choice for our family.

Every time I paid the bills, and every time something broke and had to be repaired or replaced, I sort of second guessed my decision, but I knew that spending more time with my kids—as opposed to spending more money on my kids—was still my preference. Our situation wasn't one in which I'd earned an extra income and was taking it from our household. We wouldn't miss what we hadn't had. But I did think if I had a paying position outside the home, my presence and guidance would be missed, and my absence could possibly have a negative impact on our family. Careful budgeting made it possible for us to make ends meet.

I felt privileged to be the one who witnessed my children's firsts and thought it was of significant importance that I understood their language when nobody else understood a word they said. It was important for me to let them know they could depend upon my presence for their happy and sad times, and that I'd be there for their times of trial and accomplishment. I wanted them to know I'd be available when they needed me—especially when they needed guidance and praise, and healing kisses and hugs. Those children were the culmination of the love Jacob and I shared, and we cherished every moment we had with them.

Sometimes, though, the simple things of life caused me to doubt the wisdom of my parenting skills. I didn't always make wise choices, and when that happened I paid the consequences. The kids often asked for pets. At various times, they had fish, a cat, a turtle, numerous dogs and some litters of their puppies, a butterfly, a rabbit, and a variety of birds. The lovers of fowls, reptiles, and animals always seemed to depend a little too much on the adult female of their own species to perform the tasks they always promised they would perform without having to be told to perform them. Being a mother and a former animal-loving kid, myself, I knew what to expect, but I often fussed and complained and reminded those little work-shirkers of all their empty pet-nurturing promises. Then knowing I'd probably end up doing it anyway, I worked along with and taught the kids, and did whatever was required to care for our pet population.

Of all the pets the kids could own, I figured a bird would probably be the easiest and least time-consuming. It had been my experience that the fish tanks needed cleaning too often; the cat hairs needed vacuumed away too often; and the dogs and puppies needed taken out to do their business too often. So, as far as I was concerned, a bird seemed like a pretty good pet choice. Boy was I wrong!

Bob and Bitsy's neighbors were looking for a new home for their blue parakeet. The neighbors enjoyed traveling, and finding bird sitters wasn't always convenient. They mentioned their dilemma to Bitsy, who happened to be one of their bird sitters, and she told them her grandchildren might like to have the bird. She called me and said: "Cassie, Mont and Jeannie have a parakeet they'd like to give away. They said they'd give the cage and everything that belongs with the bird to someone, if they could just find him a good home. I told them the kids might want him, but that I'd have to call and check with you, first. If you want him, we'll bring him up this weekend."

What a thrill! We'd actually considered buying a parakeet, but with all the first-time purchases required when buying a bird, it wasn't economically feasible at that point. "Sure, we'll take him. I think the kids would love to have a bird—especially a free one with all his stuff—and he can't be much trouble."

The following weekend, Henry moved to our house. Henry was a pampered parakeet, as was evidenced when Bitsy and Bob delivered to their grandchildren: Henry; Henry's gourmet selection of foods; an assortment of Henry's worldly goods; and Henry's cage, which was round, a whopping four feet tall, and looked like a parakeet hotel. Everyone who lived in our house was excited.

After spending a few days with Henry, we were out shopping, and the kids decided Henry needed some other worldly goods and some more food. We still had the new-pet-owner thrill, glow, and contentment, so when we went to the pet area of the store and saw a green parakeet, we thought she was just the thing old Henry needed to keep him company. Everyone was just so excited!

We took Henrietta home to Henry. Henry's parakeet hotel provided plenty of room, and when we placed Henrietta in Henry's cage, the birds seemed to be as excited as we were. They made all sorts of bird noises—in many degrees of clarity and in many degrees of noise factors. They reached decibels that might have warranted federally recommended hearing protection. What we initially thought of as beautiful chirping bird sounds quickly became annoying ear-splitters.

By the time the birds moved in with us, we'd built a house and had plenty of room but still couldn't find a good spot in the entire house in which to keep those chirping, wing-flapping, seed-scattering vultures. Several times a day, those birds fluttered their wings and fanned birdseed out of the parakeet hotel. Several times a day, an area of our carpet was covered with little colorful parakeet feathers and with bloomin' little parakeet seeds. Several times a day, I vacuumed.

Jacob and the kids released the parakeets from the parakeet hotel every chance they got, because they wanted to get close to the birds and teach them how to talk. The only thing they taught the birds, however, was that when they were out of their parakeet hotel, they were free. They were free to sit on their owners' fingers and shoulders long enough to poop. They were free to fly off to the nearest curtain rod to poop again. I spot cleaned and vacuumed, and laundered clothes and curtains.

During the daytime hours of the summer months, it made sense that the parakeets might like to have their hotel moved to the porch, where they could get some fresh air, sing, chatter, and flutter, and where I didn't have to be so concerned with the cleanup—and I was pleased when the weather was nice enough to take the parakeet hotel outside. Too often, though, our kids and their friends opened the cage door and reached in to stroke the pretty birdies, and a few of those times the birds sought freedom from those loving little hands, hopped right along the kids' forearms, flew out the door, and sought their flight to wide open spaces.

Jacob and I found ourselves coaxing those colorful parakeets from trees, from bushes, and from neighbors' yards. One day after one of the birds had flown the coop, a man who lived about a mile from us called to say he'd captured a parakeet and had been told it might belong to the Thomases. Adults who whistle, chirp, tweet, beg, climb trees, hang from tree limbs, search through bushes, and mutter under their breath, do attract attention—and their inane behavior apparently causes the loss of a parakeet to become news throughout the community.

I thanked the man for calling and told him I'd be over to retrieve the bird. When I arrived at his house and explained what a difficult time we'd had chasing the bird, the man who was an admitted bird-owner himself, held the delinquent bird in his arthritic hands and demonstrated a wing-clipping technique, which he promised would prevent the bird from flying.

Hallelujah! I guess I missed that page of wing-clipping techniques in the bird-owners manual. I probably lost my place when I had to stop so I could go clean up bird poop.

When we kept them in the living room, the birds nearly drowned out any conversation—especially one on the telephone. It seemed that the ring of the telephone startled them into some sort of a frantic chirping-and-squawking din. Many evenings we turned the television's audio up louder and louder in our effort to hear above the racket of those parakeets—those ones that I'd thought would be such easy-to-deal-with pets. The birds turned up their volume to compete with the television's volume. They clicked their beaks against their worldly-goods mirrors. They scampered up-and-down their worldly-goods ladders. They performed aerial acrobatics from various hanging perches. They pecked. They picked. They scratched. They clawed seeds from the bottom of their cage and from the food containers, and they scattered those seeds all over the place. Their feathers flew. They rang their little worldly-goods bells. They drove me nuts.

One night when guests were expected, I moved the parakeet hotel into the master bedroom so we could visit and discuss something other than the joys of parakeet ownership and the practice of audio competition. After our guests departed, I covered the cage with a sheet and went to bed.

The next day, I decided to clean the cage before moving it out of the bedroom, and six-year-old Meeghan climbed up on my bed to watch the usually mundane task. But that morning I decided to try a different approach. I thought if I'd take the sweeper wand—minus any attachments—and run it around the bottom of the cage, I could vacuum away all those seeds, feathers, and poop, with a lot less trouble than reaching in and trying to collect them all in the paper as

I folded it together while also fighting off the vultures. Every time I'd previously maneuvered the tray out from the bottom of the cage or maneuvered the folded crap-filled paper out through the tiny cage door, I'd spilled at least part of the contents and had to get out the sweeper, anyway. The way I saw it, exercising my new approach would simply eliminate a step. With Henry and Henrietta up on their ladders, I began vacuuming. It was going pretty well, and I was more than a little pleased with myself. Meeghan even looked as if she were impressed with my innovative idea.

Then quite unexpectedly, Henry got curious and jumped down from his perch on the ladder. It all happened so quickly. Henry hopped toward the slightly tilted wand as it scooted across the paper on the bottom of the cage. I turned and jerked the cord to unplug the vacuum. When I turned back around hoping that I'd avoided a disaster, Meeghan was screaming: "Oh, Henry! Oh, Henry!" I'd been a little slow, but I wasn't entirely too late. Most of Henry had disappeared into the end of the wand, but he hadn't surrendered—I could still see his little parakeet head. As luck would have it, Henry's outside diameter was exactly the same circumference as the inside diameter of the sweeper wand. His little parakeet head bobbed up-and-down, and he squawked his little lungs out until he almost drowned out Meeghan's screams.

The most important thing was that Henry was still alive and kicking, so I figured I'd simply remove him from the sweeper wand and all would be right with his world. Much to my chagrin, I discovered it's quite difficult to grab a squawking, bobbing, pecking, and madder-than-the-dickens parakeet by the head and pull him from a sweeper wand, and I was afraid I might break Henry's scrawny neck if I pulled or twisted too hard. Henry wanted out, but he didn't seem to want *me* to take him out. He was most uncooperative, and it didn't help matters any that Meeghan had progressed from a screaming-and-crying Meeghan to a jumping-up-and-down-on-the-bed Meeghan. I was truly at a loss.

I tried to console Meeghan and assure her that everything was going to be all right even though I wasn't so sure of it, myself. I made an effort to console Henry, who wanted absolutely nothing to do with me. Then I consoled Henrietta, who thought she had to get in on the act. With all the squawking, screaming, crying, bobbing, and jumping, I wondered whether my innovative idea had been such a good one, after all. I needed some time to think. I needed some time to pack and to run away from home. I needed to be reasonable.

I exhausted every effort to remove that ungrateful Henry from the wand, but not before he'd pecked away nearly an entire knuckle section of my pointer finger and most of my thumb's bottom pad. I thought I should just tell Meeghan to leave the room—and then I could turn on the sweeper. I knew I could get Henry out of the sweeper bag, but I wasn't exactly sure what the inside of the hose looked like, and I wasn't exactly sure at what rate of speed Henry could comfortably and safely travel in reverse, so I wasn't sure how many bird pieces I'd have to remove from the bag. I nixed that idea. Henry was relentless, and I couldn't blame him for being upset—I'd have been concerned and vocal, myself, if I were in his predicament—but he never shut his beak. Finally, I had another brilliant idea.

With what was left of my bloody stubs, I removed the hose from the suction end of the vacuum cleaner, attached it to the blower end, and turned the sweeper switch to the off position. I plugged the sweeper into the wall socket, held my breath, turned the sweeper on, and Henry shot about three feet through the air, bounced off the wall, and landed safely and soundly—well, nearly soundly—at least he was alive. The only problem he seemed to have incurred was that his tail feathers had been sucked out.

Parakeets evidently use their cluster of tail feathers as a balancing tool, because until his feathers grew back—and they did—when Henry leaned slightly forward, he continued to go forward until his beak hit the bottom of the cage, and then he forced himself back up to a position that made him look surprisingly like a mini-version of Foghorn Leghorn. I always thought he looked like he was cussing and mumbling in my direction every time I saw him do it. He reminded me of those tacky orange-colored dodo birds I'd seen bobbing up-and-down in the back glasses of cars.

After a couple more years of living with the birds, we knew we'd have to face the inevitable, and as we all knew would eventually happen, Henry died. The night before his death, the two birds engaged in something, but Jacob and I weren't sure if it was a fight, sex, or a fight about sex. Anyway, at the end of the commotion, Henry acted like he couldn't get around as well as usual, but there were no visible signs of an injury. Henry just lay on the bottom of the cage. On instinct, we moved the parakeet hotel into the master bedroom that night, just in case Henry didn't recover from whatever had happened. In the wee hours of the morning, I crawled out of bed and checked the cage. The little blue parakeet lay quiet, still, and stiff. His legs and feet pointed straight up. Even after all the hassles we'd been through together, I was saddened by the sight of him and already missed the little vulture. I woke Jacob and asked him to do something with the bird.

"What do you want me to do with him? It isn't even daylight. I don't want to go out in the dark to bury a bird."

"Well, just get up and take him out of the cage. Put him in a bag, or something, and put him where the kids won't find him when they wake up." Having taken care of my end of that matter, I crawled back into bed and watched as Jacob crawled out.

He removed the lifeless bird from the cage and carried him out of the bedroom. Jacob returned a few minutes later and slid back into bed. I was grateful he'd taken care of that project; I hated to handle the dead stuff. We dozed off.

We awoke to Meeghan's shrill, shrieking voice. "Oh, Henry! Oh, Henry!"

We heard her running feet coming from the direction of the laundry room, through the house, and down the hall toward our bedroom. We sat straight up in bed. I looked at Jacob and demanded, *"WHAT DID YOU DO WITH THAT BIRD?"*

Jacob said, "I put him in a bag, like you told me to do, and I put it on top of the dryer."

Well, I couldn't blame him. He'd put the bird in a bag, and what were the odds that Meeghan would go into the laundry room to get her sandals as soon as she got out of bed? Jacob had no way of knowing that Meeghan would be curious enough to open the bag and find the bird. By the time I had it all reasoned out, I was holding Meeghan in my arms, and from the deepest recesses of his messier-than-messy bedroom, a squinty eyed, messy haired J.R. emerged.

I sat down with the two sad little children and explained: "Henry's soul has just flown to Heaven. We all knew Henry was injured, yesterday. Now, he'll not hurt and suffer, and that's a good thing. We're sad, but don't you agree that it was much better to have had Henry and to have loved him, than never to have had him at all? Daddy will dig Henry's grave, and you can make a little cross for it. We'll all sing a hymn for him. Henry's a little bird, so it would be appropriate for us to sing 'I'll Fly Away.' A little later, we'll have a proper funeral for him. We'll just wait a while until Daddy's ready to get out of bed. He's really tired right now, because he was up taking care of Henry very early this morning."

Once they'd calmed down, we found a small shoe box to use as Henry's coffin. When I went into the laundry room to place Henry's bagged body into the box, I understood why Meeghan had thrown such a fit when she'd initially found Henry's body. I should have been more specific with Jacob and mentioned using a brown paper bag, because there lay Henry—just at Meeghan's eye level—on top of the dryer—in a clear plastic sandwich bag—quiet, still, stiff, and with his feet stuck straight in the air.

~~The picture of our precious babies went into the album. Two kids, a wife, and a mini-menagerie never drove Jacob over the edge. He remained emotionally supportive, and he always did his best to provide for us. I thank God several times each day for giving Jacob to me. If he weren't the kind of person he is, I don't think we could have survived some of the rough times. I found the picture of Jacob that was taken upon his return home from his first day on the job at the coal mine.

CHAPTER NINETEEN

M ajor and numerous changes took place for our family during the years of 1975 through 1987. Jacob worked for an oil company from shortly after his military discharge in 1970 until 1975. The oil company where he'd worked for those five years eventually found it necessary to send him to work away from home, and after a few weeks of that and with no end in sight, Jacob decided to seek other employment.

The coal companies in our area were hiring, and even though he knew that type of work would be a major change, Jacob also knew if he worked close to home, at the end of his workday he'd be able to spend his free time at home with his family instead of in some motel room wishing he were with us.

Changing jobs was a difficult decision for Jacob to make, though, especially because outside influences pulled at him. Many people advised him that because he'd already worked at the oil company for five years, he should stay with that company for which he worked, no matter what. For us, however, his being home with the family was important. We finally decided we couldn't allow anyone who didn't actually live in our house to influence our final decision, determined that it was ultimately our choice, and we knew we'd have to face whatever challenges and consequences followed our decision.

As we expected would happen, our family struggled together through what we recognized as the norm for coal miners: strikes, layoffs, temporary shutdowns, and closings of some West Virginia coal mines. Due to necessity, we became fairly good money managers and did what we could to get through the bouts of unemployment that each lasted for periods of a day, a few days, a few months, for several months, and in one instance for about three years.

On the first day he reported for his new job in 1975, I worried about Jacob—not so much for his safety—but I wondered whether or not he'd be satisfied with the outcome of our decision. That evening when he returned home, the kids and I met him at the door. He'd showered and changed at work, of course, but he brought his miner's gear home with him because he wanted to show us how he looked when he wore it. He buckled on his leather miner's belt with the loops and attachments that were used to carry tools, and he dropped his light-attached hard hat on his head. In one hand he held his new, round, shiny, aluminum, three-sectioned lunch bucket. The top section was designed to hold a homemade baked cake, but on that day held pre-packaged lunch cakes. The next section was designed to hold his main course that consisted, that day, of bologna and cheese sandwiches and potato chips. The bottom section was designed to hold drinking water. Jacob looked rather different wearing his miner's gear, but at least he was smiling when we met him at the door—and that was an encouraging sign.

During dinner, Jacob said: "I have to tell you, Cassie, about halfway to the mine I almost turned the truck around and headed home. I've gone through tunnels in Vietnam, but I'd never been in a coal mine, so the reality of what I was about to do started to sink in, and I was a little concerned about what I'd be walking into. For a few minutes, I wasn't quite so sure I was doing the right thing."

My heart skipped a beat, and I felt like it sunk a little within my chest. Then Jacob smiled and continued. "I knew I'd made the choice, though. I'd already resigned from the oil company, and I knew I had to support my family. I knew I'd have to stick with the plan." Then he gave a little laugh. "But, you know, when I went into the mine, it was nothing like I'd expected it would be. Instead of being black, everything was white with what the other miners told me was rock dust. The interior of the mine looked like long white halls with other connecting white halls. It wasn't what I'd expected at all."

"That surprises me. I always pictured everything as being black—walls of coal."

"I did, too. I was surprised."

I had to ask: "Were you afraid to go inside the mine? I mean, were you worried about the roof falling, or anything? It seems that everyone who opposed your job change mentioned that possibility when you talked about applying for a job at the mine. I just wondered if it worried you."

"Well, I'll be honest with you. I was a little leery about going in, but once I was in there it didn't really bother me.

"I worried that you might be afraid of what could happen in the mine—concerned enough that you'd be sorry you took the job."

"Well, I thought about the possibilities before I applied at the coal company. I didn't just jump into this without thinking it through. I thought about the times I'd been in some sticky situations in the oil fields. I thought about the times I'd traveled icy and snowy dirt roads out on those ridges when I worked at the oil company; and that was no picnic. I thought about surviving Vietnam and coming home. So—I figured I could deal with the coal mines, at least for a while, and see how it goes.

One night during dinner, Jacob said: "Kids, I thought about something pretty interesting today. You know that astronauts have gone into outer space and walked on the moon—and Neil Armstrong is famous for being the first astronaut who walked where no man had walked before. Well, I got to thinking that in the coal mine, as each cut of the coal is made, we're doing something pretty big, too. Instead of walking far *above* earth's surface where no man has walked before, we coal miners are walking far *beneath* earth's surface where no man has walked before."

During Jacob's first few months at the mine, we experienced wildcat strikes that lasted a day or two out of many workweeks, but it was easy to adjust to irregular amounts of income, especially because Jacob's hourly rate of pay as a coal miner was nearly three times what he'd earned in the oil fields. Within a few years, the oil companies' rates of pay caught up with the coal companies' rates of pay, but for that period between, the substantial wage difference tremendously helped us. We knew when Jacob went to work at the mine that we'd have to prepare for wildcat strikes, for contract negotiation strikes, and for the inevitable layoffs or shutdowns at the mines.

When Jacob had relatively steady work, we had what we liked to refer to as good financial times, but when he didn't work at the coal mine for any period of time, we still managed to keep our heads above water. Even when we weren't sure what amount would be on each paycheck, we managed, and we made sure our kids had the necessities.

During those layoffs and strikes, we took advantage of Jacob's time at home and enjoyed sharing conversations on the porch during warm weather and around the fireplace during cold weather. I quilted while Jacob and the kids worked jigsaw puzzles, and we all played board games and card games. No matter whether it was warm or cold outside, we had to stay prepared, so we cut, loaded, hauled, and stacked several cords of wood for the fireplace. We played together and worked together. Having Jacob home with us, as opposed to working out of state, was well worth making sure we financially managed. We treasured our time together.

Our financial lifestyle paralleled that of many families in our area, and even though layoffs were to be expected, it still seemed that the actuality of their timing always came unexpectedly. One night while I waited for Jacob to return home from his afternoon shift at the mine, I turned on the television and heard on a local news station that the mine where Jacob worked would lay off the men as they left their work location at midnight—and that the mine would be closed for an indefinite period of time. I thought: *"Jacob's still in the mine and hasn't even been told, yet."*

When he arrived home expecting to give me the disappointing news, I explained that I'd already heard about the closing on television, and Jacob was a little surprised. We discussed changing some immediate plans to use money from our savings to work on the home in which we lived. We could wait. We were comfortable enough living in it and working on it when we could, so another delay was simply another delay.

The first year of that layoff wasn't too difficult. For the first six months Jacob drew unemployment benefits, and we dipped into our savings for the next six months. Jacob was eventually called to work at a different mine that was owned by the same coal company, so his company service and benefits weren't lost. He worked there for a few years, and then he was laid-off again in 1984.

By that time, J.R. was a freshman in high school, and Meeghan was in the seventh grade. As usual, we thought we were about to experience another one of those inconvenient, but somewhat prepared-for, periods of unemployment. We weren't overly concerned and didn't expect the current layoff to be lengthier than the last few had been, so we tightened our belts.

In our area, many families earned incomes from the coal mines, smokestack construction, chemical plants, aluminum plants, or steel mills, and they learned to deal with bouts of unemployment. Although it might seem strange to people who don't experience our sorts of lifestyles, we had many reasons for wanting to stay with our coal companies and plants, and to stay in our homes and maintain that sense of familiar community.

Most of our relatives lived in our area, and it was difficult to think of moving away from them. Our children were familiar with the school system, and their friendships were important to them. Our home was established. So, we just sort of rode out the difficult financial times as well as we could and tried to maintain a sense of pride and dignity.

Usually, the unemployed were entitled to about six months of unemployment benefits that were taken from a fund to which they and their employers had made contributions. Depending upon the country's unemployment figures, sometimes an extension was granted, and that provided an additional six months of benefits. We couldn't predict whether an extension would be granted, because as far as we could determine, the information obtained and used to define the rate for publicized unemployment figures was somewhat misleading.

Those unemployed folks who applied for and actually received unemployment benefits were included in national unemployment figures. Those who were unemployed and whose benefits were exhausted, however, were dropped from the list of those receiving benefits. When they were no longer receiving benefits, it seemed to us that they weren't officially counted as being unemployed and their existence almost seemed irrelevant.

During Jacob's layoff period that time, though, a six-month extension was eventually granted, and as usual, Jacob applied for employment at plants, factories, and small businesses in our area, but one drawback with being a laid-off coal miner was that potential employers apparently expected that coal miners would return to the mines if they were given the opportunity. It was easy to understand that reasoning, because many miners had built seniority along with some pension and medical benefits. Prospective employers were reluctant to spend the time and financial resources required to hire, start, and train new employees. It was likely they believed the newly hired employees would return to their former employers as soon as their layoff status changed. So the employment applications submitted by laid-off miners were usually ignored. Prospective employers seemed to view the submissions of a laid-off miner's application as the fulfillment of one requirement to draw his unemployment benefits—proof that he was actively seeking employment. It was a very difficult position for a man who wasn't sure whether he should change professions, but who knew he would if an opportunity ever presented itself.

Many well-meaning working and retired people tried to help us by passing along information when they knew someone was hiring, or when they knew someone who knew someone who was hiring—and they made sure to keep Jacob informed. Jacob was grateful and ran around to check those suggested leads for potential employment opportunities, but when he did, all but one resulted in dead ends. It was difficult to figure gasoline money into our budget, and driving around from our remote area to all those suggested dead-end positions—some of which were even out of the state of West Virginia—cost us a precious bundle of money. If he didn't try, however, Jacob knew he'd constantly answer to himself and appear ungrateful to all those truly well-meaning folks who'd sent him on what we all thought were legitimate job leads. It was necessary to follow through on the leads—he'd never find a job if he weren't out there looking for one— even though the leads and follow-ups turned out to be expensive and unrewarding.

When questioned, it was difficult for us to explain how hard it was to find a job—how hard it was to even get a potential employer's attention. Although he'd submitted applications to nearly every place within a reasonable driving distance from our home, most places kept the same application on file for at least a year. It wasn't easy to explain why office personnel would not, or could not, accept more than one application in a one-year period, and that many office workers were not authorized to hand out, or to accept, applications. It was also difficult and humiliating for us to explain that—even though we'd mailed out several résumés—many companies didn't even accept a résumé, and that Jacob had been told more than once that he would not be given a job interview just because he happened to show up and asked if it were possible to talk to someone about a job. Jacob, like so many other unemployed people, suffered much humiliation from all arenas, even though unemployment had definitely not been by choice.

As if he didn't have enough on his mind, when Jacob *was* employed, people often told him they wouldn't work in a coal mine, because: it was a dirty job; it was a dangerous job; the work wasn't always steady. Then when he *wasn't* employed, those same folks expounded upon their beliefs. Jacob was always polite and didn't respond with negative remarks about the jobs those people had. In fact, Jacob usually just remained quiet. He reminded me of my grandfather in the respect that he had a sort of quiet confidence and wasn't always compelled to explain himself or to make excuses for his career choice.

Jacob was a coal miner. He worked in the mines, where he became familiar with the dirt, the dangers, and the insecurity of it all. He also became as comfortable as was possible with the situation, and it eventually became routine for him. I feared for his life not only in the mines, but as he traveled the highways. I agreed with Jacob that when a person's time comes to die it will happen no matter where s/he is, and that we should deal with our everyday situations without a constant fear of impending doom. We agreed that if we spent too much time worrying about what *might* happen, we'd miss too much of what *was* happening. We couldn't avoid a certain amount of worry, but we decided that too much worrying seemed to show a lack of faith.

We reasoned that the world was full of dangerous lines of work and adventures. We probably wouldn't choose to be airline pilots or bomb defusers. We wouldn't choose to race cars for a living. We wouldn't choose to be thrill-seeking bungee-cord jumpers. We wouldn't choose to be mountain climbers or mountaintop emergency rescue members. We wouldn't want to be snake handlers or professional boxers. The duties of S.W.A.T. team members were out of the question for us, too. But, thank goodness for police officers and fire fighters, and all sorts of rescue teams. The list was endless—but we didn't seek any sort of compensation or satisfaction in the act of contacting the people who'd chosen those professions to inform them that we thought their jobs were too dangerous and that they should consider other lines of work. We didn't feel any sort of need to tell them that we wouldn't want their jobs. Jacob and I think a lot of us are risk takers; we just take different forms of risks. So, we just decided to politely listen to what folks had to say and to live our lives the best we could.

The first year of that layoff wasn't too difficult. After unemployment benefits were exhausted, we dipped into our savings, which had been difficult to scrape together because of the former layoffs. Jacob hadn't previously been laid-off for more than eighteen consecutive months, so we counted on his being called back to work any day. It didn't work out that way, and heading into the third year of the layoff, money got much tighter. It was difficult to determine when would be the right time to give up the fight. So many things had to be considered. I prayed that something would come along to alleviate our circumstances.

One day as I walked home from the post office, I ran across a friend who was visiting his mother. We chatted a while, and somewhere during the conversation he asked, "Well, has Jacob heard anything from the mines, yet?"

"No. Not yet. He has applications strung out all over the immediate area, but you know how that goes around here. There don't seem to be many openings available. It's been a long haul, but we're hangin' in there."

Jerry Swanson smiled. "I know what that's like. Janet and I have been without work as much as we've been with work. The construction business wasn't really something we could depend on for a full-time income, either. We were relieved when I landed my job with Amalgamated Gas Systems."

"You surely were lucky, Jerry. I wish Jacob could get a job there. He's submitted applications but never received a response. Company officials seem reluctant to even consider hiring laid-off miners. They probably think it would be a risk to spend money training people whom they suspect will leave without much notice if they get a call to come back to work at the mines where they've built up seniority and benefits. It's too bad for people like us that they operate that way, but we understand the logic."

Jerry nodded his agreement. "I know. Listen, would Jacob be interested in finding an odd job until something else comes along?"

"He would be. Why? Do you have something specific in mind?"

"Maybe. I don't know if it's something Jacob would want to do, but my supervisor Ralph Colter and his wife are looking for someone to paint their house, and they don't seem to be having much luck. You know the Colters; their number's in the phone book. If Jacob's interested, it might be worth a call."

I was elated. "Thanks for the lead, Jerry. Jacob will be interested, all right, and if it works out—every little bit helps."

"Well, good luck. Call and let Janet and me know how it goes."

"I will. Thanks, again, Jerry. I can hardly wait to get home to tell Jacob."

That impromptu conversation was one of those many gifts from God for which I had prayed. It wasn't until much later that I'd discover just how significant that gift was. When I got home, Jacob was mowing the lawn. I went inside the house, poured a couple glasses of iced tea, went back outside, walked around the house to where Jacob was mowing, and got his attention. Jacob finished cutting a strip of grass as he headed back in my direction and smiled an appreciative smile when he saw the iced tea. He arrived at where I stood, shut off the mower, and extended a tanned, sweaty arm and hand toward me, until he latched onto the chilled glass. The way I beamed, he probably thought he'd received a letter that called him back to work at the mine, and although it wasn't quite *that* exciting, it was exciting.

Jacob said, "Let's go sit on the porch; I can see you have something on your mind."

"Yes, I do! Just as I came out of the post office, I saw Jerry Swanson heading toward his mother's house…"

"And you really must have been glad to see him." We both laughed.

"Well, it was nice to see him, but you'll be glad I saw him, too, when I tell you what he just told me."

"I can hardly wait. What was it? Tell me before you explode."

"Okay; give me a chance. Jerry mentioned that Ralph and Iris Colter need someone to paint their house and that if you're interested in doing that sort of work it might be a good idea to give the Colters a call."

"You're right; I'm glad you ran across old Jerry. I'll call this evening after Mr. Colter gets home from work. Well, I'll give him time to have dinner and relax a while, and sometime before bedtime I'll give him a call. Boy, wouldn't it be nice to get that job?"

"I knew you'd think so."

"We've painted our own house several times over the years, and we've painted some for family members, so I reckon we could paint somebody else's house."

"Jacob, I lie in bed so many nights and pray for some kind of work to come along before our savings account is depleted. I've always believed that everything happens for a reason, and I guess this is one of those things. I don't usually understand why some things happen to us, and I admit that sometimes I question some of those things, but then I think about how at least our kids and you and I are healthy and happy, and those are the important things to us. As long as we're healthy, we can deal with these financial inconveniences."

Jacob smiled that sexy crooked smile and said: "I know we're healthy enough to paint a house—and I do agree with you. Somehow, we've always managed to make it through, haven't we?"

"I figure that maybe God's going to give us a house to paint, and I feel very comfortable with that. It would be a blessing. Any job that allows us to stay in our home and provide for our family, even if it's only for a little while longer, is a welcomed gift."

We finished our iced tea, and Jacob went to finish mowing. J.R. was out and about mowing for a neighbor, and Meeghan was working in the house, so I grabbed the weed-eater and went to help Jacob with the yard work.

That evening we could hardly contain ourselves as we waited for a proper time to call Mr. & Mrs. Colter. We were excited just at the thought of possibly being paid for painting their house!

Around 8:00 p.m. Jacob walked toward the phone. "I think I'll call the Colters. They've surely had their dinner and aren't in bed yet."

I followed him to the phone so I could get his immediate reaction to Mr. Colter's response.

He dialed the number. "Hello. Mr. Colter?" .... "This is Jacob Thomas." .... "I'm fine, thanks; how are you?" Jacob waited for Mr. Colter's response.

"Mr. Colter,..." .... "Okay, Ralph—the reason I've called is that my wife Cassie was talking to Jerry

Swanson today, and he mentioned that you might be looking for someone to paint your house. If you haven't already located someone to do it, we'd like to be considered for the job." .... "Oh, you haven't? Well, like I said, we'd appreciate it if you'd consider us for the job." I waited along with Jacob as Mr. Colter made a few comments. I wasn't sure what they were; I could only guess from the responses Jacob eventually gave.

"Thanks a lot, Mr. Colter." .... "—Ralph." .... "We can start as soon as you want." .... "I'd have no idea about that; I'm sure that whatever you would consider fair would be fine with Cassie and me." .... "Okay, we'll come out and look at the job, and we can discuss it then, if it's all right with you." .... "Sure, tomorrow will be fine. What time would you like us to be there?" .... "That's fine; we'll see you at 10:00 a.m., then." .... "Thanks a lot, Mr. Colter. We really appreciate this."

Jacob hung up the phone, looked at me, and smiled. We reached for each other and held on tightly. We were possibly one step closer to a job, which meant we were also one step closer to some income.

"Well," asked Jacob, "if we actually get the job, would you like to be my painting partner? I could use a good hand, and I think I already gave Mr. Colter the impression that we're a team."

"I noticed you used the words 'we' and 'us' while you talked to Mr. Colter. I'm honored that you asked for my assistance. Would I like to help? You bet I would! Let's tell the kids; they'll be so excited." We did; they were.

The next morning, Jacob and I counted the minutes until we could drive out to the Colters' house. Mr. Colter greeted us with such enthusiasm that I wasn't sure which of us was more excited. He was obviously pleased to find—and we were definitely glad to be—his house painters. He filled us in on what he wanted to have done and showed us around the place. We learned that the Colters weren't actually living in the house. Because of Mr. Colter's position, and because his immediate presence was essential in the event of a company-related emergency, he was required to live a few miles away in a house that was owned by the company for which he worked.

"Iris and I were glad you called last night," said Mr. Colter. "We've had a difficult time finding someone to do this job."

We were glad we'd called, too. Then we took care of a little business. We discussed and agreed upon a flat rate that pleased all concerned parties. Mr. Colter made it easy for us.

"If you want the job, it's yours. I took the liberty of calling the hardware store this morning and ordered some supplies." He laughed and added, "Don't let that make you feel obligated or anything."

Jacob was somewhat taken aback at how easily everything had fallen into place, but he pulled himself together and said: "No, sir. If you're ready for us to start, then we're ready to start."

"There's a little catch," added Mr. Colter. "I'm going to have to ask you to take your truck into town, if you don't mind, and pick up the supplies."

"Sure, I can pick up those things this morning and start the job as soon as I get back, if that's all right with you."

"That's fine, Jacob. I hoped you'd be willing to do that. I'll make sure you're compensated for the gasoline." He held up a hand to stop Jacob's beginning of a protest. "And by the way, I gave the salesman your name and said that if you were the one who came in for the things I ordered, you'd have my permission to pick up anything I might have forgotten. I have an account there, so you be sure to check the order, and if you can think of anything I've missed, just get it and bring the invoice copy back with you. Well, I think that pretty much takes care of everything. I'm going to go now. If you need anything, you know where you can reach me."

"Thanks, again, Mr. Colter. We'll paint your house as if it were our own."

Mr. Colter shook Jacob's hand, looked him straight in the eye, smiled, and said, "I believe you will, Jacob; I believe you will."

It was just that easy. We got the job! While we worked on the Colters' house they found other odd jobs for us to perform, and they must have been pleased with our work, because when the exterior painting was completed, they asked if we would consider painting the interior and finishing some new interior doors and installing them. We decided the additional work was another gift from God, and I actually thought the Colters were our own personal angels.

We loved working for them and did what we could to show our appreciation. We didn't do big things— we couldn't afford big things—but we did extra little things, like polishing the brass on the old doorknobs. We scoured and cleaned the bathroom and kitchen. We vacuumed the carpet and cleaned the windows. Even though they were just little things, they were things that Mr. & Mrs. Colter noticed, and they never failed to express their appreciation.

They kept us busy for several weeks—from exterior to interior and from basement to cistern. They seemed glad to have us, and we were definitely glad to have them. Before each task was started, we agreed on a flat rate and felt comfortable with that. We were able to take our time and do a conscientious job without fear of appearing to run up the tab. But, we didn't dawdle; we kept busy.

As each task was completed the Colters paid us, and we were able to live fairly comfortably with the knowledge that it wouldn't be long until we received each job's payment. Ralph and Iris were always kind, and when they drove out to the house every once in a while to look over our progress, they didn't appear to be looking over our shoulders. They made us feel like they came to admire our work.

We were almost sad when the work for the Colters was completed. Before we left on the last day, the Colters drove out with a check for the last of our work. We were shocked to find that they'd insisted on adding a little extra to the agreed-upon rate, "Because," as Mrs. Colter said, "we're so glad you did this work for us. We're more than pleased with what you've done." The Colters had a way of making us feel as if we'd done them a favor, even though working for them had actually been an answer to our prayers. As we drove away, we glanced back at the finished product, and I offered a silent prayer that more jobs would come our way.

Some people who'd driven by the Colters' house while we were painting the exterior, stopped and asked if we'd be available to do other painting jobs, and Jacob had explained: "We can't make any commitments until we're finished with this house, but if you'd like, give us a call, or drop by our house if you still need someone after we're done here, and we can talk it over."

Word soon spread that we were available and that we performed a conscientious job, and we got a few calls for painting jobs. We soon discovered that each new job was an additional blessing. We felt a profound sense of purpose when we had some reason to get up each morning and get started on a project. We had a satisfied sense of accomplishment when we completed each job, because we knew we'd done our best. We were desperate to stay in our home and were proud to have any kind of work that enabled us to stay there.

One painted house led to another, and we made it through another summer and early autumn. Our kids mowed lawns, cleared hillsides, and on rainy days when Jacob and I couldn't paint, Meeghan and I cleaned houses for folks in the community. The kids helped us as much as they could with our own household chores. J.R. did nearly all of our mowing and vehicle washing, and Meeghan did most of the laundry, cooking, and cleaning. We were each a part of the team.

Jacob and I have a profound work ethic, and one thing that could never be honestly said about us was that we weren't willing to work. We'd always explained to our kids that no matter what people do to earn a living, as long as what they do is moral and legal, and as long as they don't intentionally hurt anyone in the process, they have no reason to be ashamed of their stations in life. We explained to them that as the heads of our family, we'd set our priorities and had ultimately made our own choices to live the way we lived, and that we'd always dealt with the circumstances into which we were thrust, at least until we could find more satisfactory arrangements. At that point, we were experiencing the opportunity to practice what we'd preached, and we hoped to set prime examples for our kids. Judging by the way they pitched in to help around the house and by the way they worked for others and earned their own spending money, we were proud to learn that our children had been paying attention.

It definitely wasn't easy. We were tired and worn out at the end of our workdays, but along with our sense of satisfaction and our sense of accomplishment, we also had a sense of survival.

As tired as I was, though, I lay awake many nights, praying, asking for guidance, asking for another house to paint, asking for strength and stamina, and asking for more odd jobs. I lay awake planning menus and organizing our finances around a monthly budget of about $500. I didn't want to burden Jacob any more than he was already burdened, so I made sure the bills were always paid on time. We'd never missed a payment, and we'd never been late with one, and I didn't intend to get bogged down in some sort of quagmire from where it would be difficult to get out.

On those many sleepless nights, I devised ways to cut our expenses to the bone. In the early morning hours, I put my plans into action. I called and requested a disconnection of our television cable, and we bought an antenna, which eliminated an unnecessary monthly expense. We were very careful about the use of electricity. We limited the use of the gas clothes dryer by hanging laundry on the clothesline during the summer months and on hangers over the tops of door-facing woodwork during the winter months. We lowered automobile insurance rates by calling the insurance agent and requesting a higher deductible on our plan. When we weren't painting houses and doing odd jobs, we were often cutting firewood for the fireplace. We installed and used a wood stove in another area of our house, and that cut back on our gas heating bills.

We ate pots of pasta and buckets of beans, along with the vegetables we'd raised during the summer months, and we never went without food on the table. We even managed to put aside a miniscule nest egg in an effort to get through another winter, and Jacob took time to continue checking out other job leads.

One day Jacob ran into Larry Donovan, an acquaintance whose son worked near Washington, D. C. During the course of their conversation, Larry said: "Jacob, my son said they're hiring people for house construction down where he works. Maybe you could go down and stay with him—he has an apartment with some other guys—and he could take you over to talk to someone about a job. If there's anyone else you know who might be interested, take him with you. My son and his roommates can always make room on the floor for one or two more."

Once again, we were encouraged. Larry had steered Jacob toward another job lead, and Jacob mentioned it to John Undo, another laid-off coal miner. Jacob asked John if he'd like to go along and check out the job possibilities. We thought that if they were hired—even though it was out of our state—they could send money home to their families while we awaited a call for them to return to their jobs in the coal mine. As each day passed, we looked at it as another day closer to that call.

The day Jacob was to leave for the D.C. area, J.R. came from his bedroom and offered an envelope to his dad. "Dad, I've been saving this money in case we really needed it for something. I've put $300 in this envelope. Maybe you'd better take it with you. You might need it while you're away."

Jacob and I both knew how hard our teen-aged son had worked and had sweat in order to earn that much money, and we knew how easily he was willing to share his hard-earned cash, but Jacob couldn't accept it.

Tears welled-up in Jacob's eyes, and he wrapped his arms around J.R.'s shoulders. After a few seconds of throat-knotted silence, Jacob said: "I can't take your money, son. I know you'd give it to me in a heartbeat, and I'm not saying I'll never need to ask for it, but right now I think I'll be fine. I know how hard you worked for it, and it's really unselfish of you to be so willing to share it. I love you all the more for offering it to me. Thanks, buddy."

216

Jacob and John Undo drove off and returned home a few days later. "We located Larry's son," explained Jacob, "and he took us to his work location. I appreciate that Larry thought of me and suggested that I go down there, but even though the pay's all right, with the high cost of living down there, it just wouldn't be possible for John and me to pay our expenses and send money back home. It's not so bad for a bunch of young single guys to live together and share expenses for a small apartment and exist on bologna sandwiches, but John and I decided that if we could even find a place to rent and lived on peanut butter sandwiches, there wouldn't be enough money left over to send much home. If I have to leave here to find work, it would be better if the whole family just pulls up stakes and goes—but I hope it doesn't come to that. What do you think, Cassie?"

"I wouldn't want us to be separated, either, Jacob, and as long as we can make it, we'll go on. It was just another one of those leads you had to check out. I'm surprised after all the wild-goose chases that this one job offer even existed when you got there. I agree, though, it wouldn't be a good offer for us to accept. We'll all tighten our belts some more—and even though I'm getting sort of tired of saying that, at least we still have that option—I just hope we don't cut off our circulation." We hugged.

~~The picture of Jacob that was taken after his first day of work at the coal mine went into the album, right beside the picture of our precious babies, and I thought about how quickly our children had matured. Their ability and willingness to take on responsibility had helped to form the adults I've come to love and respect.

I stopped to think for a minute and realized I didn't have a snapshot that showed anything about the next big step in my life, but I definitely had some memories that formed a vivid mental picture for that period of time.

CHAPTER TWENTY

That winter I applied for—and received—a college grant. The cold and inclement weather wouldn't allow us to paint houses, so I decided to use those winter months to start working toward a degree in elementary education. It would take a few years to earn a degree, but we needed someone in our household to have a job that offered at least some semblance of financial security, and teaching was a profession in which I thought I'd be comfortable. Earning a living as a teacher would provide us with a more stable income and benefits that could help our family through continuing difficult financial times. I hoped to achieve my goal.

So, I went to college. I was scared nearly to death, wasn't sure I could handle an attempt at higher education, was afraid I wouldn't do well, and was especially afraid I'd embarrass myself. I wondered if my family and friends thought my quest for a degree was ridiculous, and I wondered what they'd think if I were a total washout. Then I decided that as long as I did the best I could, that was all I or anyone else could expect. What I thought of myself was what was important. It had been several years since I'd been in a classroom setting, and at the age of thirty-six I was somewhat intimidated by the young minds of my fellow students and by the brilliant minds of my instructors, but I was even more intimidated by the thought of possibly becoming homeless.

I was afraid that because of my age and circumstances I'd be unable to pull off such a feat as being successful in college. I soon realized, however, that possibly because of my age and circumstances, I had more reason to persevere and realized the importance of my endeavor. I drew from areas I didn't know existed. I saw words I'd written and heard words come from my mouth that I hardly believed had come from me. Much to my complete and utter surprise, I actually understood much of what went on around me. I identified with much of what was being said and realized that perhaps my age and life's experiences were assets. I familiarized myself with my new surroundings and realized the abundance of opportunities. Participating in my college classes became a pleasure, and visions of success danced in my head.

I gained some tremendously needed self-confidence, was pleased with what I learned, and was also pleased with my accomplishments. I wasn't the most intelligent person to walk through the doors of any educational institution, but I saw myself with at least a modicum of potential. I especially enjoyed my Speech and Composition classes and was encouraged by my instructors.

One evening after class, my composition instructor walked back to where I was gathering my things in preparation to leave. She sat down at one of the desks and said, "Cassie, I've been wondering whether you'd ever considered a career in writing." My heart pounded, fueled by excitement.

"For most of my life, nearly from the time I can remember, I've thought I'd love to have a writing career, Dr. Augustus, but I need to concentrate on a career that will give my family and me some sense of stability, financial security, and medical and retirement benefits. As much as I'd love to pursue a writing career—right now, it sounds like a pipe dream. Teaching seems to be a safer career choice. I'm looking for a job that will give me a paycheck every two weeks; I need a sure thing." We chatted a while about some of my work, and I went home with a feeling of encouragement and with a fleeting thought that a part-time writing career might actually be possible. Then I came to my senses, pushed the thoughts of a writing career toward the back of my mind, and was fully aware that I definitely needed a sure thing.

For about three of those winter months that I attended college, because inclement weather conditions prevented Jacob and me from painting and doing our odd jobs for folks in the area, and although we hated to resort to it, after nearly three years without steady employment and without regular paychecks, we sought Public Assistance. Welfare. I hated for Jacob to have to go and apply for benefits at that office, so I told him I couldn't let him go alone. We both went. And while we sat in the waiting room, I looked around and noticed that folks who looked as if they came from several walks of life sat in there with us. I thought of a quote my grandfather so often used when people made derogatory or degrading remarks about other folks. "There, but for the grace of God, go I." I had a much clearer understanding of what it meant. Unemployment figures were high; times were tough for a lot of folks.

We felt backed into a corner and weren't sure how to get out. We'd actually come to a point, after those three years, where our savings account was nearly depleted. We couldn't even afford to move.

Shortly after Jacob and I had done the dreaded deed of going to the welfare office, the topic in my history class pertained to the development and implementation of the Welfare System. Doris, who sat beside me in that classroom, looked my way, gave an expression of sheer disgust, and somewhat bitterly said: "They never should have started that system in the first place. All it did was encourage a nation of deadbeats. I think all those people on welfare should be run off. They're all a bunch of bums. Freeloaders. They're all just waiting for some kind of a handout. They don't even *want* to work for a living. Why should they? They get free food. They get free medical benefits. It just isn't right! They have no pride." Again, I recalled my grandfather's borrowed quote.

Doris had no way of knowing my situation, and I wasn't offended by her remarks. I, in fact, had privately said nearly the same things to Jacob, myself— before we found ourselves in that temporary position. I'd said, "There's work out there for anyone who wants to work." I believed that, too, but I hadn't considered every situation—including our current one—in which people who were accustomed to a certain standard of living suddenly lost their incomes and couldn't live very well on minimum-wage jobs that included no benefits, and I hadn't formerly thought of welfare recipients as anything other than "career" welfare recipients. I'd even had nearly envious and nasty thoughts in the grocery stores when I'd stood with my cart of macaroni, beans, and potatoes, and watched people in front of me unload tremendous amounts of meats, fresh fruits, vegetables, and snack foods—and then pay for them with food stamps.

I looked at Doris, who'd expressed her vehemence toward the welfare system and its freeloading recipients. I politely smiled but said nothing. I didn't imagine that I fit her idea of the typical welfare recipient. Doris meant no offense and would have been more embarrassed than I if I told her I was currently on Welfare. So I didn't give her any explanation on the way I felt about the welfare program that was helping my family through what turned out to be three difficult months. The only way I was able to cope with the reality of using food stamps and cashing a welfare check, was to justify it with the knowledge that we'd paid into government-funded programs with all the years of taxes that had been deducted from Jacob's payroll checks, and we definitely didn't plan to abuse the system.

As soon as weather permitted, Jacob went back to some painting jobs while I finished my semester. I was pleased with my progress, registered for the next semester's classes, and was honored when my speech instructor asked me to participate on the next semester's Forensics Team. My time at college proved to be a real confidence-boosting trip for me. The circumstances of the following summer months, however, led me down another path.

Jacob and I struggled while I attended that semester at college, and when the weather broke we were grateful for our few odd jobs. We set aside a small amount of money for whatever our future held, but we eventually reached a point where we believed we had to give up the fight. We had so much for which to be grateful and were glad we'd stayed in our home for as long as we had. We'd reached an all-time low the previous winter and didn't relish the thought of a repeat performance. Because of our discomfort at having done it, we didn't want to apply for welfare benefits again.

It was time to rethink our position. After careful thought and many discussions, we decided to leave our home and move to a southern state where we'd been told we could probably find jobs. Instead of Jacob leaving home alone, however, we were all prepared to leave, and we believed that as long as we were together we'd make it work.

I nearly cried when I called the college and requested that my name be removed from the next semester's roster. I left a message for Dr. Frazier to offer my regrets that I'd be unable to participate on the Forensics Team, and I knew the timing of my message would allow her to find a replacement. I hated to drop out of college and was tremendously disappointed in the continuation of our financial difficulty. I tucked away my plans to earn a degree and to find a teaching job where I'd earn a living to provide for my family. We didn't have the luxury of time and financial resources to wait for my teaching plans to reach fruition. And—I kept telling myself that everything happens for a reason.

We reached a difficult decision when the kids had approximately a month to complete their current school term. We decided to make our move as soon as we had enough money to leave. Jacob and I hated that we'd take J.R. from home just prior to his senior year of high school, and that he wouldn't graduate with those kids who'd been his classmates since kindergarten. We hated to take Meeghan from her best friend who was like a sister to her. But the kids realized the struggle we'd endured and were willing to make whatever sacrifices were necessary. In midsummer, after being paid for the completion of a few odd jobs that feathered our nest egg, we made preparations to leave home.

A major concern was what to do with our house, and we eventually decided not to put the house on the market unless or until we'd been gone from it for a year. We thought a year should give us enough time to find jobs in the south and to determine whether we wanted to stay there. We continued to hope that the added time might also be enough time to receive a callback to the coal company. We didn't easily give up.

We told our relatives of our decision to move, and under the circumstances everyone understood. Some laid-off coal mining families had already left the area. Because of their lack of income, some had lost their vehicles. Some had even lost their houses. Before those things could happen to us, we would voluntarily leave.

When I think back on it, I believe I had another one of those nudges from God. I couldn't really explain why, but I felt a strong urge—no, a profound need—one that nagged at me to call the home of Ralph and Iris Colter, who'd given us our first house-painting job. From time to time, Ralph had also hired Jacob for some contractual painting at the company where he was a supervisor, and I had an immediate and very real desire to thank Ralph and Iris for all the work they'd given us. The Colters' kindness was a major contributing factor to our being able to stay in our home for as long as we had, and I wanted them to know that Jacob and I would be forever grateful to them. I wanted them to know how much their help was appreciated and knew we couldn't leave without telling them how we felt.

The evening I called to thank them and to tell them that our family would be moving to the south, Ralph Colter sounded genuinely sorry about our situation and asked, "When do you plan to leave?"

"We're packed and plan to leave tomorrow morning. We're not taking our furniture, yet. We plan to leave it here until we find jobs and a place to live down there. So, we're only taking clothes and the necessities on this trip."

Ralph turned into what I always felt was a messenger from God, again, and provided a possible answer to my prayers. Ralph quite unexpectedly said: "Amalgamated Gas Systems has given me permission to hire two fieldmen, and I really wish I could hire Jacob, but I'm obligated to hire minorities." He paused a few seconds, and almost as if he'd been zapped, he added: "Come to think of it—I don't know if you'd be interested in this type of work, Cassie—but I know you're not afraid to roll up your sleeves and get dirty, because I've seen how you work alongside Jacob. If you'd like to be considered for one of the openings, and if it works out that you'd be hired, you'd have a lot to learn and it wouldn't be easy, but well, do you think you'd like to give it a try?"

I couldn't believe it. I figured I was about as much of a minority as was necessary, and I nearly shouted in Mr. Colter's ear: "Oh, yes, I'd love to be considered. I don't care what kind of job it is."

"Now, you have to understand, Cassie, that I can't promise you anything. It might not turn out that you'll be hired, but it might be worth a shot. And if it turns out that AGS hires you, it would be on a temporary basis pending your work performance and other company-needs factors. You'd be on a ninety-day trial period, and I don't want to give you any false hope; it could turn out that you'd never be hired on a permanent basis. During the trial period, you and your family wouldn't be eligible for any of the benefits in the company's benefit package, but of course if you'd be injured during a work-related incident, you'd be covered by Workers' Compensation." Ralph went on to explain what steps would need to be taken and that it could be several weeks before the actual jobs would be awarded, and then he added, "If you're interested,

come down to the office and submit an application—
that is, if you think you could hold off moving for a
little longer."

Even though the prospect of a fieldman job,
whatever *that* was, scared me nearly to death, Ralph
Colter's words were like music to my ears. I told Jacob
and the kids about the totally unexpected results of my
thank-you call, and we unloaded the vehicles. Early the
next morning, I drove down to AGS and submitted an
application. We picked up some odd jobs to tide us
over while we waited to hear from AGS, and we stayed
put. We wished it weren't necessary for AGS to hire
minorities in this instance, because Jacob definitely had
more experience with such man-type work, and he
already had an application in at AGS, but hiring
minorities was mandatory, so we held out for that one
thread of hope that I might get a job, and as always, I
thought that everything happens for a reason.

I wasn't afraid to work hard—and relished the
thought that maybe I'd be the one in our family who
could provide us with a chance to stay in our home. If
I didn't get the job, it would only mean that our move
had been delayed for a while, and if necessary we'd still
have time to enroll our kids in another school before
the new school term began.

A few weeks after I submitted my application, a call
came from the head secretary at AGS who said,
"Cassie, we'd like for you to come in tomorrow for a
job interview with Ralph Colter."

I could hardly sleep the night before the interview.
I was so afraid I'd say or do the wrong thing. Even
though I was somewhat comfortable with Ralph Colter,
I'd never been in the position of possibly becoming a
company employee under his supervision, and that
prospect put much more pressure on me than I'd
anticipated.

When I went in for my morning interview with Mr. Colter, he made me feel much more at ease than I thought would be possible. He covered the job description that could actually have been explained in a foreign language, because I had no idea what it meant. He asked me a few questions and seemed pleased enough with my responses. At the end of the interview, he told me just to hang in there and he'd do the best he could, but he stressed that he couldn't make any promises. I thanked him for considering me for a position with the company and explained that, no matter how it turned out, I appreciated his consideration. Then he actually thanked me for coming in. I nearly cried.

Two months later, I received a call and was instructed to report for a physical with AGS's company doctor. A few days after the physical, I was notified that I'd been awarded a position with AGS. I had been given a chance at an actual job.

AGS is located approximately three miles from our home. It's a large utility corporation that has facilities in several states. The company offered excellent pay and benefits, and I was especially impressed with its steady work history. That job was a definite answer to my prayers, and I thought about how a seemingly insignificant conversation with Jerry Swanson a couple years earlier had led me to that point. We didn't have to move away, and we didn't have to wait for someone to earn a degree to find work. We thought we were finally on our way to financial security, and I hoped and prayed that I could handle my part.

I was a thirty-seven-year-old female who didn't know whether I could meet my new job description. I had that specific trial period in which I must prove my worth, or I would be replaced. At any given time in my life, if anyone had asked me what I wanted to be when I grew up, being a fieldman for a utility company would not have been on my list. But, at that point, I was thrilled to have the opportunity to become one.

On my first day at work for AGS, I was actually so nervous that I wondered whether a move to the south was such an undesirable alternative. There I sat, with my please-be-nice-to-me smile, in a room that held one other newly hired female, about forty men, and one other woman. When Linda (the other newly hired female) and I received job orders for the day, we were assigned to George, our team leader, who soon led us to gather materials.

When I stepped into the company's warehouse, I almost thought I'd gone to a place where everyone spoke a foreign language. I heard: rubber buttons in various sizes; nails (I'd heard that one); ratchet wrenches; manufacturer's names for bottles containing something like soapy water; half-round bastard files; band clamps; anodes; anode pot; copper sleeves; powder; sparking guns; brand names for stuff that looked like tar; heavy scrapers. The list went on and on. I was literally sick; my stomach rolled; the lump I'd had in my throat all morning continued to grow; and my intestines called out to me. I defied tears to spill from my eyes. I felt totally lost and helpless. But, I wasn't homeless.

Linda and I were issued safety glasses and hard hats that we had no idea contained unhooked, adjustable liners. I put the safety glasses on, put that hard hat on my head, felt it cover my forehead and ears, decided it was much too big, and I struggled all day to keep that wobbling object on my head. Linda did the same. Linda and I received some knowing looks and silly grins, but no offers of assistance from other employees, and after we'd privately discussed our hard-hat problem, we supposed we'd have to develop enough nerve to later request smaller hard hats from the warehouseman.

Even though I was with other people, I felt so alone and so afraid. I was actually homesick and wished I were there—and was reminded of my feelings on my first day of school. I was out of my element and longed for the end of the day. As much as I wanted to cry, I decided crying wouldn't be a very fieldman-like thing to do, so I trudged forward.

Poor old George, Linda, and I, had been instructed to repair a leak in a gas pipeline, and I wasn't sure about Linda's leak-repair knowledge, but I knew I had none. We took our cue from George's halfhearted effort of motioning his hand, and even though we had no idea what we were supposed to do, Linda and I followed him to the warehouseman's cage where he requested the needed materials.

Without a word directed to his apparently good-for-nothing tagalongs, George left the warehouse and looked as if he were probably wondering what he'd done to make his supervisors mad enough to result in sending Linda and me with him. Linda and I looked at each other and supposed we were to follow him toward our assigned company truck. I had no idea where I was headed or what I'd do when I arrived there, but I was sure I'd better keep an eye on George, and unless told otherwise be sure to follow along.

The three of us traveled in the truck to a point where we left the blacktopped road and eventually reached another point where it was necessary to travel on foot. George mumbled some instructions toward us, and we sort of had an idea of what to collect from the truck, which we did, and we headed out, single file, into a wooded area. I wasn't sure if we were supposed to be there, or if poor old grumbling-and-mumbling unlucky George just thought it might be a good place to strangle and leave the bodies of two newly hired female-minority employees. I was certain nobody would ever find us, if that were George's plan. We walked for what seemed like hours. I wasn't used to wearing leather steel-toed work boots, and they quickly burned blisters right through my socks.

Eventually, we arrived at an area with which George was apparently familiar, and he began his unenviable task of teaching as much as was possible to us two sore and tired gas company know-nothings, about the process of gas pipeline leak repair. I was familiar with a shovel's use from the times when I was a kid and had used one to clean the barn and to dig in the gardens, and as an adult I'd dug around in my own vegetable and flower gardens, but I couldn't recall a time when I'd had any reason to dig for anything on a steep hillside where water trickled down at a pretty good rate.

The steep hillside was where I had the shovel that day, though, and I didn't accomplish much. I used my shovel to scoot and roll rocks from the affected leak area. And as if that weren't enough of a problem, I fought with that stupid wobbling-and-offensive hard hat that, under penalty of death, I was required to keep on my head. And judging from some of the looks I'd received that morning, I didn't think the Safety Department would have any trouble finding members for its firing squad. I tried to familiarize myself with some way to comfortably work with larger-than-I-needed-but-all-that-I-could-find work gloves, especially because working in the muddy water caused them to be so wet they further hindered my already clumsy efforts.

I was sure I understood the goal, but I wasn't sure what steps I should take to reach it. George was obviously trying not to laugh and offered any number of suggestions. Even though George turned out to be most patient, I knew that whether anyone said so or not, I was not proving my worth. It seemed that taking the job seriously wasn't going to get it done. I made every effort, but I didn't know the proper procedure. I wasn't worried about the other woman's performance; she probably did no better than I; but I was certainly worried about my own non-productive efforts. I could only imagine George's report to the supervisors at the end of the day, along with his promise to get even with them for the cruel joke they'd played on him.

I needed instruction and was glad when it was offered, even though I had trouble putting my understanding of it into a productive action. I needed experience and would be glad when I had some. I decided I'd eventually discover how all those articles with the foreign-sounding names were used, but I also realized that if George didn't jump in and physically take over, we'd all be entitled to overtime pay.

George apparently realized that, too, and when he'd seemingly tired of watching Linda and me totally humiliate our gas-leak-repairing-know-nothing selves, he quite adeptly and quickly completed the repair. He made it look so easy that I felt even more inept. When we left that first work location, I was sure I wasn't the only one who was glad we were leaving. I didn't mind being soaked and muddy, but I didn't like the fact that because of my ignorance and ineptitude in that situation, I'd not performed well. I was quite disheartened.

When the end of the workday finally arrived, I went to my car, where I felt more comfortable than I'd felt since I'd left it that morning. I actually had to struggle to hold back tears—tears of frustration at feeling so out of place and inept—and tears of relief that I'd soon be going home. I took along my hard hat, drove home, and when I stepped out of the car at my house I put on a happy face because I knew Jacob and the kids would be hoping I'd had a good day. I recalled how I'd felt the first day Jacob went to work at the coal mine and was determined not to let anyone in the world know how miserable, stupid, afraid, nonproductive, and out of place I really felt. As tremendously grateful as I was for the opportunity to work at AGS, I didn't know how I could face the next day, knowing I had to go back there.

I stepped out of the car wearing my wet and muddy blue jeans, a wet and muddy tee shirt, wet and muddy leather steel-toed boots, and holding wet and muddy gloves. To complete the ensemble, I threw on my wobbling hard hat that was covered with several smears of mud, which were the results of my hands constantly grabbing and replacing or repositioning it. I was sweaty, hillside-water wet, muddy, and stinky. My hair was a total mess. I looked exactly like I felt.

Jacob and the kids were on the porch, where they'd been anxiously awaiting my arrival. When Jacob saw my hat, he couldn't help himself; he burst out laughing and asked, "What's wrong with your hard hat?"

"I don't know. It's just too big. Linda—she's the other woman they hired—and I guess we'll have to ask the warehouseman for smaller hats."

Jacob walked over to me. It was obvious that I was his ignorant-about-such-things wife, who definitely knew nothing about hard hats. He looked as if he really felt sorry for me. He said he guessed I'd walked around all day with that wobbling hat and also mentioned that he wondered why nobody had offered any help. We made eye contact, and without having to ask, he realized how difficult my day must have been— and I knew he knew. He also understood that I didn't want him to think it had been a lousy day, so he smiled and removed the hat from my head, attached the liner that had been held inside the hat by only one of four clips, made an adjustment to the band with the ratchet knob, and placed it back on my head. Then he said, "There; isn't that better?" I smiled and made a mental note to show Linda that hat trick the next morning. We both had a lot to learn.

I was relieved and felt a sense of comfort when I walked into my home that was full of love, welcome, and dinner smells. I showered and changed while Jacob and the kids put the meal they'd prepared on the table. When we sat down, everybody was ready to hear about my day. I laughed along with the rest of my family about the hard hat and jokingly divulged a little information about my feelings of ineptitude, but I didn't go into great detail about how I sincerely wondered whether I could cope with the expected job requirements. I didn't tell anyone that I felt like a total dolt or mention that I was definitely out of my element. In an effort to convince my family that I'd make it through the little bumps in my road, I focused on my potential to learn. (I still dreaded going back.)

Jacob looked like he knew what was going on in my mind. He smiled and tried to reassure me. "Everything will be all right. You'll do a fine job. You just need some time." At that point, I wasn't totally convinced he was right.

But I went back to work, and I continued to go back for the next two weeks. I wanted to go back for a longer period than that, but it was at about that time another one of those unexpected inconveniences happened.

It started out like any other day where I was sent out on a routine leak-repair crew with a couple other experienced fieldmen. After we drove as far as we could and then walked to our remote leak location in a rural wooded area, we discovered we needed some additional items from the truck. Being the newest member of the crew, I volunteered to go back for those items.

A slight drizzle of rain had fallen. I climbed up on the back of the truck and gathered what I'd been told we needed, and as I stepped down onto the bumper, my wet boot sole met the wet bumper, and I slipped and fell from the back of the truck. I'd previously broken my wrist and some ribs, so I was all too familiar with the sound I heard when I landed.

When I hit the ground—out in that wooded middle of nowhere—I yelled, "Ah..." It doesn't really matter what I yelled. I was pretty sure I'd broken my left elbow, and even though it hurt like the dickens, my major concern was that I'd probably ruined any potential chance of being awarded a permanent position with AGS. I also knew I had to get back to the leak location with the tools. With my one good hand, I gathered the scattered items from the ground and placed them in a metal bucket. I gritted my teeth, and with my right hand I pulled my left thumb through a belt loop on the front right side of my pants, gritted my teeth again, picked up the bucket, and headed back through the woods toward the rest of the crew.

Shortly before I reached my destination I met Marvin, who with obvious concern said: "I thought I should come and see if you needed any help."

In some of the remote areas where we worked, there were always the potential dangers of snakebites, falls on slippery and steep wooded areas, and so forth, so everyone watched out for each other. Marvin added, "We thought maybe something happened to you."

In response to Marvin's concern, I replied, "I've been gone so long because I fell from the truck, and I'm pretty sure I broke my elbow." Then, because I was nervous and humiliated, I just sort of laughed.

I wasn't making a big squalling-and-bawling production of my incident, and Marvin looked like he wasn't sure whether or not I was serious. He looked a little uncertain when he said: "Well, we'd better tell Kenny and see what he thinks. He's the team leader today, and he'll have to decide what to do."

Marvin was right, but I didn't relish explaining my situation to Kenny. I felt like I was letting down the female minority—and validating that a woman shouldn't have been hired—at least not an accident-prone one.

When I acquired my temporary position at AGS, being a woman in that type of work was an unusual position in which to be. We lived in an area where the female minority was probably the only minority from which AGS had to choose—under the circumstances, Ralph Colter had little choice.

Even though my co-workers treated me with kindness and respect, I understood that didn't mean everyone at AGS thought it was a position that ever should have been offered to me or to any other female, and to be honest, I wasn't so sure about it, myself. When I worked with people who possibly weren't exactly keen on the idea of a woman working in their field, they pretty much accepted my presence as a sign of the changing times and were always polite and respectful toward me—and they gave me the benefit of the doubt. Their occasional bit of good-natured teasing was welcomed, and I easily took it in stride. I was pleased that we got along as well as we did, and I actually felt somewhat accepted by most of them.

I didn't fool myself for a second, though. I didn't think anyone else actually thought I *should* be there, even though I was glad I was. And I didn't think anyone else was glad I was there, even though I was pleased to have the opportunity to be. I knew right from the beginning that my presence might forcibly be tolerated and, for me, that would have to suffice. It hurt deeply, but I continued to smile every day and hoped my co-workers might at least *try* to understand that I had valid reasons for wanting and needing to be there.

Kenny was one who left no doubt where he stood on having me in his workforce. He proved not to be so accepting of those changing times that required hiring minorities, and he made me fully aware that he believed I had no business working in that job. Every time I worked with him, Kenny made sure he lectured on that topic before the workday ended, but I wasn't quite sure whether it was me in particular he had a problem with, or if he had a problem with *any* woman being in that line of work. I finally told him that if I'd had a lot of choices, I'd rather not have been a fieldman, either, but that because of my personal circumstances I appreciated the opportunity to try to become one.

To be honest, I made myself tolerate working with him, too, but his unkind words and ways brought a lump to my throat and tears to my eyes many, many times. Every time I worked with Kenny, when I returned home, I vented my stress by crying while I showered and prayed to God and thanked Him for creating good, kind, decent men, and for placing them on this earth. And I wholeheartedly thanked Him for Jacob Thomas.

Regardless of how I felt about Kenny Crumbly's reaction to my presence, however, I knew I'd have to bite the bullet and tell him I'd possibly broken my elbow. I figured at least he could look forward to the time in which AGS would be rid of me.

Marvin and I reached a point where we had to climb over, or in my case through, some strands of a barbed-wire fence. I brought up the rear. Marvin stepped over the fence and continued to walk ahead. I set the bucketful of tools through the fence and held up one strand of fence as I crawled between the strands. My shirt caught on the barbed wire, and I jerked to pull away. My thumb fell from my belt loop and my arm flopped around like it wasn't a part of my anatomy. I suppressed a moan, gritted my teeth, used my right hand to pull my left thumb back through my belt loop, swallowed down the nauseous feeling, and continued my journey.

When we finally arrived at our destination, I didn't have to explain anything to Kenny. Marvin filled him in, and Kenny said we'd report it when we got into the office.

We completed our assigned task, eventually arrived at company headquarters by quitting time, and when I went inside to report my injury, the office staff took a quick look at my swollen and bruised arm. They took down my information, and one of the supervisors accompanied me to the hospital's emergency room.

X-rays confirmed a broken elbow, and I was informed that I'd also sustained an extensive amount of muscle and tendon damage to my wrist and hand. It was necessary to wait three days for the swelling to subside before my arm could be casted. I felt like a complete incompetent, and for the following six months, I was off work for the healing- and physical-therapy processes.

When I eventually returned to work, I was afraid I'd be treated in a less than positive way, but my fear was totally unfounded. Some of my co-workers even teased me about finishing out my workday with a broken arm.

In my brief time with AGS, I'd already discovered that the actual workings of the industry were quite interesting and was genuinely eager to learn any aspect of the job. I was also grateful to anyone who willingly took time to teach me. I understood—more than anyone else—just how important that job was to me, and I hoped my accident and ensuing six-month time off hadn't jeopardized my position. I definitely didn't want to lose my job.

Eventually, my co-workers understood that I hoped to have the opportunity to stay for as long as AGS would allow me to stay, and we sort of settled in with each other. As each day on the job passed, the other employees patiently assured me that they didn't know all about the utility industry when they started to work there, either. They made every effort to teach me what I needed to know to properly and safely perform my work duties. Good old-fashioned work ethics, well thought-out ideas, caring, and an appreciation for a busy workday ran rampant throughout my work location.

Each day's work assignments placed different people together and sent them to do various daily tasks, so it wasn't long until I'd been on a job with just about everybody else at my work location and was soon exposed to quite a variety of work tasks. When I became more at ease with the other employees, and when we had some idea of each person's personality and work ethics, it wasn't long until I was good-naturedly teased about being an old woman in a man's world. I was yelled at, laughed at, and laughed with. I knew, for the most part, that no real intention of cruelty or harassment entered my co-workers' minds. Our senses of humor made the day pass quickly and proved to make the work much more enjoyable.

The fact that we all got along so well helped to alleviate the times when we worked in adverse weather conditions and on difficult location terrain. During the next few months, my work assignments varied. I mowed company properties. I painted, which sometimes included surface preparation by using a sandblaster on extremely rusted areas. I performed janitorial duties. I walked pipeline rights-of-way to check for gas leak indications, repaired leaks in gas pipelines, and helped to install new pipelines. I checked the pressures on gas lines and learned some oil

239

and gas well-tending duties. I learned various other maintenance duties and dealt with the public. I became quite comfortable with my work situation and found it amusing that, initially, I'd been so intimidated and overwhelmed by it all.

I became fairly comfortable with the situations in which I found myself and continued to be grateful for the job that had allowed my family to stay in our home. Some things I thought I'd never learn soon became run-of-the-mill for me. It quickly became natural to scrape mud from my work boots, to use leather gloves while I worked, and to wear a hard hat and safety glasses without being uncomfortably aware of their existence.

I initially thought I'd never remember the names of my new co-workers, and by the time I accomplished that feat, I was also familiar with the names of those mysterious items in the warehouse and with the names of those items in the toolboxes on the company trucks.

Eventually I learned to recognize pipe and fitting sizes on sight. The first time I was sent back up a hill for a specific fitting, I didn't know a collar from a nipple, and rather than ask for a briefing, I clawed and crawled my way back up the hill, found the truck, opened the toolboxes and filled my pockets with every size and type of fitting I could find. I scooted back down the hill to the leak location, emptied my pockets, and said I wasn't sure which fitting I was to bring back, so I was prepared not to have to go back up that hill for another one.

When my co-worker explained the fittings to me, it was a lesson I hoped never to forget, and I didn't have to make very many additional trips up-and-down those steep rights-of-way on other jobs. Determining what fitting was required quickly and easily turned into a fairly simple task.

With proper training, I performed more duties than I'd expected to perform. I couldn't lift as much as the strongest man who worked at my location, but I reasoned that neither could any of the other people who worked there—that's what made him the strongest—so I pushed myself and lifted more than I thought I could. I helped others when I could, and others helped me when I needed help. I had great respect for the others who proved their worth, and I made every effort to prove mine. It paid off, and I was eventually awarded a permanent position with full benefits at AGS.

My co-workers and I realized there were valid reasons why and when people should report incidents of discrimination and harassment. We understood the importance of such true occurrences, but we also understood that people should make clear determinations in respect to each incident, to know when a joke was just a joke, and to know that certain words or actions weren't always evoked by feelings of discrimination or concocted to intentionally offend or humiliate another person. We understood that pranks were pulled on each other, no matter what the gender, the age, or the job title. I was glad my co-workers knew I had a sense of humor and could take a joke.

Derrick soon became almost like a younger brother to me. I didn't tell him very often, but I respected his experience and knowledge concerning the gas industry. I also appreciated that Derrick was more than willing to teach me what he believed I should know to contribute to and perform in a safe environment. On the other hand, he liked to tease and joke around—almost to the point of good-natured torture, if there is such a thing— and he was never satisfied until he got a reaction from me. He kept me on my toes. It took some time, but I learned to distinguish between what was of true importance and what was just Derrick's way of finding out how gullible I was. The thing about Derrick was that I understood his intentions weren't mean—they were a mixture of teasing and teaching and maybe a bit of frustration and seriousness. He wasn't mean, but he liked to give the impression that he could be. I saw right through him, though.

One day when Derrick and I were assigned to a specific job location, he said, "Cassie, you drive the truck; I want to see how you handle it."

I didn't think his request was strange. I'd driven the company's trucks for as long as I'd been there—a company driving test was actually mandatory. So, we loaded the truck with supplies, and I confidently jumped in the driver's seat. Many of our work locations' roads were difficult to travel, and they were particularly nasty during the winter months, after heavy rains, and during the spring thawing periods.

I managed just fine—until we eventually came to a wide muddy area in the road where Derrick startled me when he suddenly yelled, "Go to your left!"

I didn't know what he'd seen that he thought required quick action, and I think I'd have been okay if he'd kept his mouth shut and allowed me to make my own assessment of the road conditions. But, I have a problem with that right and left thing. I'm not stupid, but as stupid as it sounds, I really have to stop and think about which is my right and which is my left. I've read that it's not an uncommon female trait, but I don't understand it. Of course, I went to my right, instead of to my left as I'd been instructed to do. As soon as I did it, I knew what I'd done, but we were already there. We were stuck in the wide, deep mudhole that I'd already seen was there. I'd allowed myself to be startled into making a stupid move.

Derrick, being his usual self, flapped his arms and loudly reacted with: "I said to go to your left! What's the matter with you? Don't you know your left from your right? Now you've done it! We're stuck! You got us into this mess! Now you're gonna get us out!" Then he sat in stone silence. I think he actually fumed.

I couldn't help my reaction to his tantrum; I grinned and suppressed a laugh. I received the treatment I'd expected but also knew it was just Derrick's way of being Derrick. I never took him seriously when he ranted, raved, or fumed. I just waited for him to get over it and thought my reaction probably ticked him off, too. I tried to drive the truck out of the mudhole. Then I *TRIED* to drive the truck out of the mudhole. Then I *REALLY TRIED* to drive the truck out of the mudhole. I rocked the truck back-and-forth and tried to get some sort of traction. That *TRYING* business didn't help Derrick's disposition. The deeper we went, the madder he looked and sounded.

I knew that if worse came to worse, we could always winch ourselves out, so I wasn't too concerned. I'd been a passenger in a few company trucks where some of the guys had driven us into similar situations, and a winch came in handy and got us out of our predicaments. I didn't even feel bad about being stuck in the mud.

So, as Derrick flapped his arms and his jaws, and as I smiled, I also tried to drive out of the mudhole. Other than a lot of flying mud, not much happened. Finally, as I knew he eventually would, Derrick took over with: "Get out of the truck! Just get out of the truck! You're just digging us in deeper. Get out of the truck! I'll show you how to get us out of here."

Arguing with Derrick wouldn't correct the situation—and, anyway, I couldn't argue with him when I knew he was right—so I stepped out of the truck and into nearly knee-deep mud. Derrick jumped out from his side of the truck and trudged around toward the driver's side. We met, and with the waving backs of his hands, Derrick motioned for me to move. He directed me to the center of the road—directly behind the truck. He said: "Now, you stand right there! I mean it! You stand right there, and I don't care what happens, don't you move!"

Derrick slogged back through the mud and climbed onto the driver's seat. He positioned himself, and the last things I saw were Derrick's pearly white teeth shining in the rearview mirror. He grinned from ear to ear, threw the truck into gear and spun mud from the rear tires. I saw teeth; I saw mud; and I could have sworn that before my ears filled with mud, I heard the sound of rotten ornery laughter.

I saw it coming and swiveled on one foot, but I didn't leave the spot where I'd been told to stand. It wasn't that I strove to be obedient; it was that I couldn't get the other foot out of the mud; it was stuck. Mud flew from under the tires, hit and covered the entire front of my body, and by the time I'd made my complete one-footed pivot, mud had also hit and covered the entire right side and back of my body. I clawed clumps of mud from my eyelids, opened my eyes, turned back toward the truck, and again saw those pearly white teeth in the mirror.

I spat mud from my mouth and laughed and laughed. I really laughed because I'd been gullible enough to stand right behind the truck, just where Derrick had told me to stand, and I knew Derrick wouldn't have pulled that trick if he hadn't known I'd laugh it off. We were comfortable with each other. We didn't have to worry that someone was going to report discrimination/harassment. Derrick would have reacted exactly the same way if it had been one of the guys who'd done what I'd done. We both knew, too, that I might have done it to Derrick, if I'd thought of it first, and if he'd have been gullible enough to fall for it. He wasn't being cruel; he was just having fun, because

244

he knew he could. I'd have been muddy before the day was over, anyway, so there definitely was no harm done.

I liked the fact that the people at AGS took pride in their work and grew very fond of those folks with and for whom I worked. Less than a year after I became employed, Jacob was called back to work at the coal company, and even though a fieldman position wasn't my dream-come-true profession, it provided us with a dream-come-true income and a sense of financial security, so it never occurred to me to quit my job with AGS. Jacob and I believed AGS offered us much more stability than the coal company offered him. We feared another mine layoff or closing and decided my job would be the one we could rely on until I reached retirement age.

~~ Perseverance paid off and good luck came my way. It wasn't long until a dream-come-true position with AGS became available. That thought prompted me to sort through the box of pictures until I found a thick Polaroid shot denoting the time when I became "Field Clerk Cassie."

CHAPTER TWENTY-ONE

The supervisors and clerical staff at our local AGS office allowed me to train and fill in as a backup when one of the clerks was absent from work, but the chance to hold a full-time clerical position wasn't even a consideration—until a job in that department was actually posted. By that time, I was comfortable with fieldman work, but when I compared the job descriptions, there was no question which one I'd prefer. At the age of forty-one, a possible desk job looked quite attractive—even though the transition between those two particular job classifications would mean an initial and substantial cut in pay.

The posting was up for bids to those already in the clerical division, and my only chance to move from labor into clerical was to follow procedure and submit a letter of interest. We were in such a remote location that no bids from throughout the company's clerical department were received, so I was considered, tested, and awarded the position.

At that point I let down my guard, became confident that I'd work in the office until retirement, and envisioned an even more secure financial future for Jacob and myself. The possibility that Jacob might have another loss of employment was even less ominous. I looked forward to working at a job I loved with people I enjoyed and looked forward to Jacob's early retirement with me providing additional household income.

Moving into the new job wasn't as difficult as I'd anticipated, because the women who trained me had been so open and giving. They didn't have know-it-all attitudes or make me feel like they were talking down to me. They treated me like I'd hoped to be treated, with kindness and respect. They did whatever was necessary to fill me in and make me feel like a part of the process. They each made me feel welcome and taught me the ropes from their own unique perspectives and job descriptions and, because of that, the transition was a relatively smooth one for me.

I loved my office position and working with Lydia. Lydia had enough experience and knowledge of the business to run the place, and she was willing to teach me what I hadn't previously been exposed to when training and filling in. She had a wonderful sense of humor, and her presence in the office made me look forward to going to work every day. We easily developed a great working and personal relationship, and when I considered working with Lydia every day for many years, that prospect, too, seemed almost too good to be true.

It wasn't long, though, until I became aware of that old familiar feeling that things *were* almost too good to be true but attributed it to the fact that, because I'd had a certain feeling of insecurity for so many years, it was just hard for me to believe I wouldn't have to worry about it anymore—it wasn't easy for me to relax and be comfortable.

We began to notice that headlines in our local newspapers and some headline news topics on TV focused on businesses downsizing to cut expenses. It was rather unsettling to read about it happening in other companies, because we were aware that once something got started, if it sounded successful to other companies' officials, they often tended to follow the lead and implemented the same technique to cut their own expenses. Downsizing too quickly became a word we heard and read too often, and it seemed to be becoming a trend. Even though it definitely was a sign of the times, I hoped downsizing would stop before it got to where Jacob and I worked.

When rumors of downsizing began floating around AGS, I was glad Jacob *hadn't* been hired there, because if he had been, we'd be in another precarious position. It seemed that everything did happen for a reason, even though it had taken nearly eight years for us to understand why I, rather than Jacob, had been hired at AGS.

I wanted to believe that only jobs in other AGS locations would be affected and recalled that, during my orientation with Amalgamated Gas Systems, the spokesperson made me proud when he said our location was the hub of the company. With that thought in mind, surely my work location's facilities were too important to be sold. Rumor became reality. Other company offices closed. Employees were categorized and lumped under headings like: Relocation Employees, Surplus Employees, Refused to Relocate/Self-terminated Employees.

Reality hit closer to home. Office telephones buzzed with information that our location's oil- and gas-production facilities were offered for sale. The effective contract that was quickly coming to the end of its term didn't permit actual layoffs of union employees, so some of us were labeled as surplus and lumped in the category of Surplus Employees—a particularly cruel label, under the circumstances. Some were removed from their familiar duties and were placed in other jobs and in other locations. The plan was to place workers where jobs were available, even though some of those positions were out of the employees' home state. If an employee refused an offer for an available job—no matter what it was, or where it was—he, in effect, terminated himself with that refusal. Only a certain number of positions were available, and some of those openings required specific job qualifications. Everyone couldn't possibly continue with AGS, and the reality of downsizing hit me with a sudden and forceful jolt into what seemed like unreality.

Employment almost depended upon the luck of the draw. Only certain positions in certain locations were affected. Years of service with the company, knowledge, skill and ability, pride in one's work, and work records that reflected a desire to work didn't play a role in the maze of surplussing and downsizing. Even several management supervisors were displaced and misplaced, until many were eventually terminated.

Meetings were held. Some meetings were designed to explain the cuts, but I wasn't receptive to the company's reasoning. Even though it did no good, at some meetings we affected employees were occasionally allowed to voice our opinions. Some meetings began the actual process of slowly, but surely, downsizing at our location. Some of the people in my location who were previously classified as surplussed accepted other positions, ones they knew could possibly be temporary. Some of the people from other locations were surplussed and were absorbed by our location, where they filled positions that had been left by our location's formerly surplussed employees. Downsizing was confusing. Downsizing was disappointing. Downsizing was a mess. "The Hub" became something of a holding tank for those whose futures with AGS looked less than bright.

My work location suffered cutbacks, until only one relocated supervisor was in attendance, and Victor Harmon probably was placed in one of the most difficult working positions of his life. As he explained it: "Your location's employees weren't placed in this position because you did anything wrong. I want you all to believe that you haven't failed in any way."

Victor openly expressed genuine gratitude for our efforts and voiced his appreciation for the attitude of the group as a whole. He did all he could to relieve our stress. He opened his office to anyone who needed to talk through his or her own turmoil, and he suffered along with us. Victor proved to be a gift to our workforce, and in his short stay with the group, he earned our respect and many lasting friendships.

We tried to make the best of that very difficult situation and made every effort to keep up morale. I struggled to maintain my sense of humor as I clung to the too few days I had left with my fellow co-workers. I'd known it before, but I even more strongly realized at that point, just how wonderful a local job with AGS was. Finally, more than a year after rumors about the location's demise began, those few of us who remained at our location faced our own immediate decision-making process.

When I previously heard that people from other locations were put into different positions, I felt bad for them and hoped the trend would stop before it reached my location. Those folks who were the first to move on turned out to be the more fortunate ones, because at least they secured positions within the company while some positions still existed. By the time the decision-making process reached our location, very few positions within the company remained available.

The meandering through that surplussing-and-downsizing maze didn't make any sense to me. I was unable to anticipate which turn the process might take at our meetings, where each employee's attendance was mandatory. Not all positions were affected at each meeting. But for those whose surplussed positions were those to be addressed, each person's opportunity hinged on the decision of the person who chose directly before he did. Although he had no way of knowing what position (if any) would be offered to him at the meeting, he had to anticipate the best- and worst-case scenarios and give his immediate decision before the next employee was given an option. Participation during those meetings was nearly mind-boggling, and we knew we'd continue to have more surplus meetings until we'd all been placed or displaced. It was impossible to relax, because we didn't know how long we'd be classified as surplus, whether we'd be offered another available company position, or whether we'd be downgraded from a surplussed employee to an actual downsizing statistic. It was a virtual nightmare.

I spent many sleepless nights that were sad reminders of those previous years when Jacob and I had no steady work and income. I saw the possibility of that happening again, but with us being much older and unable to perform the type of work we'd previously performed in our efforts to make ends meet. Besides thinking of financial loss, I had a true emotional feeling for losing my AGS position.

My grandfather had often said: "When you go to look for a job, look at the field of natural resources, because that's where the security is." It seemed that the two natural resources Jacob and I had chosen, however, weren't working out to be so secure for us. The times—they were a changin'.

As I followed the media, I thought of how the previously encouraging trend focused on companies that touted their hand-in-hand size and potential for employment- and economic-growth. I wondered why, all of a sudden, the trend shifted and so many companies announced that their workforces were overloaded and found it necessary to reverse their potential for employment growth. Was it some sort of simultaneous and instantaneous revelation?

I wondered if the higher echelon of AGS realized, or even considered, the personal devastation that was taking place. A finger couldn't be pointed directly at any one person who was willing to take responsibility for what was happening, and I wondered whether anyone was actually in control, or if after the ball started rolling nobody could stop it. I wondered whether following the downsizing trend was a well thought-out plan or whether it was a case of "...if Johnny jumped off the bridge...," and they thought they should, too.

Newspaper articles and television and radio news segments daily reported tragedies such as those of homes burning down, of violent crimes being committed, and of family losses in the obituaries. Even though I had compassion for those involved, unless it was my home that had burned down, unless I was the victim of a violent crime, or unless my loved one was the one mentioned in the obituaries, I couldn't possibly be fully emotionally impacted.

Reading and hearing the news concerning corporate business downsizing or other terms that translated to a reduction in the workforce didn't emotionally affect me too much either, until it was my company doing the downsizing, my company reducing the workforce, and my company offering jobs to employees who must move to other areas or face termination of employment. That's when I became emotionally impacted.

I was working for AGS, in a newly named department that seemed destined to face the most adverse change—a sort of going-out-of-business sale of the entire local facilities. A new plan was in the making. A major change would take place. And I was destined to be a casualty of that process. In the case of corporate headquarters, perhaps change within the company was considered excellent business strategy, but when I assessed it from my angle, the proposed change within my company was not something with which I so readily agreed. I was disappointed and angry, but mostly I was afraid.

I reasoned that with the threat of losing their jobs, employees had an incentive to offer suggestions on improving productivity, which would eventually increase company profits. The field workers were familiar with ways to make the business more productive, but it seemed that the company was leaning toward future hiring of college graduates. I respect higher education as a valuable tool, but I was afraid that we in field locations were incorrectly mistaken (by some) as an uneducated lot. Hands-on training and experience are also extremely valuable educational tools, even though they don't earn the students sheepskins. It was encouraging to think that the two realms of education could be productively merged for the betterment of the company and for the dignity and appreciation of all its employees.

Our field workers were among those who were familiar with and who could best explain the core of the gas industry, and they were those with the most to lose when certain judgments were made. I believed that if the core were destroyed, so too would be the lives, the hopes, and the dreams of many of my location's employees. I worried that if the core were destroyed, a trickling-down effect would eventually and almost certainly also destroy some of those who held higher positions within AGS. Convincing myself was easy; I just wished there were some way to convince someone to agree with me—someone who would stop the rolling ball.

I hoped AGS's CEO and his cohorts would reconsider what was being done and would hear—and pay heed to—our voices. I hoped when they lay down at night, those executives would imagine their names, their faces, and the names and faces of their family members on a reduction-in-workforce list. How would *they* cope? How would *they* make the transition from being employed to being unemployed? How would *they* manage without definite income in an area where unemployment rates were already high?

I hoped they had read and considered the information that was contained in the letters we'd sent to them and that our ideas and opinions would be considered and would negate the findings submitted by the outside time-study group that was hired by AGS to suggest what it considered to be the proper cuts. Based upon the results of that outside study group, we who were on the payroll had a lot to lose.

I hoped the company's executives would remember that a family went with every name on a surplus list and on a reduction-in-workforce list. A home went with that name. Hopes and dreams, and ideas and aspirations for the future also went with that name. I hoped the higher echelon would listen to the employees and would positively act upon what we had to say.

Because of our collective experience and knowledge, I thought our suggestions were worth consideration. I thought about our frustration at not being able to bring productivity to its fullest potential, because our hands were tied. We wouldn't sabotage AGS with misinformation and totally wrong ideas; we'd be jeopardizing our own future security. We were professionals. Of course, I realized that most executives received high salaries with secured retirement options and stock benefits, so the problems and concerns of the little people probably didn't keep the big dogs awake at night. It didn't really matter how I felt; and it didn't really matter what I thought; the big dogs didn't even know of my existence within the company.

At the end of each day as I lay in bed, the quiet and the darkness gave me too much time and space in which to think. I knew that in whatever way corporate decisions impacted our lives, my co-workers and I would have to deal with it in our individual ways. I wished our faces could reflect a peace of mind, again. I wished we could make eye contact without worrying that someone would see our fear, our dread, our uncertainty, and our inner devastation. I thought about how sad it was that at the end of their workdays, when the men returned from their jobs in the field, laughter seldom echoed throughout our office building.

Those quiet hours before sleep allowed me to think about how I missed seeing the guys standing around the coffee machine for that last few minutes of the workday while discussing work, hunting, sports, or telling funny stories about something that happened at home. I was sure it was difficult not only for me, but also for my co-workers to look forward to the next day's work, because we all realized each day was one day nearer to the major changes that were inevitable.

Many nights I felt warm tears slip from the corners of my eyes as I thought of the clouds of fear and trepidation, and those of uncertainty and insecurity that permeated the atmosphere in the presence of my co-workers. I knew we held onto the hope that it wasn't too late for a turnaround, and that we felt backed into a corner and experienced emotions that were almost foreign to us. One man described our situation as seeming like a death had occurred, and we were awaiting the burial. I was saddened by the thought that so many good and decent, hard-working people were placed in that position. I didn't think it should have happened, and I didn't want us to drift apart and to be forgotten for who we were. How wonderful it would have been to be recognized and to have our ideas acknowledged and considered for implementation.

When the security of the employees was threatened, and when so much stress was placed upon them, it was difficult for them to dig in with full force and to tackle the jobs at hand. People's minds strayed from their work when they had that nagging thought of downsizing in the backs of their minds. Several scheduled work hours were wasted when surplussing and downsizing became the main topics of conversation. And, as the downsizing process progressed, too much work was assigned to too few people and had the potential to create a situation that could result in a stress-related downturn in their productivity.

I thought that maybe within the next few years, some companies' main decision makers would find they'd cut too closely to the bone and would perhaps discover their companies suffered for it. I wondered whether a company's reputation and stability could remain adversely unaffected when so many people were shuffled into positions with which they were unfamiliar. I wondered how those folks, when dealing with the actualities of their nearly luck-of-the-draw positions, could exude confidence, understanding, and a working knowledge of their newly assigned responsibilities and job descriptions.

Forced to face my own reality, however, I realized that those were my personally biased thoughts and concerns—because I was involved on the disappointing downside of downsizing. I knew that in reality, the remaining employees would eventually adapt to their positions, and AGS would survive and would prosper. But, in my frustration with the situation, I let my mind run rampant while I tried to figure it all out. I didn't want to lose my financial security and benefits, and I didn't want my co-workers to lose theirs—and I knew that was my actual bottom line.

During my work hours when I looked at those men, most of whom were the sole supporters of their families, I realized they were being forced to make decisions that could alter their lives and the lives of their families, forever. I also thought about the men whose wives had their own professions. Those men had to determine how their decisions would affect their wives' careers. Some wives had earned tenure in their positions and surely didn't want to give up the careers and the positions they'd chosen. It was a mess.

AGS employees had to consider leaving the homes they'd inhabited with pride and comfort for many years. Some of them faced the possibility of uprooting their children from their familiar schools. Some of them faced the possibility of moving away from their grown children and grandchildren, and from their elderly parents and grandparents. They faced the possibility of moving from small and safe communities to unfamiliar areas and suffered with how to explain possible relocation to their spouses and children.

I heard bits and pieces of conversations in which those men debated whether relocation was the right thing to do, especially because AGS planned even more future cuts. They were uncertain whether relocation would result in a permanent or temporary status. I understood their obvious struggles with whether they should leave their families behind for indefinite periods of time, which some of them said might be the least disruptive road to take, at least until they had a more definite "feel" for the stability of their positions.

I worried for them even more than for myself, because I knew exactly what it was like to be without income, exactly what it was like to face a possible and undesired relocation, and exactly what it was like to have no idea what to do. I clearly understood my co-workers' predicament. It was obvious that employees with more than twenty years of company service, and employees with only a few years of service, dealt with their own inner turmoil. It was difficult for seasoned veterans of AGS to find themselves in such precarious and unenviable positions—especially while employees with much less service in other locations retained their job descriptions and titles. One thing was certain, though—we'd each have to come to terms with our individual situation.

Jenkins & Bronson, Inc., a company that was headquartered in another state, was tentatively scheduled to purchase my AGS location's facilities. Pending approval and finalization of the sale, Jenkins & Bronson, Inc. hired Thompkins & Richardson Company, a local contracting outfit, to operate those facilities.

Thompkins & Richardson Company offered jobs to a few of us remaining AGS employees. The jobs entailed much of the same work that we performed at AGS, so we accepted. Due to those circumstances, about a month before the closing of my AGS office, I resigned and moved into my new position. Even though I looked forward to going to work in the mornings and felt as if I'd found a new home, I still wondered whether I'd made the right decision.

My job with Thompkins & Richardson Company lasted six months. Jenkins & Bronson, Inc. turned out to be tentative buyers who decided not to finalize the purchase, and Natural Resources Group began the process to purchase those facilities. Unfortunately, for some of us chosen few, Natural Resources Group provided its own staff of field and clerical workers. I maintained the nagging feeling that I, once again, had made the wrong decision for a career choice. But I told myself that everything happens for a reason, and I continued to believe in the existence of an ultimate plan; I just hoped I'd make my connection.

I was later told that when "The Final Decision Day" at AGS arrived, some of the last of the remaining folks opted to relocate, and as I'd expected, some had no choice but to terminate. As disappointed and as sad as I was for what transpired at AGS and at Thompkins & Richardson Company, I remained convinced that everything happens for a reason, and that belief helped keep me going. It also kept me searching for whatever that reason was.

Nobody ever appreciated a job more than I appreciated my job with AGS. It came at a time when my family desperately needed it, and I'll be eternally grateful to Ralph Colter who took a chance and hired me. To have been involved in something that was so important and to have been involved with such a wonderful group of people will never be looked at in a negative way, and I'm proud to have been a part of it all.

But, even after I left AGS, the faces of my former co-workers continued to invade the dark stillness of my nights. Some of those folks occasionally kept in touch with me, and with each other, but it became difficult to keep track of those who'd relocated, especially when they continued to relocate until they found a more permanent position. After a period of time, some returned to our home state, but to different jobs and to different company locations. I wondered how their choices had subsequently impacted their lives and the lives of their families. AGS certainly lost some hard-working and conscientious, dedicated and honest employees, but it luckily retained some employees with those same qualities.

People adjust; life goes on; and there's always business as usual. My ultimate decision didn't cause any ripples in the waters of successful big business, but in my passion for the injustice of it all, I'd egotistically hoped it would. Finding it necessary to leave AGS was a traumatic and disappointing experience for me.

We former AGS employees are viable beings who are much too important to have been considered surplus by any entity, and we are a part of AGS's losses. Even though I'd hoped to work for the same company until I reached retirement age, and even though I'd hoped to reap those many benefits that would go along with that, I know that realistically AGS never promised to give me employment for as long as I wanted it.

I'm a product of the changing times and can't afford to allow those changing times to ruin my life. I remain grateful for what I had. And because I'm convinced that everything happens for a reason, I believe I'm where I am because I'm supposed to be here. I've drawn from my inner strength and have set new goals. I'm following my heart's passion and am embarking upon a career for which I long. I won't give up. I will survive.

~~Losing two jobs within those few months was disappointing, but it happened, and it was time to move on. I placed the picture of "Field Clerk Cassie" in the album, and it pleased me when I thought of how many wonderful people I'd met while working at those jobs. Many of those people earned special places in my heart, and I think of them often.

A random luck of the draw was in store for me when I reached back into my box full of pictures. When my hand emerged, it grasped a picture that was taken of a group of my old, nearly lifelong friends. Jackpot! My albums wouldn't be complete without pictures of my friends at what our kids eventually called "The Old Gals' Get-Togethers." We proved those people wrong—those ones who said we'd probably never see each other after our high school graduation.

CHAPTER TWENTY-TWO

For several years after our high school graduation, even though we thought of each other often, we nearly lifelong friends were involved with diverse career choices. Our lifestyles varied, and our experiences ranged from truly happy marriages and anniversaries to not so happy marriages, separations, and divorces. Death claimed some of our spouses, children, parents, siblings, and other loved ones. Some of us eventually returned to or started new careers that previously and for various reasons had been put on hold.

Some of us enjoyed good health while others experienced the pain and suffering of arthritis, diabetes, multiple sclerosis, or cancer. We retained fond memories and remained in contact with some more than with others, but not one of us was ever released from that memory- and time-woven cocoon of friendship.

Affirmation of that fact came in the form of an invitation to the home of an old friend who promised a cozy winter-evening's reunion with other old friends. We met, and once again we hugged, held hands, and wrapped our arms around each other—even after all those years. As we laughed, cried, and reveled in our celebration together, it was as if we had stepped back in time. In that brief interlude, although we would not have thought it possible, we became even closer.

We ate good old-fashioned country food, sang Christmas carols, and reminisced—each with her own recollection and interpretation of our past. We remembered aloud old pajama parties. We talked about trips to ball games. We discussed old boyfriends, former teachers, and principals. We laughed about former clothes styles. We recalled former hairstyles— and accepted the blame for home-permanents and haircuts we'd performed on each other that would have wrecked anything other than the most stable friendships. We reminisced about our roles in school plays. We talked about how we'd worn church choir robes while we sang "How Great Thou Art" for an eighth-grade talent show and expressed our indignation for that time when our mesh of song choice, choir robes, and angelic faces hadn't won first prize.

We fondly remembered parents, siblings, and grandparents. Our thoughts drifted back to lazy chats beneath shade trees, to walks along country roads, and to sleigh rides down snow-covered hills and knolls that surrounded our childhood homes in West Virginia. Laughter, memories, and much love filled the room that winter's night and made it cozy—as had been promised by our hostess. We were more than friends—we were nearly sisters.

Some of the contributions to the memory-filled evening were funny; some were sad; some were thought provoking; and some definitely weren't. Most of our conversations dealt with our memories of school, because those were the years during which we'd had most of our interaction—our coming of age.

A tradition began as a direct result of our first Old-Gals' Get-together, and on a fairly regular basis, thereafter, we met in the home of a friend. At one of those get-togethers, Dee Dee who'd taught school for many years, and who'd recently become a high school guidance counselor, shared a lovely story. She said: "I have to tell you this. You know how much these get-togethers mean to us. And, you know how close we've remained over the years. Well, I had a little fun with that a while back. While attending a seminar, the subject of friendship was opened for discussion, and each of those present was asked to tell about his or her best friend. When my turn came, I told those folks at the seminar that I couldn't really say I have a best friend." We old gals laughed, because we sort of guessed where she was headed with her story.

"I was amused," Dee Dee added, "when the seminar attendants looked at me with something akin to pity in their eyes. So I comforted those unsuspecting folks with my story of our group's almost fairy-tale friendship that includes several women who treasure our time together, and who share true compassion, respect, and unabashed love for each other. I further explained to them that my friends and I truly appreciate each other, and that if any one of us experiences a difficult physical or emotional struggle, the others are there for her, either with our presence, or in the form of a quiet thought or prayer. As I detailed our friendship and its longevity to the others at the seminar, I watched their faces soften with smiles, and I saw their eyes take on a wistful look. I understood. Of course, I received a multitude of comments from the group that pretty much translated to how lucky I am—to how lucky we all are."

Nancy said, "Aw, Dee Dee, you're gonna fool around and make us cry."

My friends and I have always known how special our friendship is, and on that night depending upon where we were seated, we leaned against the friend who sat nearest to us and touched shoulders, or we reached over and squeezed another's hand. A couple of the more demonstrative ones started a chain reaction when they rose, walked around the room, and shared hugs. Some of us wiped tears of appreciation and love from our eyes, and we all smiled. We were up and out of our seats by that time, anyway, so we filled our plates from the standard buffet setting that always accompanied our get-togethers, and we continued our love-filled evening.

At the beginning of 1995, we veered slightly from tradition when our Angie called a few of us and asked each of us to call a few others to relay her request that we meet at a centrally located and recently refurbished River's Edge Inn. She made it clear that she wanted us to meet in a public place, and we understood why. She had a specific reason for wanting us to keep our emotions somewhat in check and that would be more likely to happen in a public place than in the comfort of a friend's home. For Angie's sake, it was imperative that we be strong.

A few days after Angie's call, we met at the inn and started our visit in the lobby where one friend surprised us with an easel- and table-covered collection of pictures that chronicled our treasured past. We eventually dined in Victorian-style elegance and later toured the facilities.

Our hugs, conversation, and easy laughter were commented upon by some of the inn's other guests. Some of those other guests even offered to take our cameras and to snap the shots for us so we could all be in the photos. Some of those strangers spent a few moments with our group, laughed along with us and, after having heard our history, marveled at how we remained so close.

One thing that didn't come up in the presence of the inn's other guests was the reason why that location had been chosen for our get-together. The inn was centrally located and had been reserved by Angie, who five years earlier had undergone a radical mastectomy. After Angie's call for us to meet, word swung around on our grapevine of friendship that Angie planned to give us the most current details of her effort to combat her reoccurring cancer. We knew it would be better for us not to ask Angie about it. She'd give us the information when she was ready. She didn't like to be fussed over.

As we dined on that day at River's Edge Inn, we entertained each other with stories of our kids and—as unbelievable as it was—grandkids, of our spouses and siblings, and of our parents and grandparents. We discussed minor health issues that seemed to go along with us during our aging process. We discussed our employment and loss of employment. We joked about old school situations. And, as always, we didn't speak unkindly about anybody or anything. Our time together was always pleasurable.

We exchanged rolling-eye looks, knee squeezes, and bites of each other's dinner selections. We shared laughter and tears and reveled in our celebration of being together.

After a few hours of pleasure—except for that dark looming feeling of dread for why we were really there—we gathered in the lobby of the inn and prepared to leave. Some of us held hands. Some of us stood with entwined arms. Some of us stood with arms wrapped around each other's shoulders or waists. Some of us used each other as leaning posts, and some of us grinned at each other and shoved a little. It seemed that in some way we were each touching someone else.

We only made eye contact for a few seconds or so while we waited for Angie to speak. We knew she'd say something about her current health situation before we walked out and onto the street, so we waited for her to signal the beginning of that topic, which we knew she would do when she thought the time was right. Angie told us in her own time, and in her own way. The news was major; she was scheduled to have a bone marrow transplant within the next few days. We finally stood a little too quietly in the lobby.

In a voice that often broke, Angie said: "Well, I know you've been waiting for me to make the first move—and I don't want anyone to try to change my mind about the decision I've made—this whole thing is going to be difficult enough. You know how much I love all of you. And I know how much you all love me. I'm sure, given how our grapevine swings, that you already know I'm checking into the hospital next week to have a bone marrow transplant." She held up a hand, as if to stop anyone else from speaking. She swallowed, took a deep breath, and hesitated for only a split-second before she continued. "Here goes—no argument, now! You have to understand and not make this any more difficult for me than it already is. I want you to promise that you won't visit me in the hospital. I'll be isolated for a period of time, anyway. Of course, good old Gary, who's stood by me since we were in high school, and especially through all of this, will be there. I've even asked our kids not to come to the hospital. It's such a long trip to where I'll be, and I don't want to have to worry about everybody's safety while traveling just on my account. I probably won't feel much like having visitors, anyway, and there really isn't any point in disrupting other people's lives and entire households. It's too emotionally difficult for everybody—and you know me—I especially don't want you all to see me when I'm not looking and feeling my best." Then she laughed. She actually laughed.

Quite reluctantly, nobody protested. We didn't want to rob Angie of her dignity. We understood and respected her wishes, her pride, her desire for privacy, and her concern for our feelings. Nobody uttered a word. We just tearfully nodded our promise to her. We swallowed the sobs that swelled in our throats. We fought back tears. We, uncharacteristically, were unable to speak for a moment.

After several seconds of very self-controlled silence had passed, Angie opened her arms. We wrapped our arms around Angie and around each other, offered our prayers and love to Angie, and we quietly and solemnly walked to our cars. Nobody immediately drove away. I don't think anyone could see through her tears.

Following Angie's stay in the hospital, and after some recovery time had passed, we were once again invited to the home of a friend. Not everyone attended, because we were concerned that something as small as a common cold, or other slight health problems, could pose an open threat to Angie's weakened immune system. But we were all there in spirit. Angie borrowed her hostess-friend's telephone and called and chatted a few minutes with those friends who'd found it wiser, but tremendously difficult, not to attend the get-together.

Even under the most adverse conditions, Angie showed no suffering, sadness, or self-pity. She wore her makeup and wig, and exhibited her sense of humor and bravery, with much pride and satisfaction. As always, though, her inner beauty far outshone her truly stunning outer beauty. She clung even harder to her faith in God and remained confident in the fact that she had a beautiful and loving family and friends who adored her, and she knew we were thankful to have her in our lives.

Within the next few months, cancer again took a toll on our Angie, and malignant brain tumors were discovered. Other than for one friend who lived near her, Angie again requested that none of us visit her. She said she didn't want us to remember her as we might see her in her last weeks of pain and suffering. It wouldn't have been a bother to us to be with Angie after she'd lost her hair; it wouldn't have been a bother to us to be with Angie when she was unable to laugh and freely chat; it wouldn't have been a bother to us to travel to spend time with her. But, Angie's dignity and the time she had left with her family were important to her. There was so much more to Angie than her illness. Once again, although tremendously difficult, we respected her wishes. We sent her cards, called and checked on her well-being, and we kept each other posted on her condition. Angie spent her last quiet and special moments with her family until November 1995 when she lost her battle with cancer.

Even as she'd anticipated and planned for her death, Angie unselfishly thought of others. In an effort to accommodate her family and friends, she'd requested that her funeral service be held in a centrally located city, which was near where we'd all been together for the last time at River's Edge Inn. We friends met at the funeral home where, once again, we made eye contact, whispered in hushed tones, and wrapped our arms around each other.

But, we had lost our joy.

If a funeral service can be thought of as having been beautiful, hers was. We friends believed Angie had written the words that were spoken by the minister, because rather than eulogizing her, the service seemed to pay tribute to those whom Angie loved. Loving and appreciative references were made to her family.   And loving and appreciative references included us friends as an integral part of her family; a reference was even made to how our get-togethers had impacted the quality of her life. It didn't surprise us that Angie would have wanted it that way. Even when facing her own immediate death, it was typical that Angie would be thinking of others.

To face our group the next time would be nearly unbearable without Angie, and while at the funeral home, one friend suggested that we should meet soon because, as she explained it: "Prolonging our next time together will make it even more difficult." Within the next few weeks, we met in a public place and were all too conscious of the fact that Death had become an unwelcome intruder upon our circle of friendship.

I know, as all my friends know, that until the last of us is gone, we will continue to exchange smiles, to hold hands, and to wrap our arms around each other as our friendship envelops us. We will continue to count our blessings, and we will cherish every moment.

~~I still find it hard to believe she's gone. Angie's example is a tough act to follow. Knowing how Angie handled her life, but even more how she handled her faith and acceptance when she faced the knowledge of her own future pain and suffering, the potential effects of her illness on her family and friends, and her ultimate death at an early age, I felt ashamed for pitying myself because I'd lost two jobs within a few months, and I felt bad that I had difficulty adjusting to my empty nest. I thought of how difficult it must have been for Angie to know she was leaving her beloved husband, her two grown children, her grandson, and the unborn grandchild she knew she'd never see. I hunted and searched through the pictures of my kids and other family members. It was time to empty the picture box, to finish filling the albums, and to start writing.

CHAPTER TWENTY-THREE

Granddad was right. It was nothing short of blessings to be given a wonderful and understanding husband and the opportunity to rear two healthy children who matured and became independent adults. Those blessings fill my heart and feed my soul.

Because our children and grandchildren are so far away, and because we see each other only once or twice a year, my emotions didn't allow me to move quickly through the stacks of their pictures. I savored each one and allowed my emotions to flow. I laughed, cried, remembered, and wiped away tears of joy and sadness. The process was quite cathartic and helped me to work through my pent-up emotions and move ahead. It became quite clear that, unlike Angie, I'm blessed to still be alive to enjoy my children and grandchildren, even though we must adjust to the miles between us.

The pictures nearly summarized my life. One picture led to another picture. One memory led to another memory. Questions led to understanding. Understanding led to acceptance. Acceptance led to an even stronger sense of peace.

I was reminded of the day I left my childhood home and my non-nuclear family to start a new life with Jacob—that day when I heard my grandfather's heartbeat as he held my head close to his oversized chest—and my interpretation of that day's thoughts and feelings had proved to be true—a part of us, indeed, is always with each other even after one's death.

When each one's death was imminent, it was almost as if my grandparents had some sort of premonition. Some of the last words Grandma Maddie weakly spoke to me as she looked through faded blue eyes were: "Cassie, honey, I love you as if you were my daughter, and I want you to know my time is near. When I'm gone, please don't grieve for me; be happy for me. I'm very old; I'm tired; and I'm in more pain than I sometimes think I can bear. You wouldn't want me to continue to suffer. You know that death is just the step that leads us from this life into another, and I welcome that eternal life. When you think of me, remember how much I've loved you, and remember how much you've loved me. Be happy with those memories."

I do remember—nearly every day—I do. And, I am happy for those memories.

When Granny Rose Hunter discovered she had only a short time to live, she accepted it much better than Pappy could accept the thought of losing her. Pappy held Granny Rose's hand, and the entwining of wrinkled hands wearing wedding bands that had been exchanged more than twenty years before, reminded me of their beautiful life together—one that could so easily never have been. Pappy said, "Oh dear Rose, I do so wish I could take your place."

Granny Rose, who was still a beautiful lady, looked at the man who had been so good to her, and she undoubtedly knew that if it were possible, he truly would exchange places with her. She squeezed his hand, but her strength was nearly gone. Her eyes still twinkled when she looked at her husband and said: "Oh, Isaac, I love you dearly. You have given me a wonderful life. But, please don't wish that you could—and I know you so willingly would—precede me in death. You wouldn't want me to suffer the grief of losing you."

Pappy and Granny Rose had lost former spouses to death, so he understood exactly what she meant, and he knew she was right. He would not want her to suffer the agony of another loss. Pappy did not have long to grieve. He passed away two years later, and as I looked at those pictures, I knew I'd always value his strength and courage—and miss his presence.

Several years after my grandfather's death, I heard that my long-absentee father had died and was sadly reminded of how hard my siblings and I had tried to become an integral part of his life. We decided to shift our efforts, however, when Daddy matter-of-factly told us that he wanted nothing to do with us—that he didn't want to see us, and that he didn't want to hear from us. By that time, we were adults and decided to honor his wishes. We'd never expected anything from him except some of his time and attention. We didn't want money. We didn't want to take his time or love from his other children. We just wanted to be acknowledged and wanted to acknowledge him. Even though I'd never truly known him, I was somehow saddened by the news of his death. It was sad that we children had never gotten to know his other children—our very own siblings. It was sad that our father had chosen not to know all of his children, grandchildren, and great-grandchildren. I used to joke that if he'd taken the time to know us, he might have liked us—we weren't *that* bad. I was saddened, too, that he was the type of man who hadn't seemed to care, and I continue to find it amazing that someone with his personality was my grandfather's son. I was also sorry that I'd never had a real chance to properly thank Barbara for the kindness she'd shown me when my grandmother passed away.

I picked up an old black-and-white picture that was full of the faces of relatives who'd gathered for a traditional annual Christmas get-together at the home of Aunt Mary Kate, who was one of Pappy Hunter's sisters. The picture helped remind me that even though I'd seen most of those relatives only a couple dozen times in my entire lifetime, and even though I didn't share a strong emotional bond with them, I did feel a definite kinship toward them, most probably because Pappy, through his storytelling, had kept me aware of them from the time when I was a child. I think I actually imagined most of them as children, because of my grandfather's retelling of his own childhood stories, which included the childhood stories of his siblings. I recalled the feelings of those evenings when I sat with my siblings around our grandfather's chair and listened to his stories, while we waited like a bunch of hungry animals as he peeled and cored those home-grown, crisp, sweet-tart apples in his old pie pan and then passed the bright white and juicy, taste-bud delights down to us.

The albums. My thoughts snapped back to the task at hand, and as my eyes scanned the pictures of those grandaunts and granduncles, second cousins, and all the rest, the picture of our family gathering that elicited several memories was lovingly placed in the photo album, along with the others that also had taken me through another memory-filled evening.

With Jacob at work, with our kids so far away, and with only loving memories of so many of the deceased folks in the pictures, I felt the emptiness of heart and of home. But, with my plan in the back of my mind, and with my determination to carry it through, I continued to place those pictures into my albums so I could get on to the next point of organization on my list.

Finally, the album-filling and picture-hanging tasks were completed. The house had already been cleaned until it almost sparkled. The bookcases were organized. It seemed natural to hope that someday those bookshelves would hold some of my own works.

I wanted to write and to be published and was ready to put my plan into action. Jacob knew I'd had a desire to write since I was a child, but when I talked to him about a home office, our ideas of a home office were somewhat different.

As Jacob put it: "You have the whole house."

He didn't understand why I needed an entirely separate room for an office. So, I patiently explained. "The roll-top desk in the living room is a beautiful piece of furniture; it isn't a scattered-papers holder."

Jacob didn't look impressed with that information. He didn't say it, but he looked like he wanted to ask: "Your point would be?"

Convincing Jacob that I needed a separate space for my project meant I had my work cut out for me. "The computer station is in J.R.'s old bedroom, and it's in the way when the kids come home to visit. I don't expect you to understand, but when paperwork and books are scattered all over the computer station and J.R.'s bed, if someone unexpectedly drops by for a visit and has to pass that bedroom door on the way to the bathroom, all that clutter is right out in plain view, and it's embarrassing for me when that happens."

Jacob, as usual, didn't interrupt. From years of experience, he knew I'd eventually wind down, and he patiently waited for me to reach that point.

I gave it my best shot. "When I need a reference book, it nearly always seems to be in the extra bookcase that's in Meeghan's old bedroom, and that means when

I'm working on a project, I have to run up-and-down the hall several times, and it breaks my train of thought. The L-shaped secretary's desk in our bedroom takes up too much space in there. And, if that's not bad enough, when you're working the midnight shift and have to sleep in the master bedroom during the daytime, I can't have a bell-ringing and talking-computer and a printer making racket in the next room, and I can't rummage around through the desk in the master bedroom, and I can't just keep tiptoeing up-and-down the hall to Meeghan's bedroom in my effort to keep from disturbing your rest. So, please just give me a corner of the garage. The kids are gone; their vehicles are gone; and their old parking places are just collecting junk. I'll clean the garage. I've already figured that if I take a 12-foot by 16-foot section of the outside corner, I can have two of the windows in my office. We'd still have your shop area and room to park three vehicles." I stopped. That was about as convincing as I could be, and by that time I was nearly out of breath.

Jacob smiled that sexy crooked smile, looked at me with love in his eyes, and because I'd like to think he still finds me irresistible although understandably exhausting, he said: "Okay. Figure up the materials you'll need, and we'll go pick out what you want to build your office."

We got started on my office that week. A neighbor helped us finish the room and move my office furniture into my new special space. I re-cleaned and rearranged the rooms from which my office furniture had been removed, cleaned and organized my office, stood back, scanned the area, and smiled.

I bought self-improvement tapes, read several books about the how-tos of becoming a published writer, and I started to work. I brainstormed, outlined, made notes, and thought things went well. I wrote, read what I'd written, and decided things hadn't gone as well as I'd originally thought they had. I edited, put aside what I'd written, and stayed away from it long enough for it to seem almost new to me again. Then I reread it, re-edited it, rewrote it, and did my best to fine-tune it. Most of all, I prayed for guidance.

When I worked on my manuscript, I had happy days. When I wasn't spending time in my office, I thought about spending time there. I wrote my thoughts on scraps of paper in every room in the house and wrote notes in my car. I kept a small flashlight, a notepad, and a pen in my nightstand drawer so I could write down those ideas that seemed to come from nowhere in the middle of the night.

I performed the normal routine of running a household. I wrote. I tended my lawn and flower gardens. I wrote. I shopped. I wrote. I went to the post office. I wrote. I went to the bank. I wrote. I talked on the telephone with family and friends. I wrote. I read. I wrote. I traveled. I wrote. I thought about writing. I wrote.

Nearly everywhere I went, I ran across friends, former co-workers, and acquaintances. When they asked me what I was up to and whether I was bored with not working anymore, I honestly replied: "Oh, I'm not bored. I'm staying busy. It seems that I don't have enough hours in the day to finish everything I'd like to do." Sometimes people looked at me as if I were insane. But, what I'd said was true. I'd worked my way out of feeling a little too sorry for myself. I had a purpose and was on a mission.

Time passed, and people continued to ask what I was doing with my time, so I decided to validate my plan. I eventually developed enough nerve to tell folks that I was writing and prefaced my answer with, "Don't laugh when I tell you what I'm doing." Then I actually spoke the words. "I'm writing."

To my delight, most people said how great that was, that they hoped I'd sell my work, that they'd like to read it, and they requested that I keep them posted on my progress. I was pleased to have such feedback and would usually say: "My book might never sell, and if it doesn't that's all right, but writing is something I've always wanted to do. I've dreamed of becoming a published writer since I was a little girl, and now I have the time and the opportunity to pursue that dream. If nobody wants to buy my story, then my manuscript will be something my kids and grandchildren can leaf through someday, and maybe my work will be of interest to them—at least they'll know I wrote something in an effort to reach a goal."

My confidence and enthusiasm grew. I carried rough drafts around the house and out onto the porches with me. I *felt* like a writer. I continued to read and to edit. I wanted my manuscript to be as good as I could make it without the aid of professional help.

As my manuscript took shape, I deleted several of the stories I decided to use in a second novel—one about friendships. Jacob constantly encouraged and urged me to complete my first novel and to start my second one.

When I ran errands or received guests, it was apparent that people actually had taken me seriously when I'd told them I was writing, because even after much time had passed, folks still politely asked me how my book was coming along.

I usually responded with: "I'm still working on it and hope to finish it before the end of the year." For having asked, those folks gave me a boost. I plodded along, worked into the wee hours of the mornings many times, and on the many mornings when I woke early, I dressed and went to my office, just as if I were going away from home to work—just like I had a real job. I set up office hours around Jacob's work schedule. For about a year, I made myself accessible to others when necessary, but explained to my family and friends that I had to be serious in my efforts to complete my work, or I'd never finish. They respected my time and space, which meant that most visits and phone calls were made before or after my irregular self-imposed office hours that were arranged around Jacob's schedule.

Many people were politely curious and asked me what my novel was about, whether it was a true story, and whether I had chosen a title. I explained that my story reads a lot like a memoir but it's really not one. It's a story about an ordinary woman's journey through life's good times and difficult times. It's about how she deals with adversity, and how she eventually pursues her dream. I told them that some parts of the story are based upon truth and some parts aren't; but the whole story sounds like it *might* be true. I explained that some parts were drawn from my own experiences, and some were drawn from other women's stories. Some parts are just plain exaggerations and some parts are bald-faced lies. I explained that in my effort to bring out some emotions, I invoked poetic license and added things I thought made the story more entertaining and interesting and went back and word-painted a few pictures.

People laughed with me when I told them that because it's my story, I figure I can tell it however I want to tell it.

When it came time to choose a title, however, I was a little stumped. I considered several options but didn't feel exactly right with them. Finally, I stumbled upon a title choice during a conversation with my sister Sammie.

Sammie and I were discussing how we both love reading and how we often escape into our books. We talked about how we often put ourselves in the leading character's role and picture ourselves in those surroundings. We discussed our favorite books and our reasons for hard cover or paperback preferences. We discussed how we treasure our books, how we'd loaned books to each other and how, even though Sammie didn't want her books back after she'd read them and passed them along to someone else, I always wanted mine back.

I said: "Sammie, I've loaned or given away many books, and I've even thrown away some, because I didn't have a place to store them at the time. I wish I still had every book I've ever read. When I read a book, it becomes a part of me. I always want to keep my books, because they're a part of the comfort and relaxation in my life. Some stories are like pleasant memories. I have favorites, of course, and even though I'm anxious to finish a book, I'm almost sad when I come to its end. The feeling I derive from the book lingers with me for a day or two after I've read its last word. It sounds egotistical, but after I've read some books, I've even had the unmitigated gall to *hope* that I could possibly write something that's as good as what I just read. And, when I finish a book that brings me pleasure, I put it on the shelf and think that I'll save it and recommend it to others, but I won't loan that one out, because I'm afraid I might not get it back—it's a keeper. Wouldn't it be great to write the kind of novel for which you'd like to be remembered—one that's a keeper?

"Even though some of the things I'm writing about are based on what really happened in my life, and even though much of the story is absolutely true, I've changed too many details for it to be considered a memoir. After all, who'd want to read a memoir about an old nobody? But, I hope the readers—especially the ones who happen upon the book and don't know me well or at all—will believe the main character is the author and *think* it's all a true story, even though it's not. I don't want them to wonder if it's real, but to suspect it is. I want my story to flow, to grab the readers' attention, and to take them along on the journey. I want them to feel it when my main character's challenges start with a fear, a need, or a necessity. I want them to root for the protagonist when she's forced to overcome her next challenge and to hope she'll be all right. I want them to be relieved when she adapts to and overcomes those adversities.

"I want to stir the readers' emotions. I want them to see what's going on in the story, to feel it, to respond to it, to smile and cry—to identify with it. I want them to understand the process and to learn something from it. I want them to know the people in my story and to see the surroundings. I want to trigger memories from their own lives—give them a reason to remember and something to think about.

"Most folks read a book only once, so their first reaction elicits their only emotional responses. I only have one shot at this. I want them to enjoy it so much that they get lost in it. I want them to keep moving from one page to the next until they look up at the clock and say, 'Oh, my gosh! I didn't know it was so late.' I want them to hate to put the book down and to be sorry when it ends. I want them to say: 'I'll hang onto this book. It's a keeper.' And, I really hope it is.

"Above all else, I want the readers to know that no matter what happens in their own lives, they can work through it. I don't want them to take any of life's blessings for granted. I don't want them to ever lose hope.

"A word that summarizes the gist of what I hope to convey isn't a commonly used word, but I like it. Vicissitudes. It simply means: the ups and downs and changes experienced in a lifetime. When applied to what I've written, I think the word vicissitudes is relevant. Every moment of every life is a vicissitude— it fits here."

Sammie understood.

Dear Reader:

If you made it this far, thank you for hanging in there and for giving me your time. I'll be the first to admit I'm more of a "teller" than a writer of stories, but I hope you enjoyed what you read and that maybe you identified with at least parts of the story. Even though the original manuscript for this little finished product that spans several years was written nearly twenty years ago, many of the events and issues, and the thoughts and emotions, are timeless and remain relevant in today's society.

Dealing with life's adversities isn't easy, but we can always dream, move forward, and continue to count our truly meaningful blessings. As our cycle of life continues—it's a good idea to have faith that everything will work out.

About the Author

Debbie Ice lives with her husband Tom and their little hairy dog Gidget, in a small town in West Virginia. She fell in love with Tom the first time she saw him—and they've been happily married for nearly 43 years.

Debbie has a great love for life and an appreciation for every day it offers. She has an overactive sense of humor and has always wanted to be a storyteller and writer, but while researching and discovering differences between "telling" and "showing" a story, she became so confused that her confidence level dropped to a point where she realized she didn't have what it takes to be a *real* writer. She accepted that she could remain a wannabe writer, followed her gut instincts, and told the story the only way she knew how. She wrote in her own voice and decided that her book would probably only be read by a few family members and friends, anyway—and they already know she's an amateur and wouldn't expect much from her.

After many years of indecision and the addition of a few more grandchildren, she desperately hoped to bring this nagging project to an end and have a feeling of accomplishment. At the urging of her daughter who asked what she had to lose—especially at her age—Debbie bit the bullet, sucked it up, retrieved the nearly twenty-year-old manuscript, fought the urge to update it, decided to self-publish it, and worked hard to make it happen.

She hopes her family members and friends will enjoy the story, recognize the truth from fiction, and remember that this book's not meant to be a memoir.

She's currently working on a book about friendships—a subject that's near and dear to her heart.

www.ingramcontent.com/pod-product-compliance
Lightning Source LLC
Chambersburg PA
CBHW031207020726
47499CB00002B/521